Kent and Katcha

Espionage, Spycraft, Romance

Larry and Rosemary MILD

Magic Island Literary Works • Honolulu, Hawaii • 2024

Interior book design by Larry Mild.
Cover design by Larry Mild

Library of Congress Cataloging-in-Publication Data
 Mild, Larry M.; Mild, Rosemary P.
Kent and Katcha: Espionage, Spycraft, Romance
Mild, Larry M.; Mild, Rosemary P.

ISBN 979-8-9863864-0-9
First Edition 2024

10 9 8 7 6 5 4 3 2 1

Dedication

For our wonderful daughters—
Jackie and Myrna

For our beloved grandchildren—
Alena, Craig, Ben, Leah, and Emily

For our precious great-grandchildren—
Kai, Oliver, and Luna

For our marriage—
Soul mates, partners, lovers

Acknowledgments

We could fill an entire volume with the names of all the family members, dear friends, and acquaintances who are loyal fans of our books, essays, and short stories. And you, our readers, are all precious to us and give us the ultimate push to continue our writing.

Our special thanks and hugs to:
Hawai'i Fiction Writers and the National League of American Pen Women, for their friendship, encouragement, and advice.

Diane Farkas, our close friend, for her outstanding proofreading skills.

Books Coauthored by Larry and Rosemary

The Dan and Rivka Sherman Mysteries
- **Death Goes Postal**
- **Death Takes A Mistress**
- **Death Steals A Holy Book**
- **Death Rules the Night**

The Paco and Molly Mysteries
- **Locks and Cream Cheese**
- **Hot Grudge Sunday**
- **Boston Scream Pie**

Adventure/Thrillers
- **Cry Ohana**
- **Honolulu Heat**
- **On the Rails, The Adventures of Boxcar Bertie**

Short Story Collections
- **Murder, Fantasy, and Weird Tales**
- **The Misadventures of Slim O. Wittz**
- **Copper and Goldie, 13 Tails of Mystery and Suspense in Hawaii**
- **Charlie and the Magic Jug and Other Stories**

Science-Fiction Novella
- **Unto the Third Generation**

Also by Rosemary
- **Miriam's World—and Mine**
- **Love! Laugh! Panic! Life with My Mother**
- **In My Next Life I'll Get It Right**

Also by Larry
- **No Place To Be But Here, My Life and Times**

Table of Contents

Table of Contents (Continued)

Disclaimer

Kent and Katcha: Espionage, Spycraft, Romance is entirely a work of fiction. The plots and events therein are of the authors' imagination and invention. All characters therein are fictitious and any resemblance to persons living or dead is purely coincidental. A few real locations have been altered to accommodate the narrative.

Dialogue

Our story takes place in Russia and Finland. As one might imagine, most of the dialogue in our story would be in Russian and Finnish, languages neither we nor many of our intended readers comprehend. Out of necessity, all of the dialogue herein is written in English. However, some Russian words and phrases are used for story enhancement.

LIST OF CHARACTERS

Kent Peter Brukner—U.S. secret operative—alias George Thermon—alias Major Anatoli Todorev of the Russian Federation Army—alias Oleksander Kroschenko.

Kent's family—parents: Clinton & Clara Bruckner; brother: Gregory.

Katcha Nadia Kroschenko—Kent's Russian girlfriend/companion—a café server.

Oleksander (Olexi) Kroschenko—Katcha's father, currently serving time in prison.

Mavis Anne Dowd Kroschenko—Katcha's mother, a British expatriot from Sussex, England.

Sergei—Deep-cover operative—real name unknown.

General Uri Molitkov of the Russian Federation Army.

Colonel (Polkó) Polkóvnik Korashnev—Gen. Molitkov's aide.

Sergeant Ivan Brezkovny—Colonel Korashnev's aide.

Provost Sergeant Dolupan and his corporal, Ivan.

Fellow prisoners—Pyotr Bohinkin, Andreivich (Andrei) Troshky, Pavel Ilyan, and Grigory Parkovich.

Mikhail (Miki) Reigozhin, Camp lieutenant.

Captain Veloboro and Sergeant Lev at Camp Obuchat.

Yakim Kondreatyev—Katcha's uncle, a bus driver.

Major Dmitri Federov of the FSB, a Federation policeman.

Lyudmilla and Boris Ilyachenko and their children, **Stepan** and **Tatiana**, Katcha's cousins in St. Petersburg.

Mikhail and **Natasha Kamynina**—Lyudmilla's nosy neighbors.

Captain Ilitskova—Russian Border Police (PSFSB Rossii)—official at Helsinki ferry.

Ralph Ebernath—assistant station chief at Helsinki's U.S. Embassy—alias Victor Volkov.

Laura Tipton and **Beth Lindstrom**—U.S. Embassy staff.

Adrik Troshevsky, Vadim Ostanyuk, & Sasha Puttonyos—Dmitri's henchmen in Helsinki.

Captain Vyachesslav of the tramp freighter *MVC Maersk II*.

Tapio—Helsinki taxi driver.

Komisar Eero Koskinen—Chief Inspector of Finnish Federal Police, plus Sergeant **Jaako Heikkinen** & **Sergeant Ksenia,** Federal Police.

Lily Monahan—Special operative.

Valerie Huhta—Hospital nurse.

Chapter 1
Step into Peril

Moscow. Wednesday, May 20, 1992

Those who commit their lives to espionage are cut from a different bolt of cloth than the rest of us. Maybe only God knows why they pursue that kind of life. Is it a strong sense of duty to their country? The need to contribute on a grand scale? The potential for thrills and excitement? The urge to be wild and reckless? Or does it boil down to a feeling of personal accomplishment at any cost?

On the downside, the profession is inherently dangerous and lonely to the point of despair. Any chance of public appreciation or acknowledgment is shrouded in the depths of secrecy.

The tradecraft is vast, the training is grueling, complicated, and often difficult to master. The professional spy, or secret agent, is an actor's actor. He or she must be able to reside in a foreign country as an "inserted" person: like a native, fluent in the language and versed in the culture with neither flaw nor lapse. There can be no offstage moments to let a guard down. A rare blend of intelligence, ingenuity, athleticism, quick wit, resilience, and discipline may be required for unpredictable situations. Assigned to accomplish such improvised magic, perhaps these agents might more accurately be called soldiers of sleight-of-hand.

* * * *

Kent Peter Brukner had just finished his training as an operative—a spy, if you will, with an unnamed intelligence organization based somewhere in Virginia. An American citizen, he was on a special mission, his first, to compromise a Russian Federation Army facility.

The new government called itself the Russian Federation, replacing the ruthless Union of Soviet Socialist Republics. Triggered by the dismantling of the Berlin Wall in 1989, the federation appeared to have ushered in a more peaceful era. The tricolor flag, thick horizontal stripes of white, blue, and red, replaced the Soviet hammer and sickle. Mikhail Gorbachev became the first president of the federation, engineering the thaw of the Cold War and the lifting of the dreaded "Iron Curtain." But Boris Yeltsin replaced Gorbachev as president, and the United States felt a critical need to continually take the temperature of that New Order. Kent Brukner was one of a select few charged with that mission.

Kent wasn't using his real name, of course. His current identification and Russian travel visa provided a cover name, George Thermon, and a different vocation: as an American senior salesman for Ingleman's Department Stores in the United States. His intended purpose was to sell Ingleman's high-end men's clothing and specialty items to Russian department stores. Russian citizens were now craving all things American—after years of deprivation under the drab, restrictive Soviet Union. George's leather briefcase contained elegant product catalogues, a notebook, contract forms for orders, and swag, small giveaway items like ballpoint pens. He had a reasonable mastery of the Russian language, lacking only the seasoned intonations.

On May 20th, a few minutes before midnight, his plane, Aeroflot Flight 22303, landed at Moscow's Sheremetyevo SVO Airport. "George" picked up his bag and cleared customs in forty-five minutes. A taxi took him into the city, to the Ibis Budget Moscow Panfilovskaya, a midsized hotel where he would blend in among throngs of tourists and businesspeople. Once settled in room 303, he showered, then slept off the jet lag for the rest of the night. Early in the afternoon of the new day, he left the hotel and saw the structure's lower stories in daylight for the first time, noting that they were a pleasing pink brick and the upper half yellow brick. But he forced himself to focus on his mission and sought out a somewhat dilapidated public phone booth a five-minute walk away. He made two calls with a precise number of rings and a designated delay between the calls. George neither spoke nor heard anything during either call. Walking back to the hotel, he ate supper in the coffee shop, returned to his room, and waited—for a response from "Sergei," a deep-cover operative he'd never met. George's two phone calls had initiated a prearranged meeting with the operative for the next morning.

Law-school dropout Kent Brukner, alias George Thermon, was about to embark on his new life. And deep down, he felt uneasy.

* * * *

Sergei arrived the next morning at ten o'clock, a short fellow with a trim beard and thick-lensed glasses. He knocked at George's hotel room door as a delivery person for a florist, carrying a long white box, but much wider, as if designed for multiple floral arrangements.

At that meeting in his hotel room, George received key tradecraft materials, a detailed briefing, and most important, yet another identity. For this mission he would no longer be George Thermon, but Major Anatoli Todorev of the Russian Federation Army, and he was given the necessary credentials to prove it.

Sergei wasted no time with pleasantries. He drew up a straight-backed chair and spread the contents of his florist's box on the bed: a military uniform; a security access pass; a pair of neutral-lensed glasses; a lock-pick set; a bugging device; a roll of electrical tape; a glue stick; and a 9mm Makarov pistol. The neatly pressed wool uniform looked smart. Brown with an olive-green hue, it bore the rank of major in the Russian Federation Army. The access pass was, without question, the most critical item: an "official" identification card for Major Anatoli Todorev. George tried on the glasses. The likeness on the ID card wasn't perfect, but the photo was "close enough for government work," as the cliché goes. In a chilly voice, Sergei said, "Try on the uniform. If it doesn't fit,

3

you won't look authentic." George followed directions and checked his six-foot-one frame in the full-length mirror attached to the closet door. Quite impressive, he decided, especially the stately officer's hat. Sergei permitted himself a brief smile of approval.

The bugging device measured two-by-two inches and a quarter-inch thick. Sergei explained, "It's sound-triggered to record any voices in a room and go active to burst-broadcast its contents—but only when an encoded radio trigger targets the device at pseudo-random times between one and five a.m. local time." Sergei fingered two wires protruding from the base. "These need to be connected to a 220-volt, 50-Hertz power source. The broadcast will be received at an undisclosed location that you have no need to know about."

"Sergei," said George, trying to keep his voice steady so as not to betray his annoyance. "At first glance, this device looks like its size and power requirements severely limit the locations where it can be hidden. A wall socket is out of the question. Why can't the device be smaller and operate from a battery?"

Sergei had a carefully rehearsed reply, as if he'd heard this objection before. "The size and power are both related to the need for long-distance transmission. Live power will ensure extended access by the end-user. Besides, a battery will go dead eventually. And by the way, George, nobody said anything about a wall socket. Use your imagination. You'll figure it out."

His clipped response signaled "End of discussion." Sergei moved on to provide the address and floor plan of the targeted Russian Federation Army building and the location of General Uri Molitkov's office. His final instruction: "Wait for the weekend, when there will be fewer employees around." Reaching out to shake George's hand, he said in a softened voice, "Good luck, my friend."

Chapter 2
Forbidden Access

The Russian Federation's Army Annex Number Three was located in a Moscow suburb behind double rows of chain-link, barbed-wire fencing ten feet high. The complex of four six-story buildings sat behind an acre of green lawns and dense trees, blocking any invasive viewing from outsiders. The ring of green lawn circling the trees enabled the area just inside the fence to be surveilled from well-placed guard towers. A single manned gatehouse outside the fence provided access and egress for any individual and any vehicle with the necessary credentials.

The date chosen for George's mission was carefully keyed to the absence in the building of General Uri Molitkov. At four o'clock in the afternoon, George Thermon stepped into the role of Major Anatoli Todorev, in full uniform with combat ribbons and medals. He had decided on four o'clock because after-hours security might be more intense, but possibly less strict during the weekend.

Adopting a confident stride, "Anatoli" arrived at the Annex Security gatehouse, manned by three uniformed personnel. He had carefully planned how he would deal with the lock-picks and bugging device. The lock-picks were nonmetallic clear plastic, which he had stuck just under his military webbed fabric belt. He was able to fit the device neatly inside the slightly oversized belt buckle. As required, he removed the belt and placed it in a basket and sent it through the X-ray machine, along with his Swiss Army pocketknife and briefcase. As he had predicted, the bug's metallic content was insignificant compared with the ferrous content of the buckle as far as the X-rays were concerned. His preparations allowed him to pass successfully through the security magnetometer.

The photo likeness on his fake identification card was close enough that the major was given a security badge to hang around his neck. This particular badge granted passage into certain spaces and dictated exclusion from other spaces inside the building itself. Kent Brukner, alias George Thermon, now Major Anatoli Todorev, had gained entry to a highly sensitive military facility. He went through another successful badge check just to reach the reception desk.

He stopped at the desk for directions to the twenty-four-hour library. "For research, of course," he told the female clerk at the desk. *It's as good a place to wait as any*, he thought. *Hang out until the daytime work force leaves and the remaining personnel traffic becomes more manageable.*

Anatoli strode briskly through the first-floor halls, receiving and executing salutes along his way, as he headed to the research library, located at the end of a first-floor corridor. Entering the reading room, he nodded to the librarian, who barely raised her head. Most of the two dozen wooden tables were occupied. Browsing through the stacks, he randomly chose five large tomes and set them down on an empty table at the back, where no other visitor was even close. Seated with head and shoulders bent in intense concentration, he buried himself in the books and took notes, giving off a convincing image of a serious researcher.

* * * *

Anatoli remained in the library until after midnight when the number of other visitors had dwindled. Initially, he took a small packet containing an antiseptic wipe from his briefcase and, as he read, wiped his prints from the book covers, as well as from each page he had read. When he was ready to leave, he wiped clean and tore up his notes before tossing them in a wastebasket, even though the subjects and details were of such a bland nature that they revealed nothing.

Leaving the library, he started toward the fire stairs, intending to walk up three flights. But this was a gateway to spaces denied to personnel with his particular badge. A female *serzhánt*, or sergeant, stood guard at the nearby first-floor elevator. To avoid her spotting and remembering him, Anatoli waited in one of the perpendicular corridors opposite the fire stairs until he saw that she was distracted by some activity at the other end of the corridor. He then silently slipped from his hiding place across the main hall, and up the fire stairs unnoticed.

From the fire stairs, he peeked into the fourth-floor main corridor, hoping the coast was clear. It wasn't. A *yefréytor*, or private, was guarding this floor's elevator and main hall. Major Todorev waited for a distraction and got lucky when the private bent in the opposite direction to buff a spot on his shoe. Anatoli seized the opportunity and darted into one of the many secondary corridors. The sign revealed that he had landed in *Koridor pyat'*, or Corridor Five. Sergei had briefed him on the layout. The Russian Federation Army's Advanced Deployment Planning Section occupied Corridors Five and Six on the fourth floor on either side of the elevators. General Uri Molitkov occupied a double office midway along Corridor Five. Anatoli had landed in the correct corridor. It was just opposite the fire stairs.

Affixed to every door were shiny brass plaques bearing names, ranks, and functions in the Deployment Planning Section. Moving down the corridor, checking plaques, Anatoli proceeded to Molitkov's office. He examined the wooden outer door and lock—a simple push-button activated from inside. He slipped a long, thin Swiss Army knife blade between the wood molding and the door jamb at the height of the latch and pushed against the angled lock tongue until it retracted enough to spring the door open. After gaining access to the room, he locked the door behind him. He assumed this outer office to be for the secretary and tried the door to the inner office. This lock proved a bit more sophisticated. Anatoli selected two suitable picks and had the door opened in about forty seconds. *Not my best time,* he thought.

The huge challenge now, and the entire reason for his exploit, was to plant the bugging device. That wasn't so easy. He thoroughly surveyed this inner room, the general's private office. It had a surprisingly elegant feel to it. A plush oriental rug. Three oil paintings in gilded frames of heroic Russian military scenes. And a large, highly polished mahogany desk devoid of any evidence of toil. No inbox or outbox, no file folders of any kind. Anatoli tried the drawers. They were all locked. It took him several minutes to locate a place to plant the bugging device. He was sorely reminded of its serious size and extended power requirements. Then he spotted the perfect candidate: a large ceramic table lamp with a cream-colored shade. The ceramic was finely decorated with a wraparound Chinese scene. It sat atop a three-foot-high wall-to-wall bookcase behind the general's desk. Its large bulbous shape and wide base could easily house the bug package; power was certainly available inside.

Anatoli unplugged the lamp, lifted it from its perch, and inspected its base. Then he removed the shade and bulb and laid the lamp down on the general's desk, thankful for all the working space on the near-empty desk—only a calendar/pad, a stapler, and a roll of plastic tape. The base of the lamp was covered with a protective felt pad backed by a stiff cardboard disk. His knife blade made a neat slit around the periphery of the glued disk, exposing the interior of the base, and revealing more than adequate space for housing the bugging device.

The lamp's power cord entered through a three-eighths-inch hole near the five-inch opening in the base. Anatoli pulled more of the cord inside the hole to make a working loop for himself. Using his knife, he separated and stripped the two wires of insulation, and spliced in the two power leads from the device. That took six minutes. Next, he reinsulated these connections with a strip from his roll of black electrical tape, and stuffed the working loop and the device inside the lamp. Using his glue stick, he resealed the cardboard disk to its ceramic base.

Anatoli collected and stowed the waste material in an envelope, pocketed it along with his trusty knife, and turned out the lights. He passed through the secretary's office and out into the hall, closing the door behind him. He took a few steps—and then it hit him. He hadn't pushed the button on the inside knob to re-lock the outer door. He spun around and placed his hand on the knob, poised to open the door a crack so he could slide his hand in.

He froze. The door to the office across the hall had swung open.

Chapter 3
The Challenge

Colonel Polkóvnik Korashnev, or Colonel Polkó as he was known to his colleagues, blinked twice and shifted his rear end in his swivel chair. Feeling achy and sluggish well after midnight, he thought he heard a noise in the corridor, but dismissed it as his imagination and the grueling fatigue of an eighteen-hour work day.

Colonel Polkó was about to make some clever supply train decisions that night that would enable innovative troop movements over the next eighteen months. These secure assessments would keep NATO and the Western nations from knowing exactly where the strategic strength of the Russian Federation Army was positioned at any given point in time nor what they were planning.

Kent, acting as Major Todorev, would be responsible for harvesting those assessments.

Colonel Polkó served as General Uri Molitkov's second-in-command and so had an office directly across the hall from him, midway along Corridor Five. The general headed the Russian Federation Army's Advanced Deployment Planning Section.

The colonel sat behind his desk dictating a supply-chain support diagram for Sergeant Ivan Brezkovny to draw on the wall's whiteboard. This intricate diagram of text-filled geometric figures was an integral part of a Power-Point presentation he was planning for the general. The diagram was only one of many, and the written part would take more than a week to get down on paper. Polkó's timing was good. General Molitkov had begun a two-week vacation at his Black Sea dacha the day before yesterday.

After the completion of each diagram or illustration, Sergeant Ivan transcribed it to a computer to document the final version. The sheer length of the colonel's innovative project prompted him to work on it after hours, as there were far too many interruptions and other pressing duties during the workday. This was Ivan's pet project, his path to further promotion—at least that's the way he saw it.

"Now draw a line between those two rectangles," said Polkó. "It will show the necessary chain-of-command connection."

"Here?" asked Ivan, pointing with the black marker.

"No," replied Polkó, changing his mind as he'd done dozens of times before. "I think it might need another step in between. Let me think about it for a minute."

The two men looked at one another, reacting to an unfamiliar noise.

"What was that?" asked Ivan.

"Sounded like it came from the hall," replied Polkó. "Probably nothing."

"There it is again, and it's coming from the hall," said Ivan. "Do you want me to check on it, sir?"

"Yes. There shouldn't be anyone else in Corridor Five this time of night."

Ivan set the black marker on the whiteboard ledge and hurried through the outer room and out the hall door. He stopped short.

"Halt! Halt! Please!" yelled Ivan. "Colonel! There is a major here trying to access the general's office!" Gathering his wits to appear respectful, he turned to Anatoli and said, "The general isn't in, sir. Can I help you with anything?"

Polkó appeared in his doorway with his sidearm

drawn and pointed at Anatoli. "May I see some identification, Major?"

"Yes, sir!" Anatoli snapped to attention and pointed to his badge. When he saw that it was not enough for the colonel, he pulled out his ID card from his wallet.

The colonel studied both, then asked, "Major Anatoli Todorev, what possible business could you have in the general's office?"

"The general asked me to pick up a file for him."

"And just what file is that?" asked Polkó.

"ARN3205, sir," replied the major, sharply.

"And just where and when did you see General Molitkov?"

"At his home this afternoon," Anatoli replied without so much as a flinch.

Polkó's smoky gray eyes turned to slits as his face took on a satisfied sneer, showing a mouthful of crooked teeth. He had no intention of telling the major that General Molitkov was at his vacation dacha.

Reading Polkó's expression, Anatoli stiffened. *Damn! Sergei told me something about the general being at his dacha and it slipped my mind. Too late now. I blew it.*

"Sergeant Ivan," the colonel barked. "Call Security and have them come up here with restraints. Tell them we have a security breach on the fourth floor."

"Yes, sir." Ivan dashed to the phone in the outer office.

Polkó's eyes narrowed. "Major Todorev, neither your pass nor your ID grants you clearance to enter the general's office. In fact, you are not even permitted access to anywhere on this floor. Who are you and what are you after?"

At this point Kent alias George alias Anatoli knew he was already in the hole and thought it best not to answer any more questions. His silence angered the frustrated colonel.

"By the time Security gets through with you you'll sing like a bird," said Polkó. "You are not a real major, and I highly doubt that you are even a member of the Federation Army. Your speech, your pronunciation, tell me you may not even be Russian-born. Your silence confirms you're a Western spy, and you will be treated like one."

Sergeant Ivan returned to the hall and reported, "They're sending up a team, sir. I've also typed up a brief summary of charges for the incident."

"Excellent," said Polkó.

They heard the elevator doors slide open and a minute later, two hefty men in uniform appeared at the end of Corridor Five, a provost sergeant and a corporal, both wearing sidearms. They took charge of the prisoner by slapping restraints on his wrists and took the time to learn about the attempted break-in.

"Did the major actually access the general's office?" asked Dolupan, the provost sergeant, a short, squat man with a thick Stalin-like mustache.

Ivan shrugged. "I really don't know. I doubt it."

"Of course not," snapped Polkó. "We caught him tampering with the door lock. He hadn't gotten inside yet. A good thing, too. The general's office is full of sensitive material."

"What was he after?" asked Dolupan.

Sergeant Ivan shrugged, then said, "State secrets, plans you don't have the clearance level to know about."

Polkó scowled and shook his head.

The burly corporal gave Anatoli a shove in the small of his back to direct him down the corridor to the elevators.

A few minutes after the prisoner had been taken away, Ivan glanced down at the general's door and saw the major's briefcase still standing there. Examining the contents, he found nothing incriminating, so he dumped the few items into a trash basket and latched onto the nice leather briefcase for his very own.

Chapter 4
The Provost's Office

On the first floor, the two security men conveyed the major to the provost's office, a three-room, three-man clerical facility charged with building security. Usually it was staffed by a the provost captain and his two noncommissioned officers.

"Stand at attention," ordered Dolupan as they entered the office. "What is your name?"

Silence.

"Who do you work for?"

Silence.

"What were you after in the general's office?"

More silence.

"Oh, you'll talk when the provost captain gets through with you."

The prisoner shrugged and half-smiled.

"Shouldn't we search the prisoner?" asked the corporal.

"We'll conduct a full strip search just as soon as I contact the captain," said Dolupan. "He may want to do his own interrogation. Keep an eye on him." He disappeared behind a partition to make a phone call for further instructions.

"Prisoner! Go wait in the corner 'til we're ready for you,"

ordered the corporal.

Kent, handcuffed and still in the major's uniform, retreated to the appointed corner and sat down on a folding chair facing the corporal. The moment he settled into it, he felt something unpleasant brush against his face—the coarseness of an army field overcoat hanging on a coat tree next to him. At first it annoyed him, but soon he noticed a large overcoat pocket within reach. With a furtive glance, he saw the corporal turn away to pour himself a mug of coffee and slowly decorate it with three heaping teaspoons of sugar. Taking advantage of this, Kent half-turned to his left and painstakingly emptied his own pockets into the overcoat pocket. With the metal cuffs cutting into his wrists, the task required subtle maneuvering—almost, but not quite impossible.

The corporal was taking his time stirring his sweetened coffee as if it were the only reward he would receive all night. He eventually turned to face the prisoner and perched on the nearest corner of his desk. "You're a disgrace to our army. Take off that major's uniform."

Kent thrust his fists forward, showing there was no way to remove his clothes as long as he was cuffed.

The corporal realized his mistake, but needed Dolupan's okay before removing the cuffs. Five minutes later, Dolupan reappeared from behind the partition, shaking his head and mumbling a string of choice cusswords.

"What's wrong?" asked the corporal.

"The captain went home sick and there's no one over there to do a proper interrogation. I don't know what they expect me to do with this prisoner. The interrogation clerk suggested we get him over to Cell Block 2B, so they can ship him off to Camp Obuchat out in the boonies. He thought the camp had professionals that could do the interrogation for us. I don't know much about that camp, but I like the idea. Get him off our hands."

"Well, we've got to search him anyway," said the corporal. "Is it okay to take the cuffs off now that you're here?"

"Yes, I'll watch while you remove them. But, first, get a set of prison garb for him to wear, the largest sizes you can find—he's one big guy. You'll find a bunch of them in the uniform closet."

The corporal returned with a pile of prison clothes, laid them on the desk, and turned toward the prisoner, who again extended his cuffed fists. Pulling a key from his key ring, the corporal unlocked and removed the cuffs. He stepped back and ordered, "Stand up and remove your clothes. Everything! And be quick about it."

Kent stood and began the humiliating process of stripping, dropping each article of the uniform as well as his underwear on the floor in front of him. Standing stark naked before them, he covered his privates with his hands and waited, silently cursing himself. His temporary cover as Major Anatoli Todorev was blown. The Russians were a long way from learning who he really was and who he worked for, but even so, they would eventually find out. *Dammit. Why didn't I memorize Sergei's credible cover story so that I might have actually fooled the colonel?* An ugly thought crossed Kent's mind. *Did he actually tell me the correct details about the dacha? How trustworthy is my deep-cover operative? Was I actually being set up?*

"Now do a quarter turn," ordered the corporal. "Again. Now bend and touch your knees. Stand straight. Turn again. Again." He picked up the prisoner's pile of clothes and tossed them on the desk for a probe through the uniform pockets and a check for false linings.

"Good. He's hidden nothing," said Dolupan. "Get him dressed now."

The corporal grabbed the stack of prison clothes off the desk and threw it at the prisoner's feet.

Kent began pulling on the fresh pea-green underwear, gray-green denim trousers, and a chambray shirt with broad green and white stripes. When he had finished, the corporal sent him back to the same corner with its coat tree. While the corporal fumbled about, searching once more for the cuffs, Kent quickly retrieved his belongings from the pockets of the greatcoat, a much quicker and easier task this time without cuffs on. As long as his hands remained free, his thoughts focused on formulating an escape plan, but even this idea was short-lived. The corporal found the cuffs beneath the pile containing the major's uniform and proceeded to re-cuff the prisoner. Dolupan added a set of chained leg irons to completely hobble the prisoner while in transit. All hope of escape had suddenly evaporated.

The phone rang twice: "Provost Office, Sergeant Dolupan here. Yes, sir. We'll have him ready and outside for you."

"Who was that?" asked the corporal.

"The lieutenant over at Cell Block 2B. The clerk's office told them we have a prisoner to ship out to Camp Obuchat. They already have four other prisoners. Two guards and a driver are leaving on an armored prison bus at 5 a.m. this morning. He wanted to know if he should send the bus here to pick up our prisoner. You heard what I told him."

"But we have learned nothing about him," protested the corporal. "We could get into deep shit making the decision to transport him ourselves."

Sergeant Dolupan scowled. "It's the middle of the damn night, 2 a.m., corporal. I don't want to be responsible for this creep while we wait for some big shot to make up his mind. I'm supposed to go home on leave tomorrow, not stay here and watch scumbag prisoners. I can always say it was the captain's office and cell block lieutenant who authorized him to be shipped out. Besides, I'll send Sergeant Ivan's paperwork along, and they can do all the interrogating they want at Camp Obuchat. His report lists all the charges."

"What about the colonel and sergeant on the fourth floor?" asked the corporal. "What if they ask about the prisoner?"

"They won't ask," said Dolupan. "By tomorrow those two big shots will have forgotten all about him. They were in too big a hurry to get rid of the prisoner so they could get back to doing whatever they do." He cleared his throat and muttered under his mustache, "If anything at all."

Chapter 5
The Armored Bus

The next morning, just after daybreak, a Mercedes armored bus pulled up to the building's side door and tooted its horn. Dolupan and the corporal unlocked the door, pushed the prisoner outside, and shoved him onto the bus. The leg irons forced Kent to hobble in short, painful steps. The two local security men remained on the pavement and watched through the smudged windows of the bus: the American spy being cuffed to the seat rail in front of him. Glad to be rid of the troublemaker, they obtained a receipt for the prisoner and the bus rolled away.

Kent's gut cramped with a sickened feeling. The bus was ancient, armor-plated, and hard riding, with windows so dirt-smeared he could hardly see out. He had no idea where they were headed. Probably to some high-security prison camp, maybe in eastern Siberia. Escape? With the leg irons still on, and the two feet of chain linking him to the seat in front of him, escape was impossible. The prisoners sat in zigzag fashion—zigging across the center aisle and zagging back, always leaving an empty row in between to discourage any fraternization. The two accompanying guards sat right behind the driver, sometimes chatting, often dozing. Food was brought to the prisoners; stale sandwiches and tepid water, but only at fueling stops. Toilet breaks meant a guard's unchaining a prisoner from the seat rail in front of him and re-chaining it to a rail next to the toilet in the tiny, smelly restroom at the rear of the bus with only a crude curtain for privacy.

The numbing, endless ride left plenty of time for self-reflection and, worse, a sense of hopelessness. Kent lowered his head and brooded. *I was never really interrogated and I never had a trial to convict me of anything. So why am I headed to prison? How did I get this deep in shit anyway? I have no one to blame but myself. I forgot to set the outer door latch in the general's office. I made a noisy exit and got caught red-handed. I can't let them know that I'm Kent Brukner, but there has to be a record of me landing in Moscow as George Therman.*

George Thermon became tired of the muddy view outside his window, as the bus rolled through mostly deserted flatlands, and willingly ignored the ugly circumstances inside the bus as well. Closing his eyes, squeezing them shut, he became even more self-reflective. *How did I wind up on this bus?*

* * * *

But how Kent Brukner wound up on that bus went back a lot farther than the night he was arrested—all the way back to a medium-sized farm just outside Jefferson, Iowa. His parents, Clinton and Clara Brukner, raised two sons, Kent and his brother, Gregory. Older by four years, Greg grew into the role of farmer, almost a clone of his father. He loved working with the cows, sheep, and pigs, a dozen or so of each, as well as plowing and harvesting the sixty acres of wheat. Being taller and the better looking of the two boys, Greg married and settled down to help on the farm when he was just nineteen, a year and a half out of high school. Clara Brukner battled cancer for six years and passed away when the boys were in their teens.

The thought of being saddled to farm life repelled Kent. He had an itch to do something more with his life. His lean, hard, limber body enabled him to attain several track and field records at Thomas Jefferson High School. A 3.8 grade point average attested to his quick-witted intellect. The combination led to a four-year scholarship to Iowa State University in Ames.

At the insistence of his father, Kent majored in pre-law, but he had a flair for languages, primarily Russian, so that became his minor. During his junior year, he sailed through the LSAT exams and was accepted into the ISU's College of Law. Clinton was both proud of and pleased with the decisions both his sons had made.

Despite all of Kent's successes in high school and college, a roguish streak lurked inside the boy, causing his parents endless aggravation. In high school he grew his hair so long it flopped over his shirt collars. In his sophomore year, Clara discovered a stash of marijuana joints in his sock drawer. His father had ranted and preached. "Iowa boys just don't behave that way!" Even Kent's decision in college to minor in Russian language sent a stab of fear through his dad. But now, as Kent was about to enter law school, Clinton felt his younger son had finally buried the rogue and rebellion and joined the mainstream of "good people."

During first-year law, Ailene White, a cute brownette he met in torts class, caught his eye. And soon she locked her attention on him as she struggled to focus on the current case law. The other men in her class struck her as too intense, too competitive. She liked Kent's flamboyant sweep of light brown hair over his high forehead. His wide face, slightly rounded cheekbones, inviting lips, and laugh lines around his mouth gave the impression of a man with a sense of humor, even irony. What started as casual dating, often studying together, turned into passion. Ailene brought him home to meet her parents. He brought her to the farm to meet his father, Gregory, and Greg's wife. Clinton seemed quite pleased with Ailene and assumed that the two would eventually marry.

But three months into Kent's second year of law school, Ailene detected a sense of restlessness in the love of her life. Her intuition proved correct. A visiting recruiting agent from an un-named intelligence organization captured his attention and lured him away from his law studies. Kent had admired the clandestine profession since he was a kid. The recruiting agent promised a life of glamor, purpose, world travel, and excitement. Ailene, rocked to the core, argued against his decision. She had envisioned a pleasant, predictable lawyerly life for the two of them. When he confessed that he had already accepted the job, she broke up with him for good. His father was also furious with his son's decision and came close to disowning him. When he withdrew from law school and left home, they weren't even speaking.

Kent was sent to a northern Virginia facility branded familiarly as The Field. For the next eighteen months he learned the skill set known as tradecraft. It included disguises, stealth, weapons, martial arts, survival, diplomacy, interrogation techniques, electronic devices, and other tools of the spy trade. Time was made available to polish up on his Russian language skills as well. The more he learned, the more he wanted to learn, and most of the hands-on and intellectual skills came easily to him. Often he was given hypothetical problems and tested for proficiency, speed, and ingenuity. His class of prospective operatives graduated in January 1992. Of the eight who started with him, only five made the grade.

By the end of January, Kent had been flown to Paris and assigned to the U.S. Embassy there. His work was mostly clerical—crosschecking names and places appearing in the city's Russian language media. By April 1992 this work bored him. Then an agent who was scheduled to go into deep cover abroad broke his leg in a bicycle accident. Because the mission was time-sensitive, the chief of station scrambled to find a replacement. Kent's fluency in Russian brought his name to the forefront. "But Boss," the deputy station chief argued, "Brukner's had no experience at all in the field." The chief decided to go with him anyway, arguing that Kent was a quick study.

A week later, with his head packed full of briefings, the young, inexperienced agent found himself in seat 3C aboard Russian Aeroflot Flight 22303 headed for Moscow. His papers said that he was now George Thermon.

* * * *

The armored bus chugged through miles of treeless plains as far as the eye could see; tall, untamed, weedy grasses. Rubbing away a bit of dirt from his window, Kent saw birds circling high overhead. A hawk swooped down with lightning speed, caught a crow midair, and flew off with the flailing victim.

The armored bus screeched to an unexpected halt, jarring Kent Brukner alias George Thermon from his self-reflections. His view out the smudged window revealed nothing to justify stopping *here*. He watched one of the two guards leave his seat and get off the bus. He heard a bit of arguing, none of it intelligible. Then the second guard joined the first one.

Two soldiers with sidearms boarded the bus. The first one grabbed the chin of the closest prisoner and yanked it up to study his face. Satisfied, the soldier moved to the succeeding prisoners. *Are they looking for me?* Kent wondered. *Have they discovered their screwups and want me back in Moscow? Shit. I'm really in for it now.* Genuine surprise, then relief came when his face didn't match the one the soldiers were looking for. Disappointed, they left the bus and the two guards climbed back on. As soon as the bus pulled onto the road from the shoulder, a military vehicle zoomed past.

Chapter 6
Camp Obuchat

After being confined on the prison bus for forty-eight hours, two days straight, even the chain-link fence and weathered wooden sign of Camp Obuchat looked preferable to the prisoners. The sun struggled to peek through thick clouds, matching the bleak mood and morale of five souls contemplating a life of undetermined imprisonment. The bus stopped outside the steel gate and waited for a sentry to board. A camp guard in an army uniform exchanged paperwork with the driver, then directed him to pull up to the entrance of the first building, the camp headquarters.

The two guards on the bus removed the chains linking the prisoners' cuffs to the seats. Still in cuffs and leg irons, their wrists and ankles raw from the rubbing of the metal, the five prisoners hobbled off the bus, through the personnel gate, and up to a graveled space in front of the main building. The bus turned around and parked outside the fence awaiting orders, the driver unaware that the folder, containing the summary charges, had slipped down between the guards' seat and the bus bulkhead and wouldn't be discovered until many months later. The gate clanged shut and the prisoners, watched over by the two guards, were left standing in the damp early morning air for the better part of an hour.

Kent struck up a conversation with the much older man standing next to him. He learned that the man's name was Andrei. To his relief, Andrei was talkative and spoke quite an educated Russian. "Want to know what the camp's name means? *Obuchat* means 'teach, train, discipline.' If I have to guess, we're now somewhere in the foothills of the Ural Mountains. I've heard the camp was constructed to house German prisoners of war during the 1940s. Now it's supposed to be a temporary place for political dissidents, malcontents, misfits, and crazies." Andrei looked at Kent with a wry expression. "Meaning the powers-that-be haven't decided whether to hold a spectacular trial, or simply send us here to rot and be forgotten altogether."

Suddenly, they heard the screeching tweets of mouth whistles. A couple dozen prisoners poured out of two adjacent buildings that looked like a barracks to Kent, and formed two lines in front of them. A lieutenant and a sergeant stepped forward. The sergeant ordered the five prisoners who had just arrived to stand at attention side by side. Reading from the newly acquired paperwork on four of them, he barked out their names as an initial roll call.

"Pyotr Bohinkin!"

"Da!"

"Andreivich Troshky!"

"Da!"

"Pavel Ilyan!"

"Da!"

"Grigory Parkovich!

"Da!"

Seeing a fifth prisoner standing there, he shouted, "No name!"

"Da!" said Kent after a brief hesitation. *He means me. I'd better be George Thermon here.*

The sergeant looked Kent over and cracked a crooked grin. "I don't give a crap what your whole name is or even who you really are. Unless you give me a first name to call you right now, your name is shit and that's the way you'll be treated from now on."

"George Thermon, sir!"

"George Thermon!"

"Da!" he responded again.

"You're American, aren't you?" asked the lieutenant.

Kent responded with silence, convincing the lieutenant that his assessment had been correct. He ordered the leg irons off the prisoners, and the two guards worked their way down each row, one removing the irons and the second one collecting them. Meanwhile, the sergeant moved to the front of the adjacent buildings and took roll call of the men standing there.

Kent's training led him to constantly take stock of his situation, surroundings, position, and resources—always considering the escape possibilities. From where he stood, he estimated this building to be about thirty feet wide by eighty feet long—noting that its length was parallel to the main gate, as were all the buildings adjacent to it. Twisting his head, he could see there were other buildings just like this one, at least three in a column and five in a row. Gray, neglected, unpainted and aging wood everywhere. At the front of the camp there were two thirty-foot-high guard towers just inside the barbed wire fence corners; he assumed there were two more at the rear of the camp. This would mean each tower had a clear view of two sides or one-half of the camp's perimeter. At least fifty feet of surveillance space separated the nearest buildings from the fence. He estimated the overall fence was twelve feet high, comprising many strands of continuous barbed wire stretched between six-by-six posts eight to ten feet apart.

Once all the leg irons had been collected, the lieutenant turned to one of the bus guards and ordered him to move the newest group to the third building over from the headquarters. They filed up four wooden steps and went inside.

Kent found himself in a large room with thirty double-decker bunk beds, fifteen on either side of the main aisle. An open washroom—sinks, showers, and latrine troughs—stretched across the rear of the room. Six zombie-like men of varying ages and sizes slumped on their bunks at the opposite end of the room as the new arrivals entered their new dormitory. These six were the old-timers, the men who'd been there for, perhaps, years, lost and despairing as evidenced by the dullness of their expressions. Kent noted that his group's arrival had been anticipated. He saw five empty bunks, each with a pile of prison garb, bedding, and a ditty bag, which he hoped was full of personal items such as soap, toothpaste, toothbrush, and shaving gear.

The two guards departed and hurried out to the bus; the driver had received orders to drive back to Moscow. They couldn't wait to get away from this godforsaken place.

In the dormitory, Kent's new friend, Andrei, chose a lower bunk. Andrei made up the bunk, stretched out on top, and immediately fell asleep.

Kent selected the lower bunk next to his friend's, He put his bed in order as well—all the while doing some serious reflecting. Thank God for that army overcoat's pockets and dumb provost corporal. He sat down at the far end of the mattress, the end closest to the wall, and furtively opened his Swiss Army pocketknife. As quietly as possible, like a surgeon at work, he carved a hole in the end of the mattress, just large enough to poke his hand in, and pulled away a fistful of stuffing. Glancing around to make sure no eyes were on him, he stashed away his knife, watch, passport, and five 50,000-ruble notes, then neatly replaced the mattress stuffing and propped his pillow tightly against the wall.

Brooding over his situation, Kent had to face the fact that George Thermon had been unmasked—as an American spy, caught impersonating a Russian army major, and there was a price to pay: imprisonment, a punishment he somehow had to subvert. He felt a grim sense of satisfaction that he had frustrated his captors. "George Thermon" turned out to be an unknown soul as far as the Soviet legal and penal systems were concerned. They had arrested him, all right, but he hadn't been fully and properly processed. Even his body search had been badly bungled. Due to hasty, sloppy handling, there wasn't a speck of paperwork about him anywhere in those systems. Apparently, Colonel Polkó had neglected to write up a full security-breach report. From what Kent had overheard, Polkó's aide had scribbled only a few details. The scant document of summary charges written by the provost people hadn't made its way to the camp office Unknowingly, it was on its way back across the countryside aboard the armored bus. The incident, soon forgotten, the principals too busy, too disinterested to follow up.

Kent was simply George now and he believed his captors had no way to prove otherwise. He knew that getting caught meant undergoing intensive interrogation, and a strong chance of enduring torture, too. So far, he'd avoided everything but a few harmless questions. Oh, he'd been threatened to reveal much more, but those threats had never materialized. He remembered what Andrei had told him—dissidents, malcontents, misfits, and crazies. So why George Thermon, the neutralized spy, remained unchallenged, and wound up here at a remote camp in the boonies remained a mystery to him.

Settled uneasily in the barracks, Kent, aka George Thermon, did some quick arithmetic. He counted twenty-three prisoners assigned to the first barracks and his group of five recent arrivals was assigned to the second barracks, along with six more seasoned prisoners. That meant that a captain, a lieutenant, two sergeants, ,and twenty-two guards watched over thirty-four prisoners housed in two buildings. He also heard from one of the guards that in recent years the outmoded Camp Obuchat never held more than three dozen prisoners at one time. Kent saw the camp as ridiculously inefficient and a huge waste of military manpower. *Why in hell do they even keep this place open? Surely, they have other camps that are run more efficiently.*

Ironically, the prisoners were left to themselves for the first day, so they mostly flopped around on their bunks. At first, they avoided going outside because they were unsure just what was off limits. Then they saw the more seasoned prisoners roaming around the open area between the fence and the buildings. They soon learned that they were free to be in this open area at the gate end of camp if they weren't on work or physical exercise detail. The areas between the buildings were forbidden, as was wandering and idling near the fence.

On the second day, all eleven men in Kent's barracks were marched outside and put through physical exercises for an hour: push-ups, jumping-jacks, and running in place. Standing there, once the calisthenics were finished, Kent looked skyward and made another important observation. The sun had risen in the east over the camp gate and would eventually set in the west over the rear of the camp. Any sort of escape would necessarily be toward the west. He made a mental note. The prisoners spent the rest of the second day cleaning and scrubbing their barracks. An inspection followed.

On the third day, a guard with a huge head and no neck marched the eleven men around to the rear of the camp—to a long, narrow, garden patch, about two-hundred-by-forty feet, Kent estimated. He read the small Russian signs on stakes identifying the vegetables, with some sprouts, lettuce, and cabbages beginning to show their heads. The carrots, beans, potatoes, and beets were underground.

"Listen up, goons!" boomed No Neck. "This garden patch raises all the vegetables you and the staff eat. One prisoner team takes a turn at gardening every three days. Today's tasks will be weeding and irrigation channeling." He led them toward the southern edge of the patch to a decrepit woodshed containing gardening tools. Unlocking the shed, he chose one prisoner to hand out the tools to the others. Squinting in the sunlight, No Neck pointed out two guards, automatic rifles at-the-ready, keeping watch from opposite ends of the patch. He bellowed, "Don't go getting any funny ideas about using the tools for the wrong reasons. You even walk too close to those guys you'll wind up in their sights. The tools will be padlocked away in the shed at the end of each workday. "

On the fourth day, the eleven were marched to the camp kitchen and put to work doing manual food preparation and clean-up for all three meals. As the weeks passed, it became clear to Kent that each type of duty repeated every third day.

As chance would have it, there came a day when Kent was

chosen to hand out the gardening tools. While lifting a rake off its hook to hand to Pyotr, he accidentally knocked it against the rear wall of the shed. Looking down near the dirt floor, Kent saw a glimmer of sunlight leaking into the shed where the bottom of a rear board had rotted. He intentionally bumped the board next to it with his foot and, sure enough, more light shone through. He continued to pass out tools, and at the end of the day, collected them, stored them, and padlocked the shed as ordered. But he had also collected another valuable piece of intelligence to build his escape plan. At that moment, the plan was merely a jigsaw puzzle in his calculating mind.

Other than the three-day cycles, one day seemed pretty much like any other, intensifying Kent's resolution to make an escape. At first, he thought about partnering with another prisoner during the planning, but his four roommates were a sorry lot and far too undependable.

The original six prisoners kept to themselves, so Kent could never get a decent feel for their trustworthiness. The only social one in the bunch was their leader, Vladimir, who talked their ears off during idle evening hours, whether anybody was listening or not. But Kent decided the man was too much of a dreamer and at the same time too obsessed with Russian politics to be of any practical use to him. *Besides*, Kent shrewdly thought, *one of those six could be a plant.* He couldn't take a chance by confiding in any of them.

Of the four others in his own group, Pavel was just plain nuts. Babbling in disconnected phrases, he was too far off his rocker to deal with. Andrei proved socially and mentally capable enough, and his language skills definitely would have been an asset. As a native and self-described intellectual, he spoke excellent Russian and English. Kent's Russian, although fluent, was limited; weak in conversational lingo and not good enough to discuss philosophy, literature, and the arts in depth. But sadly, Andrei was too frail physically to participate in any breakout scheme. Antisocial Pyotr wanted nothing to do with anyone. He argued all the time about anything just for the sake of it. Kent and everyone else avoided him like the plague. Belligerent Grigory always had to be in charge, refusing to take orders from anybody, even the guards. As a result, he was beaten regularly. Sadly, Kent and Andrei were the only ones who related to one another. Kent knew he was entirely on his own. The challenge he faced as he calculated his odds, surveying and assessing his surroundings, was not to appear to be doing these things. So stealth was a necessity.

Chapter 7
An Escape Plan

While under constant and heavy scrutiny, Kent focused on formulating a viable escape plan. In a matter of a few weeks, that plan evolved as he casually acquired the information he needed.

Two guards armed with automatic rifles patrolled the perimeter on foot every forty minutes. All the buildings were constructed of aging wood from the World War II era. In some respects, the camp was not high security. Nevertheless, the guard towers presented a formidable obstacle. Each four-legged tower held one guard, who wielded a powerful sixteen-inch spotlight, as well as an excellent variety of automatic weapons. The guards changed every six hours. Mounted on the inside corner of each tower, the spotlights moved almost automatically, in specified search patterns that conformed to regular timed intervals. The blinding beams not only swept the fifty-five-foot surveillance space between the perimeter fencing and the outer buildings, but also lit up the facades of those buildings.

Kent keenly noted something odd about the towers. They had been installed as an integral part of the perimeter fencing. The rows of barbed wire were nailed to the three outside supporting tower legs or posts, thus putting the corner ground spaces out of

31

view for anyone stationed above in the towers. Kent decided this illogical design might be to his advantage.

For several weeks, he had been studying every inch and aspect of his barracks. The only door was barred each night from the outside with two-by-fours. The lack of a second door at the other end of the barracks—in case of a fire, for example—reflected the government's total indifference to the safety of its prisoners. Obviously, escaping through the only door was out of the question. Kent knew that any surveillance, any exploring, any tinkering would have to be done long after "lights-out"—most likely after midnight. To the left of his bunk stood two empty bunks that extended out from the wall parallel to his. Behind the farthest one he discovered a waist-high window, almost totally hidden, one of only four in the entire building. It faced away from the nearest tower spotlight. The first time his eyes surreptitiously landed on it, Kent saw wood screws in rotting wood, securing the window lock. They would be no match for his Swiss Army knife's screwdriver blade.

One night, silently, slowly, when all the other men were asleep, he loosened the screws, so the keyed window lock could be rendered useless in a matter of seconds. Another night, long after midnight, he removed the window lock, slid the window up inch by inch, and, little by little, pried the heavy hardware cloth away from the window frame with the knife blade. The hardware cloth was not really cloth, but made of three-sixteenths wire mesh that was power-stapled to the wood frame. He left the top row of staples intact so the cloth would still hold and appear to be in place. On the night of his attempted escape all he would have to do was bend it out of his way. He wiped the perspiration from his brow when he was done and listened for any disturbance he might have caused, but all he heard was an asynchronous chorus of snoring and heavy breathing from the other prisoners.

He now had his initial escape plan. It took shape with a reasonable chance of not only survival, but also the promise of freedom. All he needed now was the right night to execute it—a moonless, starless night. Of course, that might even involve traveling in the rain or severe storms. The weakest link in his planning would come after the initial escape—navigating from the camp to the West, some three or four thousand miles or maybe more through unknown and unfriendly territory. He'd have to tackle that part as he encountered it. Early on, during an idle chat, Andrei had made a calculation that it might take some thirty-six hours by car to reach any western border of Russia, traveling at conventional speed limits. But at this point that information was of no use to Kent—he didn't have a car.

Even the best of plans come with unexpected hitches. It was his group's day for kitchen duty, and Pavel was given a paring knife to peel potatoes. As he peeled, he gruffly sang an old sea chanty. Annoyed by his raspy voice, one of the Russian undercooks shouted, "Shut up, you lowlife!" Pavel sang on. The undercook slapped him across the top of his head, knocking him off his stool onto the floor. The undercook turned and walked away. Pavel slowly rose from the floor, enraged, and ran at the undercook ready to plunge his paring knife into the man's kidneys.

Kent envisioned the outcome. Security would be tightened ruthlessly just before his planned escape, He decided to intervene. He grabbed the thrusting arm and brought it down harmlessly to Pavel's side. Then he stared directly into the frenzied guy's face and shook his own head, "No!" Pavel struggled for a few moments, but Kent held him tightly until the undercook was out of the room and out of sight, never knowing that he had been in mortal danger. In Kent's grip, Pavel eventually calmed down.

"Why did you stop me?" he whined.

"How long do you think you would have lived if you had stabbed him?"

"I don't know and I don't care," Pavel replied. "The bastard had it coming. He didn't have to hit me." He wrestled free of Kent's grip, returned to the toppled stool, and righted it, then picked up a spud and began peeling as though nothing had happened.

"You fool," said Kent. "I just saved your pitiful life."

Pavel looked up at him. "Thanks for nothing!"

Kent returned to the sink and the filthy stockpot he'd been scrubbing.

* * * *

Forty minutes later Kent felt a hand on his shoulder. He turned around to face a guard named Lev, one of the two sergeants who ran the kitchen.

"What's up?" he asked.

"I saw what you just did," whispered Lev. "I commend you for keeping the peace. And yes, you undoubtedly saved the man's life. I was about to shoot him."

What's with this guy? Kent wrinkled his brow. *Why is he complimenting me?*

"I see you are curious, nervous about my motive," declared Lev. "Don't worry. I'd like to ask a small favor of you."

"I'm a lowly prisoner," said Kent. "Not in any position to grant favors."

"My lieutenant wants to talk with you," said Lev.

"Now?"

"Yes, now!" said Lev, tossing him a towel.

Kent froze, wondering, *What the hell did I do wrong now?*

But Lev calmed him. "I told my lieutenant what you did here and he was impressed."

Kent wiped his hands and rolled down his sleeves as he followed the sergeant out of the kitchen to a small building near headquarters at the front of the camp. From the outside it looked as sterile as any of the other buildings. Lev led him up the steps to the lobby, knocked on the first door, and heard "Enter." Kent did a double-take. *This is an office? More like an apartment.* Unlike his own rough, neglected barracks, he discovered a decor almost sumptuous with traditional furnishings: a polished, uncluttered oak desk; wall-to-wall pearl-gray carpeting; and upholstered armchairs. The far end of the room opened to a sitting room and bedroom. The lieutenant, his uniformed collar unbuttoned, sat relaxed next to his desk in a velvety-gray wing chair facing a matching settee. Kent guessed him to be in his early fifties. His face narrowed to a receding chin. Clipped dark brown hair descended to a widow's peak. His eyelids were a bit hooded as if tired. The corners of his mouth drooped slightly, an overall appearance of disappointment. He looked up from his reading and motioned for Kent to sit on the settee. One manicured hand went to his chin as he studied the prisoner.

"You may leave us, Sergeant," said the lieutenant. "I'll call you when it's time to return him."

"Why am I here?" demanded Kent, speaking in Russian.

"I am Lieutenant Mikhail Reigozhin." He spoke in English.

"I know that," said Kent, switching to English. "But why am I here?"

"I would like to converse and practice my English language with you."

"May I ask why you would want to practice English?" asked Kent.

"My military career is limited, as I have been passed over several times for promotion. Even now, I've been relegated to a prison camp assignment. When my current tour of duty is finished, I would like to teach Western literature at one of our better universities."

"I see, but what does this have to do with me?"

"One, aside from Andreivich, you are the only prisoner who speaks English. And two, Sergeant Lev told me of your skillful handling of a situation in the kitchen this afternoon. Why did you save the undercook's life?"

"Life is hard enough here in camp without impulsive off-the-wall craziness," said Kent. "I didn't want to stir up more trouble."

"Exactly my point," said Mikhail. "You're not a trouble-maker. Now if you will agree, you will spend every third afternoon here in my office. Each time you have kitchen duty, Sergeant Lev will escort you here and we will talk literature."

"But literature is not my forte," said Kent.

"You have read books, no doubt?"

"Sure, lots of them, but I'm no authority on any of them."

"No matter. Then you and I have an arrangement?" asked Mikhail.

"I'm willing, sir, if you are," replied Kent.

"I've heard quite a lot about the American author Mark Twain. What do you know about him?"

"Well, for starters I can tell you about his most famous novels, *The Adventures of Tom Sawyer* and *The Adventures of Huckleberry Finn.*"

"Excellent!" Mikhail smiled. They spent the afternoon discussing Mark Twain, including his essays in *Roughing It.* Based on the success of their first session, more sessions followed: on J.D. Salinger's *Catcher in the Rye*; Harper Lee's *To Kill a Mockingbird*; and F. Scott Fitzgerald's *The Great Gatsby.* Kent began to enjoy these encounters. They reminded him of his carefree college days and, better yet, took him out of kitchen duty. The lieutenant even provided hot tea in a glass with milk, a cinnamon stick, and crescent cookies, and sent him back to the barracks with books from his own collection. Kent enjoyed reading them between sessions. Through these discussions, the two men got to know each other quite well. One might even say they had become friends, calling each other Miki and George.

One afternoon session took place on the very night Kent had planned for his escape. The lieutenant eagerly focused the entire discussion on Herman Melville: *Moby-Dick, or, The White Whale*; *Typee*; *Omoo*; and *Billy Budd, Foretopman.* Kent dared to suggest comparisons of Captain Billy's mutinous predicament and sympathetic feelings to his own imprisonment—and Miki's sympathetic feelings for him. Miki wasn't at all offended, but he stopped in the middle of a sentence and stared hard into Kent's eyes.

"You're planning an escape attempt, aren't you?"

Kent gasped and replied, "I don't know where you got such an idea, Miki."

"George, there's something different about you today. I just can't put my finger on it. As your friend I'd strongly advise against it. Even if you do manage to get outside the fence, the geography you'll face is just too menacing. You won't find any help out there either."

Kent shifted in his chair and chose his words carefully to suppress his alarm. "Miki, I won't lie to you. I've thought about it a lot. I still think about it. But I haven't got a workable exit, or resources, or the guts to tackle thousands of miles on foot with a posse out for blood on my tail. But I'll warn you now—all that could change somewhere down the road. So, my friend, are you going to turn me in for even thinking such things?"

"Of course not, George. You are entitled to have your dream, just as I am entitled to mine."

Chapter 8
Breakout?

Stunned and disturbed by Miki's astute perception, Kent shelved his scheme to escape that night. His training as an agent conjured up all kinds of implications. Should he take the lieutenant at his word? Or was Miki's literary friendship a ruse? Did he actually intend to tip off the guards? Or worse yet, did Miki plan to have him shot by a firing squad in front of all the other prisoners as an example of what happens when you plan to escape? To his relief, the lieutenant took no action. But Kent waited uneasily. What if Miki changed his mind and turned him in to further his own sorry static career? Would he receive a promotion for exposing an American spy? Kent could only hope that their bonding was stronger than Miki's sense of duty. He set his plan back in place and waited for the next time the cloud conditions were favorable— a heavily clouded, moonless night.

Kent never closed his eyes during the night he intended to escape. He lay in his bunk watching and listening for hours—until he heard enough snoring to convince himself the entire complement of prisoners was sound asleep. Kent slowly sat up. It was now or never. The rookie agent knew he would have to draw on his raw training to free himself from this blasted prison. Otherwise, he would shrivel up here and die. And nobody would know or care.

The rains of the past week had stopped that morning after exactly fifty-two days of his imprisonment. He assumed the ground had dried sufficiently, so he selected this very night for his escape. He waited just long enough for his eyes to become accustomed to the dark before swinging his feet onto the rough, grainy-plank flooring. Dressing quickly in prison garb, he emptied the precious items from his mattress cache into his pockets. He moved to his chosen window—behind the farthest empty bunk on the side of the building facing away from the nearest tower spotlight. According to plan, the already loosened wood screws securing the keyed window lock allowed him to render the window unlocked in a matter of seconds.

The escapee started to slide the window up, but hesitated, sensing someone standing close behind him. He turned around and found Pavel, the mentally deranged prisoner, hovering there in his underwear, staring him down. Wild-eyed, with dirty, tangled hair and beard, he didn't speak at all. Instead, his arms and hands jerked back and forth, trying to convey some sort of a message. As near as Kent could make out, Pavel wanted to accompany him on the escape and didn't care how he was dressed. Whispering, Kent tried to convince him to return to his bed before he woke the rest of the prisoners and killed his escape plan altogether. Pavel merely looked confused. As a last resort, Kent reached into his food-stash pocket, retrieved a large hunk of bread, and held it out to the distraught man. Pavel snatched it, stuffed the whole crust, a heel of a loaf, between his teeth and turned away. The gift seemed to satisfy him. He shuffled off and climbed back into his upper bunk.

Convinced the deranged prisoner posed no further threat, Kent turned his attention back to the unlocked window. He slid the lower half up to meet its top mate and pushed the hardware mesh out of his way. Head-first, he wormed and wriggled his six-foot-one body through the available space. With chin tucked against his chest, he curled his body into a somersault position and dropped five feet to the freshly hardened ground. *I made it! Nothing bruised or sprained.* Taking in gulps of air, he sprang to his feet and gazed for a few seconds into the moonless, starless night, trying to adjust his eyes to the unknown spaces beyond. *No time to lose.* He scurried some forty feet toward his target at the end of the building. In the murky dark he couldn't see the target, but knew it was there: a huge green trash dumpster. As he reached out, the solid cold steel object soon fell into his touch, and he dropped behind the safety of its bulk.

One wrong move would light up the entire camp and trigger the alarm system. He knew full well what the dreaded alarm would sound like as it revved up from a basso roar to a high-pitched soprano scream. He could only imagine what the punishment would be if he were caught. But the alarm hadn't sounded—yet. *So far, so good.* No one knew he was missing, except maybe Pavel.

In the next instant the entire world in front of him exploded into blazing spotlight beams. The light source, a powerful lamp mounted atop an open thirty-foot-high tower, slowly sharpened into a narrow beam, an oval spot that explored the ground floor of the exposed buildings. The well-defined spot quickly leaped to the left edge of the farthest building, then began to pan to the right, creeping over every facet and detail of the gray wooden surfaces. The beam flew to the left once more, moved to another set of windows, and panned across that naked building. Kent's chest ached as he held his breath. One more sweep would encompass the ground floor of his building and his dumpster. He couldn't move without giving away his position. The beam performed its patterned dance in the open space between the buildings and the perimeter fence, elongating farther as it neared the east-end fence tower.

With the seconds hand of his luminous Timex watch, he timed every leg of the beam's journey. After six exacting repeats, the fugitive figured he could risk being where the lamp was not. Picking out his next target, he fixed on a space between the tall vegetable garden rows, sheltering him from one tower, and the toolshed, sheltering him from the tower beyond it. Now he had to wait for the most opportune moment of the spotlight pattern to blend into the night. He had thirty-eight seconds to traverse this distance.

Loping through the shadows, he made it safely across with twelve seconds to spare.

The toolshed was padlocked shut, but again his preparation and fact-gathering paid off. Kent padded around the weathered woodshed and ducked into the space between the rear of the structure and the fence. In near darkness, with strong, practiced fingers, he palpated the wood where the rear boards met the ground until he found a gap created by complete rot. He shoved the fingers of his left hand through the gap, gripped one board and then the adjacent one, pulling them both outward to make a sizeable opening. Kneeling, Kent slipped inside and felt his way around in the dark until he had his hands on a shovel and rake. He pushed the tools through the opening in the shed, crawled out behind them, and reset the boards in place. Still gripping the tool handles, he knelt down behind the shed and started to count seconds. Soon he locked onto the full cycle of the search lamp's path once more.

His next target was the tower itself. He counted on the stupidly designed blind spot, where the guards could not see directly beneath their own tower. He had selected this particular tower because of its proximity to a wooded area behind the camp, and also because it was the western end of camp. Although the distance was slightly shorter this time, the guard would be more likely to hear any noise he made. But was that music coming from the tower? Most likely a radio keeping the guard company. At the opportune moment, Kent slipped out from behind the shack and started across the thirty feet toward the underbelly of the tower, hauling the shovel and rake with him. With one third of the distance still to go, the spotlight broke pattern and the beam headed downward in front of him as though it knew he was there. Kent dropped facedown, his body flat, leaving the garden tools on the ground next to him. He closed his eyes and tried to hug the lean space beneath him. *Dear God, not now!*

The beam crossed directly over his body, dallying there for seconds, totally revealing his presence—that is, if anyone had been looking down in that brief interval of time. He remained silent and immobile, expecting to hear the alarm pierce the night and awaken the entire camp. A rush of plan B thoughts raced through his mind—none of which had any chance of succeeding. The sweat beaded, rolled, and collected in his hairline, despite the cold night. Nearly a minute passed and still no alarm. *Is it some kind of miracle?*

Without warning, the beam skipped to a different building and began its random search for no one in particular. Whatever the guard's momentary distraction, he had returned to his routine.

Kent gave a quick gesture of thanks to the heavens above, sprang to his feet, and continued toward the base of the tower, dragging the long-handled tools with him. He wasn't a religious man, but he knew he'd been given another life. *They say a cat has nine lives—I wonder how many I have left.*

Kent reached the tower's underbelly and exhaled with relief. Thankfully, the radio music was much louder here. At the tower's supporting post farthest from the corner, he executed his next move. First, he fitted the rake spokes-up between the lowest barbed wire and the post. Using the handle as a lever, he pried the U-shaped nail securing the wire away from the wood. Next, he stepped on the wire and found enough slack to bring it to the ground. He raised the shovel blade three feet off the ground, took aim at slicing the wire, and lowered it like an axe with all the force he could muster. It made a single chopping sound. He froze. Minutes later, when no alarm sounded, he pulled the cleanly sliced wire section under the tower and out of the way. Kent pried the next U-shaped nail above it out, but he knew there wasn't enough slack to take it to the ground. So, using his handkerchief, he tied whatever slack he found in that wire to the wire above it. Now he had created a crawl hole at least eighteen inches high, enough for him to crawl through. After he abandoned the garden tools in the corner out of sight, he slithered through the hole, undid the handkerchief, and pocketed it. Leaving the white handkerchief might have drawn attention to his escape.

He stayed low and crawled, traversing the twenty-foot clearing from the fence to the nearest stand of trees. Kent scrambled to his feet on the dense side of the tree line and covered the ground as quickly and as silently as he could. He needed to distance himself from the camp before his escape was discovered—as it inevitably would be at the change of guard shifts.

A huge decision loomed. *But now what? Which direction should I take?* Kent had no idea where he was. In general, he wanted to head west, but the cloud cover only added to the darkness of the hour. So whatever blind distance he could manage became his immediate goal. A cluster of trees blocked his way here, another there, and hundreds more jostled his ability to travel in a straight line. At first, he tried to keep his back toward the camp's spotlights to give him an initial sense of direction. As he traveled deeper into the forest, the beams began to fade, then disappeared altogether. Now he faced the challenge of navigating by mere guesswork. He kept his eyes down to avoid stumbling over fallen branches, decaying shrubs, and twisted vines. Soon the fugitive slowed to a walk to conserve energy—and slogged all night. After the midsummer heat of the day, nighttime under the cool forest canopy felt almost welcome.

Hours later, he noticed that the trees were thinning, getting farther apart. The clouds started to scatter, and Kent welcomed the broken light afforded by a misshapen moon. Another two hours of trudging and he came upon an actual trail—a hiker's footpath. He decided to follow it. Even in the faint moonlight, his keen eyes detected something different. *Hey! Tracks of hoof marks—a horse bridle trail. Am I nearing civilization?*

Soon Kent stepped out into open fields and noticed a reddish glow over his right shoulder, an easterly indicator that he'd been heading in the right direction, west, all along. A glance at his watch revealed the actual time. 5:20 a.m. The red dawn of a new day and a reminder that the Obuchat Prison guards changed at 6 a.m. They would be out looking for him very soon.

A few minutes later, he came to a rail fence with a cross-rail gate. About a hundred yards away, the length of a football field, he gauged, he saw a complex of buildings. He'd been scrambling through rough terrain all night. Exhausted and fearful, he needed a few hours' rest, perhaps a bit of sleep, and then he'd be on his way again. The gate slid open easily. Cautiously as he approached, he identified a sprawling farmhouse with no interior lights on as yet; a red barn that might be doubling as a garage; a white stable with crisscross brown trim; and several other outbuildings. Approaching the farmhouse in prison garb was out of the question, but sharing some straw with a horse or other animals was not. He headed toward the stable.

Chapter 9
Stable-ized
The Same Day

Oddly enough, the stable door was unlocked, and Kent stepped inside. The open door allowed enough of dawn's light to see that the four stalls held three horses. Only one bothered to acknowledge him with a short whinny, then a snort. A ladder leading to a spacious loft looked awfully tempting. He climbed up, and at the top saw tightly packed bales of hay stacked on wooden pallets so air could circulate and the hay wouldn't rot sitting on the floor. He also saw a few loosely packed bales of straw. He dragged one of those off a stack and clawed it open. Spreading out the straw to make a bed of sorts, he sprawled out. After almost three hours of lightly guarded sleep, he awoke to the sound of a horse's hooves on the stable floor below. Naively feeling secure, he intended to remain in the hayloft during the daylight hours. No way would he risk being seen outdoors.

He heard boots scraping on the wooden rungs of the ladder. Kent leaped up, scurried to the far end of the loft, and ducked down behind stacked bales of hay. *Oh shit, I've come this far and now I'm about to be discovered.* Peeking out, he saw the upper half of a boy carrying a pitchfork, climbing up.

The lad continued up the ladder, stepped into the loft, and tossed his pitchfork onto the floor. Kent figured him to be a stablehand about eighteen. Clad in bib overalls with buckled straps over a long-sleeved shirt, the boy didn't bother to pick up his pitchfork. Instead, he stood at the top of the ladder, gazing down, and called out, "Have a nice ride, ma'am."

Kent heard the horse's hooves thudding on the clay stable floor. Soon the clop-clop of the hooves faded as the rider departed on the packed earth outside. The boy, rosy cheeked with tousled blond hair, turned, took a few steps, and sat down on a tightly packed bale for almost ten minutes before noticing the bale of straw that Kent had broken open.

Kent's heart thumped double-time, expecting the lad to begin an extensive search for whomever had disturbed the bale. Instead, the boy bounced over to the spread straw, pushed a large heap of it together to form a pillow, and flopped down on the comfortable bed he'd just made. With hands behind his head and knees bent and up, it seemed as if he planned to goof off, maybe even nap while the rider was away.

Kent realized he was trapped behind his chosen stack for now. *But hell,* he thought, *I can't continue my journey in daylight anyway, not wearing these prison clothes.* He knew the odds were against him and thought about possible scenarios. Even if the stablehand fell asleep, it would be far too risky to sneak around him to the ladder. And there was no way he could discern whether the lad was actually asleep or merely daydreaming. Kent couldn't allow himself to fall asleep either; if he snored, he would be a dead giveaway—with emphasis on dead.

A painful silent two hours passed. Kent's legs ached from crouching and shifting positions. He also kept nodding off and forcing himself to stay awake. Suddenly, he heard horse hooves and voices outside. The stablehand scrambled to his feet and opened a separate loft door. With his pitchfork, he shoved a bale of hay and another of straw over the edge to the floor below, then tossed the pitchfork down. That done, he bolted down the ladder before the sound of the rolling stable door was heard.

Kent inched silently toward the loft's open edge to observe

without being seen. He saw a handsome buxom woman in full riding habit sitting astride a roan quarter-horse. After a few quick exchanges, the woman began to scold the youth mercilessly. He remained respectful yet unmoved by her tongue lashing. When the woman left and shut the stable door behind her, Kent moved to a tiny triangular window near the peak of the loft ceiling. From there his eyes followed the woman as she walked to the farmhouse. At the height of day with a bright sun overhead, he had a better view of the imposing dwelling: two stories high, with an elegant stone façade on the first floor, and on the second, pristine white wood construction with two gabled roofs. Beyond the house were freshly painted outbuildings. The farmhouse looked pretty ritzy to him compared to most houses he'd seen during the armored bus trip through this region. *Probably someone important lives there*, he thought.

Kent's gaze drifted to the rear of the house, where a thin woman in a drab dress hung wash on the line. She wore a full white apron and a babushka tied under her chin. He saw sheets, pillow-cases, and nightshirts already on the clothesline, and now she hung a dress, ladies' blouses, two men's white dress shirts, a red and black checkered shirt with long sleeves, a pair of jeans, and a pair of black trousers. Kent began to wonder. *Would any of those things fit me? But wet clothes won't help much. I'll wait for them to dry, at least a little. But the longer I wait the more likely they'll be taken down and brought into the house.* He decided to compromise—wait two hours for them to dry and snatch a few slightly damp things off the line. Perversely, he wondered, *If they're well-off, rich even, wouldn't they have a dryer? Or was the power system too weak to accommodate one out here in the boonies?*

To entertain himself for the next two hours, Kent stole near the open loft edge to watch what he could see of the stablehand performing his mucking and feeding chores. It was reminiscent of a summer he spent on his Aunt Martha's horse breeding farm. That was the year he learned to ride. A shadow of sadness crossed his unshaven face. That was also the summer his mother died, and his father retreated into a shell of grief for several weeks, ignoring his two sons. His father recovered, but emerged a silent, humorless man.

Kent could only see so much from his vantage point without being discovered, but he could hear the boy at work, and remembered doing the same chores he did in Aunt Martha's horse barn. *Muck out the stalls. Dump the muck into a wheelbarrow and push it outside to a composting pit. Spread fresh straw on the stall floors. Break apart a bale of hay to feed the horses. Fill the horses' pans with feed mix and other pans with water.* He heard a door squeak open to what might have been the tack room.

The two-hour wait was almost up. *When is that freakin' kid gonna leave?* Almost as if the boy had sensed Kent's thought, he quickly washed up at the hose beside the stable, slid the door shut, and left. Kent rushed to the triangular window once more and watched the boy walk across the field to a cottage he assumed housed servants and farmhands. Kent decided, *It's now or never.* He'd been telling himself that a lot lately. His heart again quickened as he drew a mental picture of the path from the stable to the clotheslines. It was far from perfect, but he needed a new outfit in a hurry. He planned to hide behind the bedsheets while he actually pilfered the clothes. There was no telling whether someone might look out a second-story window at any unpredictable moment. It was a chance he had to take.

Kent left the safety of the stable and stole across the field, ducking behind a four-foot-high hedgerow, a wood fence, and some tall grasses. Finally at his target, he reached up, pinched open the wood clothespins, and swiped the checkered shirt and trousers off the line. He also moved some items from the end of the clothesline to the hole left by the ones he had swiped. That way, the woman in the babushka might not notice his theft right away. He was almost done when he heard a door slam nearby. Seconds later, he froze when he looked down and saw two feet facing him on the ground under the sheets. Whoever the feet belonged to, took some items off the next line over, turned to face the house, and walked out of view. More seconds passed, and he heard the door slam once more.

Kent slipped behind the last of four clotheslines that paralleled the rear of the house, and retraced his steps back to the stable, but much more slowly and carefully this time because of the momentary scare.

Once inside, he tried on the clothes. The trousers were baggy and two inches too short, ending above his ankles. *But who am I to complain?* The checked shirt, soft flannel, fit fine. Still damp, the outfit would have to do; it would dry when he walked in the late July sun. Because of the theft, he had to leave right away. That was the tradeoff—ridding himself of the telltale prison garb, but giving up a reasonably safe place to stay for a few days and nights.

Using the pitchfork, which Kent found in the tack and feed room, he hastily dug a shallow hole behind the stable and buried his prison clothes. When finished, he returned the pitchfork and checked his watch. 4:50 p.m. Gazing up, he noted the afternoon sun was still fairly high in the sky but leaning west. The fugitive walked away from the stable. He suddenly remembered the Horace Greeley expression "Go West, young man." And west he headed. Walking up a grassy knoll and down the other side to the end of the field, Kent encountered the property's rail fence, a span of it without a gate. Nimbly climbing over it, he came to a country road that went almost westerly. That was the road to be followed. Hearing a truck approach from the rear, his first instinct was to bolt into the cover of the lush fields beside the road, but he caught himself in time. He realized he needn't have worried now that he'd abandoned his prison garb. But it wasn't until he came across a small pond and chanced a look at his image in the clear, still water that he convinced himself of his genuine local appearance.

During his forty-eight hours in the armored bus to Camp Obuchat, and later during his chats with Andrei, Kent figured he had thousands of miles to travel over harsh and rough country. Here he was, starting out walking, but somehow he had to figure another way to get where he was going. Going? He had no idea of his actual destination, only a vague sense of direction. He had no means of secure communication—no way to contact a professional colleague for assistance.

Trucks, cars, and farm vehicles passed as he walked on the dirt-packed shoulder. At one point, a covered military pickup truck passed him. In the front seat he recognized two men as Obuchat prison guards. The truck reduced speed, appearing to peruse the pedestrians they passed on the opposite side of the road. Suddenly, it did a U-turn and pulled up about fifty yards behind him, near the shoulder where he was walking. The truck slowed. He could almost feel the guards' presence. *They must be giving me a thorough once-over.* He kept walking, never turning to face them. The hairs on the back of his neck stood up, filled with electricity, and he fought the urge to cut and run with every ounce of his determination. Suddenly, he heard the truck's engine rev up. He watched the truck's canvas-covered tail bed roar ahead and diminish with distance. With great relief, his breathing returning to normal, *Did I fool them? I must have.*

Nearly an hour later, with dusk settling over the sky, the same covered pickup reappeared, slowed down, and stopped across the road from him. Staring straight ahead, Kent continued to trudge past them, his peripheral vision telling him they were watching his every move. He heard the truck door creak open, and out of the periphery of one eye, saw two men with rifles drop out of the rear of the pickup. Luckily, this was the moment the fugitive encountered a man in coveralls walking toward him holding a scythe. Knowing the guards were coming, Kent abruptly stopped the farmer, if that's what he was, and engaged him in pleasantries with his best Russian, even resting one hand on the man's scythe handle and gesturing enthusiastically with the other. The guards were surely looking for him, but must have decided the two were locals passing the time of day, so they returned to their truck and sped off again to maintain their search for the seemingly invisible escapee. When the guards were out of sight, Kent patted the man on the back and continued on his way, chuckling a bit.

The farmer's grizzled face, full of curiosity, must have wondered, *Who was that nut and what did he want?*

Kent walked and walked, checking his watch. At last, his tired feet and growling stomach spoke to his mind. He needed shelter to rest and he needed to see where he was going. He had passed assorted farmhouses, a few clusters of peasant homes and businesses that might be construed as a village of sorts. Anything larger than a village needed to be avoided if possible. He needed to stop somewhere. *But in the dark, where?*

Chapter 10
The Malen'koye Kafe

He kept walking. Around seven that evening, he came upon one charming small home, yellow clapboard with a green roof and two dormer windows. As he passed it, he inhaled the alluring, salivating aroma of deep-fried *pirozhki* puffs. He spun around and walked back to look at the message board nailed next to the door. In carefully printed letters, he read: *"Pirozhki, Pelmeni, Kasha, Blini, Syrnikis, and Borscht."* Over the curtained glass door, a large sign in red and black letters announced the Malen'koye Kafe.

Despite the apparent risks, the famished escapee couldn't resist the aromas and soon found himself in a room with eight small tables, fully set with white cloths, plates, glasses, and silverware. A stout man with a thick mustache and rimless glasses sat at the table farthest from the door. He wore a uniform that Kent didn't recognize. As he worked his way across the room, the man's intense eyes seemed glued to his every movement. *There must be an alert out on me. To cut and run here would be just as bad as it was with the guards in the truck on the road.*

The portly man's jacket strained at the buttons, bulging above the table's edge. His matching dark-blue peaked cap, trimmed with gold braid and gold wings, lay on a far corner of the table. He seemed to be paying more attention to Kent than to the bowl of steaming red borscht in front of him. His spoon remained in the bowl while Kent, the new arrival, chose a table kitty-corner to the man. Kent sensed the hostile intensity of the man's stare and selected his table so the man would be forced to turn his head in order to keep observing him.

Kent had also positioned himself to keep a keen eye on the café's entrance and the six other tables. He forced himself to passively blend in rather than make a quick and telling departure. Exhaling deeply to calm down, he took note of the pine-paneled décor—ceiling, walls, and floor. The room's length extended to twice its width. Three small windows were adorned with red-trimmed white curtains. Instead of a door leading to the kitchen, several dozen strands of multicolored beads hung down from the top of the doorway.

A moment later, a sturdy young woman in a yellow apron pushed through the cascade of colored beads and approached the uniformed man's table. His expression turned from frown to smile as she delivered a round rye bread. He immediately tore off a large chunk and ripped it into smaller pieces, dropping them into his bowl of borscht. They exchanged a few words Kent could not hear. As she turned to leave, she noticed Kent seated almost squarely in front of her. She took out an order pad and pencil from her apron pocket and nodded to him.

He judged her to be about five-foot-eight and in her early twenties. As she looked down at him in a confident no-nonsense stance, he felt the closeness of her wide hips and the swelling of her bosom under her plain white peasant blouse. Looking up, a little embarrassed for staring, he immediately liked the charming face with its high, round cheekbones, and the ash-blonde straight hair falling carelessly to her shoulders. Her bare arms in short sleeves looked invitingly soft yet capable. She said something in Russian that he didn't understand, then cocked her head to one side and repeated it. He helplessly ignored her friendly greeting and ordered pirozhkis and coffee.

"I'm sorry, sir. We haven't any coffee. Only tea or beer. Oh, are you English?" This time he understood her Russian. He was about to fake it and say, "Yes," but she didn't wait for his reply. With a glint of humor in her gray-blue eyes, she said, "Ah, the American fugitive!"

Oh shit, she's already heard about me. They're on my trail. He started to rise from his chair, but she put a hand on his shoulder and said in perfect English, "You are okay in here. My mother is English and my father is Ukrainian. And I am Katcha."

"And I am Kent," he said, unsure why he'd used his real name. *Maybe the prison guards are looking for someone named George Thermon.*

A slurping sound erupted at the next table and the two turned to look over at the uniformed man. He'd taken the borscht bowl to his lips for a final slurp. They watched him swipe around his bowl with the last chunk of rye bread before depositing it in his mouth. As he chewed away, he wiped his chin with a napkin. He popped the uniform cap onto his bushy crop, dropped a few coins on the table, stood, and left the café without so much as a word.

"Does he know I'm an American?" Kent asked.

She smiled. "Uncle Yakim? Maybe, but I doubt it. Anyway, he's harmless."

"But the uniform," Kent protested. "Is he police?"

"Oh no," she giggled. "Yakim's a bus driver—my father's half-brother." She started to turn away.

"Where are you going?" Kent asked.

"If you want your pirozhkis, I have to tell Mama to put them in the oven." She slipped through the beads into the kitchen.

Soon he felt another pair of eyes bearing down on him, and sure enough, the beads were parted as an older face appeared at the opening for a few moments. Mama, he assumed.

Katcha returned and, this time, she sat down in the second chair at his table. It appeared to him she was settling in for a long chat. "Our television in the kitchen is tuned to the Carousel Television Channel. A report they keep repeating tells us of your escape, but they have no picture of you."

"They never took one, and it's just as well they didn't," said Kent. "They'd have my face plastered all over the country."

"Can you tell me what you did that was so bad they put you in that awful prison camp in the first place?"

"I'm a buyer for Ingleman's Department Store. A few days after I arrived, they arrested me for espionage. All I was doing was taking a few pictures like any tourist, but the police didn't approve of my subjects."

"You're a buyer for a department store?"

He reached into his pocket and retrieved his passport. Inside one of the pages he pulled out a business card and handed it to her.

After she read it, frown lines appeared on her forehead. "You just told me your name is Kent. This card says George Thermon. Is that the name on your passport, too?"

"Uh, yeah, but Kent is my real name."

Her eyes turned a steely blue. "If it really is Kent, then these are false papers—and you are an American spy!" Her voice had the ring of triumph.

Hell, it didn't take her long to nail me. "Are you going to turn me in?" He glanced around the room in case other diners had heard her, but thankfully, at that moment he was the only customer.

"No. Not unless you keep lying to me. Tell me who you really are."

Peasant be damned. She's got some worldly smarts. "My full name is Kent Peter Brukner, and yeah, I'm an American spy and I work for a U.S. intelligence organization. The Russian authorities caught me with my hand in the cookie jar."

A look of annoyance crossed her face. "Your hand in the cookie jar? What does that mean?"

"It's an American expression for doing something not quite on the up-and-up," he answered, then decided, *I might as well come clean.* "I happened to be in a military facility without authorization. I didn't harm anyone. They sent me to prison anyway. So I broke out and I'm trying to escape to the West. There. I've said it all. Now what?"

In spite of her better judgment, she felt a tug of warmth as she eyed him. *Nicely shaped lips that turn up at the corners as if always ready to smile. Or smirk. A big squarish head, gently sloping to a cute, unshaven chin. Thick sandy-brown eyebrows dominating, making his eyes look perhaps smaller than they actually are. Maybe an advantage in a spy so his thoughts can't be read easily.* The hint of a blush began to suffuse Katcha's cheeks. "I don't think you should be traveling anywhere while they're still actively looking for you. Maybe you should stay here for a few days until things calm down."

Kent's eyebrows shot up. "That sounds like an awful risky invitation. You'd be putting your family in great danger. Do you realize that?"

"Yes I do, but I'll talk it over with Mama. I'm sure she'll agree with me. Besides, who would ever think of searching the Malen'koye Kafe?" Katcha suddenly looked up to the ceiling and crossed herself.

"But where would I stay? You seem to have limited space to hide me."

"You could have my room, and I would move in with Mama for a couple nights," she replied.

"It's very kind of you and I appreciate the offer," answered Kent. "But what about your father? Won't he be put out?"

"Oh, no problem." Katcha shook her head so vigorously her straight hair flopped back and forth around her neck. "Things are very bad for Papa right now. He's in prison. He was arrested for speaking out. He has another three months to do before they'll let him come home."

"When did they arrest him?" Kent asked.

"Over a year ago," she replied. "It was an eighteen-month sentence for insulting a magistrate. Two men in uniform came and took him away—just like that! So unfair!" A sob caught in her voice.

A severe sentence for a few defiant words. Typical, he thought.

They heard a bell tinkle in the kitchen, and Katcha slid out of the chair to retrieve his meal. She returned with a plate of ten steaming-hot pastries, each oven-browned to a slight crisp. He cut into the first one and brought a forkful to his mouth. Stuffed with creamy potato paste, it tasted delicious, especially after nearly two months of prison food. Other pastries contained pork and beef and cabbage. He sipped local beer between his bites; beer she brought out for him because he hadn't made a choice.

Katcha sat with Kent and chatted nonstop while he ate, that is, until other diners entered the cafe. She left him to attend to them while he finished eating and drinking. When she came to clear his table, she told him to follow her. No one seemed to notice anything unusual about his movements as he slipped through the beads into the small kitchen. While Katcha deposited his dishes in the sink, he nodded at her mama, Mavis Dowd Kroschenko, and in return, received a big bear hug from her. She whispered, "Welcome!"

Kent saw where Katcha's attractiveness came from. The mother was a few pounds heavier and a slightly shorter version of her daughter, except for the facial lines that come with aging and prolonged kitchen work. Also, her ash-blonde hair had been cut shorter and clung to her head in a bob. He judged her to be in her mid-fifties.

He told Mavis, "I accept your hospitality on one condition—that you let me help out in the kitchen while I am here. But why are you both being so generous to me?"

She murmured, "Perhaps in time I will give you my answer." In a more normal voice, "Katcha will show you to your room. And yes, you can help me here in the kitchen."

Kent followed Katcha into a small hallway by the back door and up a narrow staircase to a second floor with sloped ceilings—two bedrooms and a bath. The bedroom at the rear of the house had a feminine look and smell to it. Katcha's room, he rightly assumed. This would be where he'd be staying for the next few days. Katcha left him there and returned to her waitressing duties downstairs. He sat down in a cushioned rocking chair and looked through a bunch of Russian movie magazines to entertain himself. He could hear all the kitchen activity, including voices through the thin uncarpeted flooring. He didn't quite know why, but for the first time since the escape, he felt safe. When Kent got bored, he tried the comfort of the bed. He kicked off his shoes, stretched out, and sank into a sea of softness. He couldn't fight off sleep any longer, and finally surrendered to it.

The guest awoke the next morning refreshed and found breakfast waiting for him at a tiny table in the kitchen. Mavis thought the less he appeared in public the safer it would be for all of them. A new face in the village would be news, news that might reach the authorities. As he had promised, he began his kitchen duty and was quickly indoctrinated into potato peeling, onion chopping, and dishwashing. When the last of the patrons had left in the evening, he helped Katcha turn chairs upside-down on the tables so the floors could be swept and mopped, which he volunteered to do.

Although cramped, the little kitchen had an air of efficiency. Huge pots and frying pans hung from hooks on the wall. The oak counters doubled as chopping blocks. Mama, daughter, and Kent bumped into each other frequently. However, when Katcha and Kent brushed together, they lingered a bit, smiling.

On the third day, Katcha pecked him on the cheek. but when he tried to respond, she coquettishly slipped away. On the fourth day, he again tried to kiss her on the cheek. This time she turned to him and their lips met for something more lasting—always out of Mama's viewing, or so they naively thought. From then on, their familiarity grew with customary kissing, morning and night, as well as tender embraces. Then on the eighth night, Kent climbed into bed and fell fast asleep. Hours later he awoke, sensing someone in the room—no, closer than that—actually in bed with him. He slowly turned over to find that Katcha had preferred her own bed after all and that surely included him as well. She lay asleep on top of the covers, facing away in a filmy nightshift. A crocheted afghan she had wrapped around herself to shield her from the cold night had slipped down to her knees.

Although Kent became aroused, he tried not to disturb her sleep. He fitted his broad, muscular body to the back of her form. At first touch, she intuitively backed into him, but continued to sleep anyway. He pulled the afghan up over the two of them. Some time later, during that inevitable moment, they both found their joyous undercover union. A deeper sleep consumed the rest of that special night.

Daylight seeped in through the round dormer window at the peak of the house. It was almost seven before Kent realized where he was. He found that he was alone in bed. Katcha had gone downstairs to help her mother prepare for the first meal of the day. But the feeling of warmth and contentment as he awoke was now replaced by anxiety. They'd made love without any protection. He had no condoms with him. Why would he? Several thoughts rattled around inside his mind. *Is she on The Pill? Do they even have The Pill in Russia? What if she isn't on it and gets pregnant? American spies who stupidly get involved in sexual liaisons are vulnerable to blackmail. It's happened.* As he dressed and made his way downstairs, he worked at pushing the negative thoughts away.

Mavis had prepared a plateful of *syrnika*, pancakes filled with cottage cheese, for his breakfast. Afterward, she put him to work peeling potatoes. When the last of the breakfast customers had gone, she left the kitchen to do the laundry, and Kent tackled the dishes with Katcha doing the drying. Each time she looked at him she broke out in a smile, even a girlish giggle here and there. Half an hour later, suddenly, they heard a series of tumbling thuds followed by an extended shriek.

"It sounded like Mama," cried Katcha.

"It came from outside," added Kent. "Outside the back door."

The two ran to the rear door and threw it open. Mavis lay sprawled on the ground at the bottom of five steps. Her left foot was still on the last step. Her face had turned a pasty white, her eyes were squeezed shut, and she moaned from the pain. The laundry basket lay a few feet away with the load half emptied, strewn on the walk.

"Mama, where are you hurt? What happened?"

"My ankle," she whimpered.

As Mavis pulled her foot off the step, it dropped to the ground and she let out another shriek. Kent knelt down next to her and tested the ankle with several slow, tiny movements.

"Katcha, I can demobilize the ankle with a pair of dish towels," he said.

Katcha ran inside and reappeared a few minutes later with two thin towels. Kent first tied them together to make one longer one. Then he wrapped it around the instep, crossing to wrap it around the ankle as well, pulling the foot tightly upward to an immobile position. There he tied a knot with the towel ends.

He tested it again. "How does that feel?"

"It still hurts like hell!" sobbed Mama.

He put one arm under her legs and another under the small of her back, lifted her clumsily off the ground, and started up the steps with her. She was even heavier than he expected. Katcha held the door until he brought Mama inside and set her in a chair near the stairs.

"Mama, how did it happen?" asked Katcha.

"With the basket in front of me, I couldn't see the step, so I didn't come down on it squarely."

"Mavis, I think we're dealing with a sprain here," said Kent, "and unless you want to see a doctor, we have to put you in bed for a day or two or more."

"No doctor," she snapped.

"Mavis, how are you at hopping?" asked Kent.

She stood on one leg, hopped toward the stairwell, and then grabbed the staircase railing. "How's that?" she asked.

"Great! Now put your arm around my shoulder, While you hop each step, I'll help with the power lifting."

Step by step Mavis and Kent made it up the stairs into her

bedroom, and Kent laid her on the bed. Katcha took over from there. As Kent left the room, Mavis cried out:

"Who'll do the cooking?"

"Now, Mama, don't be upset. I'll do the cooking," said Katcha.

"Then there's no one to do the serving," protested Mavis. "You can't handle both. It's impossible."

Kent came to their rescue. "Since I can't mingle with the patrons, I can try to do the cooking. I've had some experience as a short-order cook in college. Mavis, you can supervise from here until your ankle heals. I can certainly do all the prep work and I've watched you working with the pastry dough. And when Katcha's not busy serving, she can lend a hand."

"See, Mama, we have it all worked out."

"I guess I don't have any choice then," said Mavis. "You two are in charge of my kitchen."

Despite a few minor spills, a burnt batch of twenty-four pirozhki, and a cut finger, "Chef" Kent managed the kitchen quite well during Mavis's debility. And, two days later, he devised a make-shift crutch for her: an upside-down broom cushioned with a towel strapped around the straw. Mama managed the staircase twice a day—once down and once back up. Kent's master-chef career ended after four long days, and the little café returned to normal.

Chapter 11
Quid Pro Quo

Another week passed and Mavis observed the silly antics and warmth the two young ones radiated. *I don't know if I like the looks of this,* she thought. *What's really going on? Perhaps I can turn this to my advantage.* At nine o'clock that evening, Katcha's door was still open. Mavis marched in and found her daughter and Kent fully dressed, sitting on the edge of the bed, chatting. Mavis walked over to the rocker opposite them and sat down.

"I think the time has come to have a serious talk with you two," she said.

"Oh, Mama," Katcha blurted out. "We're both grownups. Besides, I'm on The Pill. You got me the prescription, don't you remember?"

"Yes," her mother replied, "but I didn't know whether you were actually taking it. I'm glad to know. My dear, I have something else on my mind."

"What then?" asked Katcha.

Mavis fixed her anxious eyes on the young man, the guest who has been so kind and helpful to them. "Kent, exactly what do you do for a living?"

"You already know what I do, Mavis. I'm a professional spy—a mighty risky business, I might add."

"You can't plan on being a spy all your life, can you? What do you plan to do when spying is all done?"

He hesitated, knowing this conversation would come up eventually, like in old movies when the father would sternly ask the young man about his intentions.

"I'll probably go back to the States and finish law school at Iowa State University—maybe contract law."

"What has this got to do with anything?" asked Katcha, her voice tremulous.

"Katcha, dear, I do believe the time is nearing when Kent will want to be on his way. Am I right, Kent, or are you planning to make a life here in Russia?"

"Well, Mavis, the hunt for my ass will die down soon—at least, I assume so, and it will be safer for me to be on my way. I can't stay in Russia. I'd spend my whole life looking over my shoulder, expecting to be arrested again."

"Have you thought at all about what will happen to our Katcha?"

"I assume she's had as much fun as I have," he said. "She was always the aggressive one, and I swear I made no promises to her. Isn't that true, Katcha?"

"That was certainly true at first," she whimpered, "but after a while, I thought we had a lot more going for us. I thought we'd have a more permanent arrangement."

Kent's eyes narrowed and he pressed his lips together before responding, as if to harden his position. "Look, I'm certainly grateful for all you both have done for me, but did you really think I was going to make a life here? Or maybe you thought I was going to take Katcha and you with me on the long journey home."

"A travel companion *would* lower your risk considerably," offered Mavis.

"What do you mean, *companion?*"

"Just that a young couple traveling together would attract far less attention than a lone man like the one they're looking for."

"Then you expect me to marry her," he said. "Perhaps I

would have under different circumstances."

"As a mother, I can only hope for marriage, but I cannot demand it," she said. "In any case, I do want you to take Katcha to live in the Free World. I gave up so much to marry her Papa. Now I want her to have what I gave up."

"Mama...."

"No, I want to tell you both a little story, my love story. How I met your papa and came to live here twenty-eight-years ago. I was Mavis Anne Dowd, a naïve, trusting nineteen-year-old stenographer from York, England. My parents had both passed away within a year of each other, and I had no siblings. All I had in this world were two close friends and my work at Grantham Machine and Foundry Works Limited. In the spring of 1963 I attended a two-week farm-machinery seminar in Paris with my boss."

She paused to button up her wool cardigan in the chilly house. "On my second night in the hotel dining room, I was expecting to eat supper alone, when the maître d' came up to me and asked me, 'Mademoiselle, we have a shortage of tables tonight. Would you be willing to share your table with this gentleman?' Standing with him was a handsome, rugged young man. In English, I said, 'Yes, that will be fine.'

"The gentleman sat down across from me and struck up a polite conversation. 'I am called Oleksander Kroschenko. You may call me Olexi. I would like very much to practice my English skills, if you don't mind.' He was a farm-machinery salesman for a manufacturing firm called Oksana Limited. It turned out we were attending the same two-week seminar. Well, by the end of dinner he was so charming he captivated me. For the remainder of the seminar, our evenings were his to romance me, sweeping me away."

Mama's eyes reflected tender memory tinged with sadness. "I fell in love. In less than two weeks, he talked me into marrying him and returning to Russia with him. Yes, I was in love, but I was only nineteen and quite naïve. I had no idea what I was giving up, nor what I was getting into. I still love your father, and had I not married him, I would not have had you, my dear. I have lived with my own marriage decisions with little regret, but I want so much more for you, sweetheart."

"Oh, Mama," Katcha sputtered, "I don't want to leave you. Who will help in the café?"

Mavis looked sternly at her daughter. "I'll hire someone, but you must make your own choice—if not for love, perhaps for a better life."

Oh my God. This conversation hit Kent like a punch in the solar plexus. A heavy silence hung over the room for the next several minutes. Mother and daughter stared at him, awaiting some verbal reaction.

"I realize you're expecting me to marry her." His voice was low and flat.

"I cannot force it," said Mama. "But I know the two of you are already intimate. I can almost feel the magic in your bonding. In any case, that is a decision to be made by the two of you. And Kent, just so you know, I would be proud to have you as a son-in-law."

"Thank you. I'm extremely fond of Katcha, and if it leads to marriage, so be it. But our relationship is new. I have no idea what our long-term feelings will be. For now, I want to continue to explore those feelings." His voice took on a hard edge. "But I'm being put in a terrible position. I would be more than willing to take her with me, but the way I plan to travel is not just uncertain, it's downright dangerous. They're looking for George Thermon, so my travel papers are no good anymore. We might even have to steal a ride on a freight train or thumb rides along the open road. Under the best of conditions there's still a huge risk for her. I'm an enemy of the state. If she's discovered abetting my escape, or even traveling with me, she's in for big, big trouble."

"Yes," said Mavis. "I know you will face hardship, uncertainty, and risk, so I will help you all I can—on one condition. Take Katcha with you, protect her, and see that she has a good life. I ask no more than that."

Kent's voice rose in exasperation. "You ask no more than

that? That's exactly what I told you I cannot promise. So how can you help us?"

"Did I just hear you say you were going to travel freight class to the West?"

"I'm listening," said Kent.

"Why not pay for a ticket and ride to St. Petersburg in style?"

"I can think of several reasons why not," he returned. "One, I have no papers. Two, I have no idea how much it will cost. Three, I'm not sure I want to reveal my face to the authorities. Four, it sounds pretty damned risky to me."

"Suppose there *is* a remedy for each of your concerns?" Mama asked.

"I'm still listening."

"You can use Papa's papers," she said. "They took him away without them. He had been working out in the yard in his overalls when the local police arrested him. His papers and passport are still on top of our dresser."

"But I don't even know what your husband looks like. And I can't believe I could pass for him in any event," Kent protested.

"A week of not shaving your upper lip, you'll have his mustache," said Mavis. "In one of his business suits, an overcoat, glasses and a hat pulled down, you could easily pass for him."

"You really think so?" asked Kent.

"I think so," interjected Katcha. "Besides, you said the authorities have no pictures of you."

"That's true, but what will your father do without papers when he comes home?" asked Kent. "And what will he do without all his clothes?"

"If challenged, he'll claim the authorities never gave the papers back to him—they must have lost them," said Mavis. "Otherwise, you can mail them back to us after you're settled. And his clothes and glasses, too."

"Another thing," Kent said, "if we're challenged along the way, won't the authorities know that the real Oleksander Kroschenko is in jail? Where will that leave us?"

"You don't have to worry about that. It was a local thing," said Mavis. "The night before he was arrested, Olexi spoke his mind for the outlawed opposition party at a local political rally. He had the courage to speak out what most of them were really thinking. That night authorities booed him, ostracized him, labeled him a radical, and arrested him the next day. The rally was all local and most of the other men there were his lifelong friends—men he drank with at the local pub. Now they even visit him in the jail and play chess with him there. Once you and Katcha are on your way and out of the region, no one will have any knowledge of Papa's misdemeanor arrest."

"Are you sure?" Kent asked. "Our lives depend on it."

"As sure as anyone can be," said Mavis. "Your travel permit will show that you will be traveling as father and daughter. Katcha has her own papers."

"It seems you have thought all this out thoroughly," he said.

"Kent, when you first asked why we were being so generous, I told you that, over time, you might judge me differently. Well, in exchange for our generosity, you will take Katcha to the West and freedom."

"Ah, the *quid pro quo*," he said.

"I'm not sure what that is," said Katcha.

"In Latin it means something for something else," said Mavis.

"A proposed exchange of items or services supposedly of equal value," clarified Kent. "Katcha will get shelter and board and a means to travel with me."

"Then you agree?" asked Mavis.

"How could I refuse?" he said. "By the way, do you have any maps?"

Katcha went to her bookcase and returned with an atlas. She turned to a page covering the part of Russia where they lived. "There," she said, pointing to a spot in the middle of the page. He marked an X on the spot with a pencil.

"What's the name of your village?" he asked.

"It's too small to have a name," she answered.

"Do you own any vehicles?" he asked.

"Papa has a car out back," she replied, "but it hardly has any petrol left and you would have to refuel many times over that distance. Besides, you would be stopped on the major highways."

"Any other way to get from here to St. Petersburg?" he asked.

"Mama and I have bicycles," Katcha offered.

"It would take weeks, maybe months to get there," he said.

"And you'd probably get lost," Mavis added. "The major highways are well marked, but the byways have *usinsk*, street names that change between cities and towns."

"That leaves air and rail," Kent said, "and air travel requires too much scrutiny."

"That leaves just rail," said Katcha. "And we will have papers to go by rail."

"Tell me, where is the nearest railroad station from here?"

"Pechora," Mavis said. "Just a few towns north of here."

"Does Papa's car have enough gas for a round trip to Pechora and back?"

"No, Kent, but I can afford to buy a few liters for you."

"I can pay my way," he said.

"I understand," said Mama. "I will drive you both to Pechora, where Katcha will buy the tickets. I'm glad we've kept you with us the extra two weeks. I doubt that the police are still actively looking for you. Oh, and another thing, I think we all should be speaking Russian from now on. You'll need to practice the language in case you're questioned. You'll be traveling as a local from now on."

Chapter 12
The Journey Begins

At the end of the third week, Mama brought out her husband's passport and travel papers for Kent. Oleksander Kroschenko, age forty-seven, six-foot-one, worked as a traveling salesman for Oksana Limited, an agricultural machinery manufacturing firm. His official photo depicted a man with thinning brown hair, intense dark eyes, a clipped mustache, and rimless glasses. A handwritten note on one of the pages mentioned his wife, the former Mavis Dowd, a British national. Kent felt only vaguely confident that Olexi's passport picture would pass for him, so he began to acquire his own mustache in earnest. Each day, he dallied in front of Katcha's mirror to see if he looked any more like the Olexi in her parents' wedding picture on Mavis's dresser. He spent most of his idle time polishing up on his Russian language skills. Now he would have to pass for one of the locals. He not only had to convey basic meaning, but subtle tones and accents as well.

* * * *

Several times each week, during the midafternoon café lull, Mavis disappeared for a few hours and visited with her husband at the local jail. The attractive, flirtatious café owner was so well-known there that she was permitted to visit Olexi inside his cell. She brought him treats, and when the lone jailer knew enough to turn away, conjugal pleasures as well. A few times each month Katcha accompanied her there for a family reunion. In all her recent visits Mavis had not told her husband about Kent and the plan to escape to the West. She feared he would strongly disapprove and might even intervene.

As the day of departure approached, Mavis thought it important that Katcha come with her to see her father—to break the painful news. She would let her daughter explain why she was leaving and that, in all probability, he would never see her again. The joy of their greeting soon turned into the agony of loss. By the time mother and daughter left the jail, all three of them were in tears. Papa cried for days afterward, and when his jailer sought the reason, Papa kept their secret.

The two travelers packed light: only one suitcase and one backpack each. Mavis had altered more of Papa's clothing so they would appear tailored to truly belong to Kent. He stuffed Papa's shaving kit, several pertinent pages from the atlas, and a compass into his backpack. Katcha packed nonperishable snacks and a first-aid kit. The day before leaving, they stowed the luggage in the boot of Papa's car.

Mavis approached her daughter with her hands cupped around a glass jar. "You will be needing money for the trip, and I have a little savings that your papa doesn't know anything about." She reached into the jar and withdrew a fistful of ruble notes. "I haven't counted it, but it may help you along the way." Choking back sobs, Katcha whispered, "Thank you, Mama," and they silently embraced.

Finally, the chosen day arrived, and the three piled into Papa's AvtoVaz Lada, a 1989 sedan. A few miles out of the village they picked up Reca-Izhma Road forty kilometers east-southeast of the town of Ukhta. As they cruised through miles of countryside dotted with lavender and poppies, a subdued Katcha noted a small pasture with a single grazing cow. It struck a chord of sadness for her. Departure meant permanent family separation and loneliness for both mother and daughter.

Mavis drove past villages of sparse dwellings with small vegetable gardens and chickens scurrying about. The longer they drove, the more it reminded her of Katcha's uncertain future. *Have I done the right thing for her or have I sent her into danger?* "I don't know about you two," Mavis said, "but I've been driving for six hours now and I need a lunch break! It's already 2:15."

"Me too," said Katcha. "We just passed a nice little café in that last block. Why don't you circle around this block and park out front?"

"Sounds good to me," said Kent. "And no one knows us here either."

Mavis made four left turns and pulled to a stop in front of the Malen'kie Kafe. One look at the sign outside and Katcha commented on how close the name was to their own café. Inside, the layout positioned a counter service in the middle and table service in rooms on either side of the counter. They seated themselves at a table in the room to their right. A friendly waitress promptly took their orders; they wolfed down roast pork dumplings, a specialty of the house, and drank weak beer.

When they got up to leave, Kent went to the cashier to pay for their meal. He happened to glance into the opposite dining room and his stomach lurched. He saw a familiar face seated at one of the tables. Pavel, the crazy inmate from the prison camp, was in leg irons and accompanied by two camp guards facing away from Kent. A hint of recognition crossed Pavel's haggard, unshaven face. Kent spun around. *The crazy fool hasn't squealed on me yet,* he thought, as he hastily paid the bill and hurried out the door to join the others. *But will he spoil everything and raise the alarm on me? He must have followed me out of camp and escaped to the south. And somehow, they caught up with him. Oh God, what now?*

Kent jumped into the car and said, "Let's get away from here in a hurry."

"What's wrong?" asked Mavis as she released the hand brake, hit the accelerator, and pulled onto the road.

"Someone recognized me in there, but I can't tell if he'll

turn me in."

"Who was it?" asked Katcha.

"An escaped prisoner with the two guards who caught him. Problem is, the prisoner recognized me. I don't know if I can trust him. The night I was about to escape from the barracks, he begged me to take him along. He's crazy, one bad hombre. We need to get out of here."

Mavis revved up to the speed limit until they encountered the modest city of Pechora, "cave" in Ukrainian. The former site of an infamous gulag under Stalin, an endearing tiny church now stood there as a memorial. On the road beside the Pechora River, birch trees lined the shore; simple barges churned along carrying their cargo. At last, they came to a wide, gray, concrete building, the Pechora rail station. Mavis pulled up to the steps. The travelers retrieved their luggage and Papa's briefcase from the trunk. Mavis and Katcha hugged and kissed and whispered for several minutes before separating for what might be the final time. Kent hugged and thanked Mavis quickly, took Katcha by the arm, and mounted the eight stone steps into the station entrance.

Kent handed one of his 50,000-ruble notes to Katcha and followed her to the ticket window, where she negotiated for two *platskart*, third-class tickets to St. Petersburg. The ticket seller, an elderly, unsmiling woman with a brisk manner, informed her, "You have two choices. One, most trains go directly to Moscow. You would have to transfer there for a train to St. Petersburg. Or you can get off in the city of Kotlas. You can transfer to a bus there and get to St. Petersburg six hours faster and a whole lot cheaper." She slid a pamphlet under the grated window containing train and bus schedules.

Kent noted a surveillance camera mounted above the window cage, pointed directly at the first person in line. He pulled Papa's gray leather peaked cap down on his forehead to just above his eyebrows, grateful that Mavis had thought to include the cap with Papa's clothes.

Quickly scanning the schedules, Katcha turned to Kent

and whispered, "Why don't we do what she recommends? Take the train west as far as Kotlas, then catch a bus to St. Petersburg."

Kent looked down at her with a trusting fondness. "You're absolutely right, sweets. Transferring in Moscow to get to St. Petersburg would give me the creeps. More camera exposure. And I'm well known in Moscow. It's too risky."

"We'll take the train and bus option," she told the ticket seller.

After perusing their papers and checking their faces against the photos, the no-nonsense clerk issued their open-seat, open-passage tickets.

Katcha noted, "Kent, there's a 7:10 p.m. train leaving in forty-five minutes."

"That's the Red Eye. Is there another one after that?" he asked.

"Red eye, what's that?"

"In the States it's the overnight travel," he replied.

"But why wait?" she asked.

"The camera planted up there," he pointed. "If they somehow recognize me, they'll assume I took the first train west."

"I thought you said they didn't have any pictures of you," she returned.

"No photographs, but there has to be some kind of artist's sketch available by now. It can't be a very good one—unless one of the prisoners won some favors by describing me."

"The next train only goes to Moscow," Katcha read. "That's two hours and ten minutes from now. Or we could wait 'til morning. There's one leaving at 8:32 a.m., but it's a much longer trip. It goes to Moscow first."

"Even so, maybe we should wait for the morning train and get off at Kotlas," said Kent.

"Whatever you think best," agreed Katcha. "But where will we spend the night?"

"That wooden bench way over there in the corner doesn't look too bad," said Kent. "It's off the beaten path, and I suppose one wooden bed is no harder than another. Why don't you go buy two cups of hot tea, and I'll reserve that bench for us."

Kent rested Papa's briefcase atop one of their suitcases and pulled both carry-on overnighters on their wheels over to the bench. He parked the bags on the floor next to him and sat down. Katcha soon returned with the hot tea and nuzzled close to him. From their vantage point, the busy station became less active with each departing train until all activity seemed to cease. Some of the overhead lighting was turned off and, in their dark corner, it appeared that a daughter had snuggled up close to her dad for warmth. It was a nervous night's sleep for the both of them—sleep broken by long stretches of wondering about their future. It was the first night of a long, dangerous journey.

Kent and Katcha awoke to the station's morning hustle-bustle, and they each scarfed down one of the ham and cheese sandwiches Mavis had packed for them. Stopping at the restrooms first, they followed the signs and made their way to the boarding platform for the morning westbound train, already in and waiting. They had to walk to the far end, where the third-class passengers boarded the *platskart* cars. *For the riffraff,* Kent thought wryly. *That sure as hell is us, for now, anyway.*

Before allowing them to board, a woman official wearing a round blue hat with two red stripes checked their tickets and passports. She lingered over them for some time—studying Kent's picture, looking up to scrutinize his features, and sensing the obvious age difference. The man in the photograph seemed much older than the man standing in front of her.

Katcha tried not to squirm. *What's the woman going to do to us?*

Kent held his breath. *Are we in deep shit? What-in-hell alternative can we come up with?*

Chapter 13
The Train to Kotlas
Tuesday, August 18

Kent tried to figure out an escape route without appearing obvious, but his head hammered with dire thoughts. *What if the woman denies our boarding? I can't just run. I've got Katcha to think about now. Is this going to be a routine scare, challenging our papers every time?* Just when he thought the worst, another female passenger burst through the line, elbowed her way ahead of Katcha, and loudly interrupted the official with a question. The angered official gave a curt reply and dispatched the rude woman to the end of the line. Turning back to Kent, she hesitated, then waved them through.

They mounted the three steel steps to the nearly empty train carriage. Kent led the way to the far end, where they deposited their luggage on shelves in a small compartment. In view of the fifteen-hour journey across the *Russkaya Ravina,* Russia's European plain, many of the rows had been made up as berths for sleeping, with one bed above the window and another, a converted table, below. The rest of the carriage had ordinary rows of double seats on both sides of the aisle. Some of these were set facing each other with a tiny table in between. Kent deliberately chose a pair of those seats, the ones closest to both the luggage compartment and the exit, in case they had to make a quick retreat. He still wasn't comfortable riding in public like he actually belonged.

Kent nudged Katcha into the window seat. He chose his seat facing her, so he could maintain a commanding view of the entire carriage aisle. They sat for about ten minutes waiting for the rest of the passengers to board. He scrutinized each one as a potential threat. When the stream of passengers dwindled, it appeared their carriage would leave Pechora only a third full. Another five minutes passed. The train didn't move. A blast from the steam locomotive, followed by the conductor's whistle, signaled that they would be on their way. But no. The train stood still at attention. Outside, a flurry of sharp police whistles pierced the air. On the platform, a group of policemen were running alongside the carriage. Two of the uniforms boarded on the exit end of the carriage and started past the luggage compartment.

Katcha and Kent froze. He gripped her hand tightly under the table, ready for them to make a run for it together. Then he realized, *Hell, I have to escape alone to protect her at all cost.* But the two policemen hurried past them, apparently seeking another target. The two uniforms stopped two-thirds of the way down the aisle and yanked an elderly man out of his seat. Decently dressed in an overcoat and fedora, he struggled at first, moaning and protesting his innocence, but succumbed after a nasty slap to the cheek by one of the policemen. They half-dragged, half-walked him back up the aisle toward the exit. When the poor man passed by, he regarded Katcha with the saddest of faces. Since Kent no longer had on Papa's cap, he had to look down and away as they passed. On the platform other uniforms regrouped to haul the victim away for an uncertain and unpromising fate.

"I wonder what will happen to him—he looked at me so forlorn and pleading," said Katcha. "But what could I do?"

"Whatever his fate, we sure can't help him," murmured Kent. "We have enough trouble helping ourselves."

The locomotive belched its basso whistle; the conductor's soprano whistle responded. After a clamor of bumping and jarring, the train lurched forward, chugging to a belabored beat at first, then a rhythmic pulsing as it gathered speed. Once the city of Pechora had slipped out of sight, the foothills of the Urals followed suit. Landscapes of deserted plains flew by. For the two travelers, boredom eventually lashed out its tentacles and grabbed hold. Katcha reached into her father's briefcase and retrieved several Russian screen magazines, soon absorbing herself in the scandals and successes of the famous. Kent tried to read one of the magazines, but there were too many special words he didn't understand—neither the meaning nor the associated nuance. He gave up and resorted to admiring the scantily dressed, full-bosomed actresses and singers.

Early in the afternoon, he looked at his watch. Just 1:30—only five hours spent, ten hours to go. Standing up, he stretched out his arms and legs in place, then paced the dozen steps to the luggage area and back several times, not wanting to walk the whole long aisle and chance someone recognizing him.

Leaning over Katcha's shoulder, he asked, "Are you hungry?"

She looked up from her reading and nodded. Kent made another trip to the baggage shelf, and extracted two of Mama's sandwiches from Katcha's backpack. He returned to their seats, and the two gingerly unwrapped the pot roast sandwiches, the thick slices of bread now soggy with gravy and onions, and munched them in silence. Conversation became challenging after a while. Each made several trips to the water fountain and lavatory in the near end of the next carriage.

Kent decided to examine what Mama and Katcha had stowed in Papa's briefcase in case some bullying authority decided to snoop. *I'd better make myself a knowledgeable farm machinery salesman.* He found company product brochures, parts lists, order blanks, instruction pamphlets, and sales swag: lined writing pads, ballpoint pens, and key chains, all bearing the company name. The brochures and pamphlets provided worthwhile reading material for him; some of the product descriptions were actually in English. The information he garnered would prove useful if his knowledge of his own company's machines were ever challenged. When he finally returned the items to the briefcase it was only 3:30 p.m., still a long way to go. For a change, he moved around the little table to sit next to Katcha instead of across from her. Soon he found her snoozing on his shoulder, and he liked that. Perhaps he should try a nap. After all, he hadn't had all that much sleep the previous night.

Kent stretched out his long, hefty legs as far under the table and the seat in front would allow, and closed his eyes, but fitful naps were broken while he wrestled with apprehension. *What's happening to me? Where is that cool spy who invaded the general's office? What's changed? Is it Katcha? Is it because I'm now responsible for someone besides myself? Get a grip, guy. We're reasonably safe now, heading cross-country on a train.* Minutes later, he fell into a more comfortable, hours-long snooze.

Kent awoke with Katcha's elbow in his ribs. "Dear! Wake up! It's 11:30! We're coming into Kotlas!" With a clanging jolt, the train stopped. The door at the opposite end of the carriage swung open and a tall, buxom woman in a khaki inspector's uniform stepped aboard for another ticket and passport check. Kent sensed something was wrong, but didn't mention his concern to Katcha. *The train hasn't made any stops, so why is another check necessary? Do they have additional information about me, a sketch or possibly a photo from the ticket booth?*

Starting at the far end of the carriage the inspector worked her way toward them. Kent noted the contrast between her inviting body and her commanding stance, her thin compressed lips and determined jaw. She took her time with each passenger, appearing even more thorough than any of the prior security checks.

They fumbled to get their documents ready before she approached, a smart move. The inspector had no problem with Katcha and handed back her papers. But under the officer's peaked hat, her sharp eyes dwelled on Kent's face, studying it, comparing it with his passport photo. He hoped she wouldn't see the beads of sweat he felt collecting on his forehead.

"Oleksander! She yelled his name to test how fast he'd respond.

Kent boldly stood up and snapped to attention so close to her she had to move back a step.

"*Da, sudarynya, tovarishch!* Yes, Madam Comrade!"

Instead of stiffening for a potential run-for-it-like-a-bat-out-of-hell, he relaxed his shoulders and broke into the broadest smile he could manage. He observed her body language as she tilted her head, then slowly shook it. In all likelihood still unsure, she handed back his papers and turned away. She had interpreted his smile as confidence of his legitimacy, a signal he'd definitely intended. He watched the woman leave the carriage at the far end as abruptly as she had appeared. He had studied her shapely form as she departed down the aisle—until he felt Katcha's elbow in his ribs once more, and this made him snicker at her mock jealousy.

While they put away their paperwork, they peered out into darkness thick as chocolate pudding. Intermittent street lamps cast weak light on silhouettes of official-looking buildings, modest houses, and storefronts locked up for the night. The train's rhythm ground unevenly. They were coming to the end of the train portion of their journey. As the train slowed to a halt at a platform, a series of signs saying "Kotlas" in Cyrillic letters came into view. They stood up, grabbed their bags, and were the first to get off the train. A public address announcement punctuated the walk into the depot. Katcha translated it. "There's a tram leaving for the bus terminal every twenty minutes on the street out in front of the depot. It's for ticketed transfers only."

They hurried outside in the murky dark and boarded early to be sure they found seats on the eight-passenger, canvas-topped vehicle. The full tram left the depot as soon as the last seat filled and arrived in front of the bus terminal twelve minutes later. Again, Katcha led the way in validating the bus transportation to St. Petersburg. They both had to present their passports and ID papers before the tickets were validated. Next, they were instructed to look up at the camera mounted above the ticket window. Kent now had two days' beard growth and Papa's hat in his favor as he complied.

His irregular sleep patterns had put some extra lines in his face and bags under his eyes, giving him the visage of an older man.

The bus connecting with their train was running two hours late, so they made good use of the restrooms to wash and refresh, with still plenty of time for a short walk outside the terminal. Off in the distance, Katcha's gaze caught the moonlit spires of the famed Cathedral of St. Stephan of Perm. She wished they could visit it. A tinge of sadness struck her. Fleeing was filled with disappointments.

Kent was eager to stretch his legs. He decided on a course of once or twice around the block. Turning the third corner, Katcha abruptly stopped.

"Oh, look," she said. "It's another charming café almost like ours. It makes me homesick."

"It does resemble yours, except it's got a glass front, and it looks like it's open all night." *Lucky us*, he thought, but then *Oh shit*. "Wait, Katcha. See those two men at a table next to the street? They're looking out at us."

"Couldn't we go in, pu-lee-ease?" she begged. "It would help us pass the time we have left."

"I can't see where it could do any harm," he lied, as he held the door for her.

Katcha chose a table near the counter. Kent stood at the counter and ordered tea for Katcha and coffee for himself. Glancing around the room while he waited for their drinks, he regarded the two men at the window table. A young, unremarkable man in a gray fedora bent over his soup, spooning rapid mouthfuls. His companion sat upright, with his back toward Kent. *Too erect*, more like military posture, Kent thought. Short black hairs marched in a monk-like fringe around the man's balding head. His tan trench coat lay folded across the back of his chair. Bending forward, he raised his hands to take a bite of his sandwich. Munching extravagantly, he turned in his chair to reach for the salt and pepper shakers. Kent's eyes fixated on the right side of the man's face. It was covered by a long, horizontal birthmark, a brown blotch from cheek to ear.

Katcha noticed her companion's fixed expression and was about to turn to look at the two men. Kent shook his head sharply, not wanting her to appear curious, which would make the two men more aware of the two fugitives. For a few seconds he wondered what to do next. It would have been much easier to just walk out of the café without their orders, but that might look suspicious. On the other hand, he had no solid indication that these men were anything more than two local workers enjoying a late-night meal.

The waitress passed their drinks over the countertop, and Kent carried them to the table where Katcha sat. Thirty minutes later they had drained their cups. It was time to return to the bus terminal. They stood to leave. Katcha's chair legs squeaked annoyingly on the tile floor. The two strangers turned quickly to observe them leaving the room. In fact, Kent felt two black crow's eyes lock onto their every movement. They belonged to the man with the brown blotch. His penetrating eyes followed them out the door.

Kent brooded. *Will this man become our eventual nemesis?*

Chapter 14
The Birthmark

Kent had an eerie feeling that the men in the café had developed an undue interest in him and Katcha. Just before turning the fourth corner back to the bus station, he hesitated for an instant and looked over his shoulder to see if they were being followed. He had always trusted his instincts and would have sworn that the man with the birthmark was a policeman of some sort, possibly even a Federation or Army cop. But not a soul appeared on the short block. The experience generated sharp feelings in Kent. Glad no one was there; disturbed that he was paranoid about being tailed.

Returning to the terminal, they happened to walk past a newsstand. Idly scanning the headlines, Kent jerked to a halt and spun around. His gut cramped. The front page of the evening paper carried a penciled sketch of "George Thermon, Escapee from Camp Obuchat." He studied it long enough to convince himself that the sketch would not betray him. Too clumsy, too vague, no mustache, even wrong about his hairline and eyes.

Katcha squealed, "Oh no!"

"Shh!" He placed his hand on her back and gently urged her forward. Pressing her cupid lips together, she suppressed any further reaction.

In silence they arrived on the bus platform ten minutes prior to departure time. They boarded and found a double seat close to the rear exit—convenient, if they needed to escape quickly. When the last passenger had settled in, a uniformed company agent boarded to check their tickets and travel papers. He left without incident. Kent looked at his watch. 1:30 a.m. He and Katcha were glad the seats were partial recliners with plenty of foot room.

The diesel bus revved up its engine to a lionlike roar and churned ahead in rumbling traffic. Even well after midnight, trucks barreled through the streets of Kotlas, a major industrial center with a pulp and paper mill and other factories. Leaving the city, the bus turned south, then west, crossing the Northwest Dvina River, then south again toward Nirksenitasa, its next big stop, a place for breakfast, borscht, blinis, and quality restrooms. The onboard facility was for emergencies only.

Katcha slept until they arrived in Nirksenitasa. She made a beeline for the restroom, leaving Kent in his seat, his head tilted back, emitting barely detectable snores. It was still dead of night—3:15 a.m. At the washroom sink, she splashed ice-cold water on her face. Now fully alert and wide-eyed, she scowled at herself in the mirror. *How stupid of me. Now I'll be awake all the way to sunup.*

Kent awoke ten minutes later when the driver tooted a warning for everyone to reboard. He rubbed his eyes and stared at the empty seat beside him. Panic suffused his large body. *Where the hell is Katcha? The bus is leaving.* He sprang to his feet and scanned the entire aisle, clogged with passengers hurrying back to their seats. Next, he knelt down on the window seat to scan the platform. It was empty. Like a shepherd counting his sheep, he checked all the other passengers as they reboarded. Still no Katcha. A half-minute later, the double doors of the bus folded closed with an air of finality. As the driver shifted into gear, Kent heard a sharp knock on the glass double doors.

The annoyed driver re-opened them. Katcha climbed on, breathless and apologetic.

He nodded, then scolded, "Don't let it happen again. I've got a schedule to meet."

"Yes, sir, sorry, sir," her voice tremulous.

Kent watched as she rushed down the aisle toward him. He sank back in his seat and took a slow, deep breath, hoping to calm down. He tried to analyze his anxiety. *Maybe I care more for this woman than I thought.* As soon as she plunked down in her window seat, he pulled her to him, right into that special nest between his left arm and the left side of his body. He held her and she soon fell asleep all the way to Totma, their next stop.

He had trouble dozing off for that entire stretch. *She worried the hell out of me.* Still agitated, Kent allowed his eyes to wander. They stopped at the aisle seat four rows in front of him. It held the man with the long brown birthmark on the right side of his cheek. *How did I miss this guy? Ah, I could only see his left side as he approached the bus door. He doesn't appear to be talking to his seatmate. Maybe he left his lunch companion back in Nirksenitasa.*

A half-hour later Brown Blotch stood up in the aisle and approached the driver. The two exchanged a few words. Before going back to his seat, Brown Blotch turned toward the rear of the bus and scrutinized every face, hesitating at each one to get a closer look. Kent swallowed hard. *Is the man actually looking for me? For us? As long as the creep remains on board, we're in fragile circumstances.* He didn't dare alarm Katcha. Her reaction might even tip off a perceptive cop.

Soon city lights flashed by their windows, melding with the orange-gold skies of dawn. The engine seemed louder enclosed by city streets and buildings as the bus navigated through Totma to the stop. There was no terminal, only a small coffee shop and a twenty-minute layover. The couple purchased containers of hot, thick oatmeal with apple bits and cinnamon and brought them on board to eat them leisurely.

The driver cranked up the diesel engine from its twenty minutes of idling to a full roar as the lumbering vehicle moved through the Totma city streets once more. Eventually, it found the

A114 Highway west.

Kent and Katcha finished their cereal. A frail-looking white-haired lady and a much younger, pretty woman next to her in the aisle seat were engaged in a cozy conversation, leading Katcha to think they were traveling together, possibly related.

"That's the way my mother and I chatted all the time," she whispered. "I wonder if I'll ever see her again." The spell was broken when the younger woman got off the bus in Vologda.

At 11:10 that morning the bus left Vologda. Shortly after, Brown Blotch left his seat, plodded toward the rear, and lowered himself into the vacant seat next to the elderly lady. Disturbed by his bulk and rigid military posture, she shrank close to the window.

Brown Blotch took the hint. Instead, he turned to Kent across the aisle and tried to strike up an exchange—in perfect English with not a trace of an accent. "Are you going as far as St. Petersburg?" he asked, with his mouth in a curl of a smile and raised eyebrows.

Kent didn't quite know how to answer. *Should I ignore him? Or I could admit to knowing English. And what language should I use, my fairly polished Russian or English? Papa's papers make me out to be Russian. Why has this guy singled me out as someone who speaks English?* He shook his head as though he didn't understand the question.

Katcha leaned over and answered in her phony English, with a heavy put-on Russian accent, "Yes, that's where we go." She rattled off Brown Blotch's question to Kent so he could give his own answer in Russian.

Kent replied with a peppy *"Da"* and thought, *Katcha has saved our asses once more.*

"Are you going as far as St Petersburg?" he repeated, in perfect Russian this time.

"Da," Kent answered. *The man's testing my skills at Russian now.* "Yes, I am going there on business, and I am bringing my daughter to see the Hermitage art." He had practiced it quickly in his head twice before saying it aloud in Russian.

"Ah, business," the man said. "I also have a business. What is your business, sir?"

Instead of answering, Kent reached for Papa's briefcase under his seat and set it on his lap. Out of the corner of his eye, he watched his questioner. *The man's showing some concern over what I might pull out of Papa's briefcase.* He sprang the clasps open with his thumbs, slid out one of the multicolored brochures and handed it to the man. "Agricultural machinery, the finest and most durable in the country," he added in his practiced Russian.

Brown Blotch introduced himself as Dmitri Federov and Kent immediately thought, *Where's the title or rank and government affiliation that goes with the name?* Dmitri leaned back in his seat and perused the brochure for several minutes. When he was done, he tried to return it to Kent, but Kent motioned it was his to keep.

After the exchange of a few more harmless questions and answers, Dmitri confided in them. "Sitting in the back of the bus makes me carsick. It's silly, I know, but I have to return to my original seat up front. He stood and strode up the aisle, gripping the chrome handles on the seatbacks.

Carsickness? Kent asked himself. *I doubt that. The man seems far too seasoned to be afflicted by such a menial malady. He's obviously a policeman of some sort—an experienced interrogator, downright shrewd and suspicious, no doubt. I have to keep an eye on the man. I hope he won't be the end of our freedom.*

Kent whispered in Katcha's ear, "The man's a cop. I think he suspects us, so we'll have to be careful."

"Do we have to get off the bus and make a run for it?" she asked. With her elbow on the armrest, she pressed her fist to her lips, as if to prevent herself from saying too much.

"No, no, I think we're good for now, but we have to be alert, all the time. I don't have to tell you how dangerous he could be."

The distance to the next stop, Cherepovets, was seventy miles away, normally a mere ninety-minute drive. The ride became more tedious with the added burden of the policeman on their minds. To make matters worse, most of the ride was through heavy road construction; they wouldn't arrive until almost two that afternoon. The driver, a gruff-voiced, red-faced man in his fifties, was in a poor temper because he was running nearly an hour late. He declared an altered layover stop, only ten minutes. Both Kent and Katcha got off to use the restrooms and returned tardy because they had to wait in line. The angry driver issued them a tongue-lashing, even though they were not the last to reboard. Because of the scolding, neither Kent nor Katcha noticed that Dmitri Federov's seat was empty.

Sharing the last of Mavis's packed sandwiches, they washed them down with the last of their cold drinks. The bus had covered another thirty miles before Kent thought to lean into the aisle and check up on Dmitri. His original seat was still empty and, a quick scan of the rest of the bus assured him Dmitri had indeed left them.

"Federov's gone," he whispered to Katcha. "Good riddance."

"I think I saw him get into a shiny new Mercedes with two other men in front of the Cherepovets stop," she answered.

"When was this?"

"While I waited my turn at the restroom."

"Why didn't you tell me before this?"

"With him gone, I didn't think it was important anymore. He isn't still a threat, is he?"

"Don't be too sure, dear. That man is cunning."

"Don't be angry with me, *moň dorogya*, my honey." She laid her head on his shoulder.

"I'm not," he assured her. "It's just that we have to be extra careful so nothing goes wrong. We have to be constantly aware and share and make use of all that we see and hear."

Kent was actually far more disturbed than he'd let on.

Chapter 15
The Bus to St. Petersburg

The 220 miles to Tikhvin proved difficult for the couple. While the moving bus temporarily shielded them from outside threats, the internal fear of the unknown and the unresolved decisions continued to eat away at the two travelers. The closer they got to St. Petersburg, the more fearsome these thoughts became, especially for Katcha. At first Kent detected a sniffle and patted her cheek with his opposite hand. It felt damp. Looking squarely at her face, he saw her fair skin and long, feathery lashes brimming with tears.

"Why are you crying? What's wrong, dearest?" He reached in his pocket and pulled out several coarse paper towels that he'd taken from a restroom, and wiped both her cheeks tenderly.

"I have so much confusion," she started in a whisper. "Where will I settle? How will I earn my living? Will you be a part of my life? For how long? Or will we ever marry? How and where will we live? I know you are a secret agent, some kind of a spy for the Americans, but I can't even begin to guess the things you have to do. So, if you leave me, what will become of me? I have no work skills." Her voice had risen almost to a whine.

Kent noticed a few passengers cocking their heads or setting down the newspapers they were reading, as if a dramatic performance was about to begin. *Oh hell.* He put an arm around Katcha and pulled her close. "Shh now." Murmuring into her ear, he said, "I will never abandon you—that I promise. I will find you a safe place to live and see that you have everything you need. I will stay with you for a time, and we will be lovers for a time. That is, until either you tire of me, or I have to leave on assignment. But I cannot commit to marriage, not just yet."

"Oh, and why is that?"

"Because," he whispered, "I will have to be away from you for substantial periods of time without explanations. Yes, hopefully, I will return in between times, too. It's the nature of—no, the requirement of—what I do for a living. It seems to me that either you'll adjust to that kind of life, or you won't. If you're still willing, we can discuss marriage more seriously, but not just yet."

"And why is waiting for you to come home so difficult for a marriage to tolerate?"

"That's just it. When I'm home I won't be able to even tell you where I've been and what I was doing. It's almost like living separate lives. There's a lot of blind trust involved."

"You can't even tell *me?* It's all *that* secret?"

"Yes."

"Exactly who do you work for?"

"I can't tell you that," he retorted, still whispering. "The work I do for them is not only secret, but often dangerous. There will always be the risk that I might not return from an assignment at all."

Her head bobbed up from his shoulder's nest and twisted to face him dead on. She met him eye to eye.

"Can't you change what you do? Find a new line of work— one that's safer, more normal?"

"It's what I do, what I've always wanted to do since I was a kid. It's what I'm trained for. I like living on a high—taking risks and beating the odds."

"You told me you're a—"

Now more than annoyed, Kent pressed his index finger to

her lips. Yes hers, not his. "Katcha, quiet! Please! This is not a subject for us to discuss here, on a crowded bus."

A storm cloud crossed her flushed face. She yanked her body sideways, and turned to the window, too infuriated to reply.

He spoke in a murmur to the back of her head. "Wait 'til we get to St. Petersburg. We'll find a place to continue this conversation, but not 'til then."

Katcha had no response except prolonged silence, and Kent had no desire to make matters worse. They rode the remaining 170 miles without speaking. As the bus neared Tikhvin, she sat back in her seat and they began to converse again on frivolous subjects as though the subject of their futures didn't exist. But it did exist in the backs of their minds ready to rear its ugly head at any time. Tikhvin was a thirty-minute stop because the bus had to refuel. They sat down at a cafe table and ordered *medovic*, a slice of honey cake, with their tea. They munched and sipped quickly until the bus returned to the boarding platform. A double toot of its horn and everyone reboarded. The air sizzled with an uplift in spirits among the passengers as the last leg of the long journey came within their grasp. The A114 Highway ended with a southerly turn onto Highway E105 at Novya Ladoga and from there to downtown St. Petersburg.

At last, near dusk, at 7:40 p.m. the big city's sights came into view—silhouettes of tall buildings, monuments, parks, and rushing traffic. Finally, the bus terminal loomed into view. The bus loudly screeched to a stop within the confines of the building. They got off, collected their luggage, and endured yet another examination of their papers as they entered the terminal. Katcha suddenly stopped short in the middle of the waiting room.

"We have come so far already, and I have never heard you once mention how we are going to leave the country. Do you have a plan to get across the border, dear?" she asked.

"Not really," he replied, looking straight ahead. "Honestly, I didn't think we'd make it this far."

"Stop joking!" she said with a swift punch to his upper arm.

"It's not a thing to joke about. I know you have a plan. So out with it now!"

"Actually, I have three viable plans that we need to discuss later. There's still a lot of tough distance ahead of us before we cross into Finland. We have to figure out which crossing—bus, train, or ferry—brings about the least amount of scrutiny from the authorities. It's complicated, and we need to do a little research into it. Meanwhile, we'll need a place to stay for a few nights while we work out the details."

"Where did you have in mind?" she asked, turning to face him.

"We can't go to just any hotel, inn, or boarding house without being challenged," said Kent. "We'd have to surrender our passports and papers. And the proprietors are likely to hold onto them until we pay the final bill."

"Also, proprietors are required by law to report the check-in of all transients to the area *politsiya*," reminded Katcha.

"And the politsiya have been known to pick up and hold onto passports on a whim," he added. "We just can't afford to take that chance."

"Well, we can't stay here in the bus terminal—it's much too busy and well lit," said Katcha. "Someone might recognize you."

"So what's the alternative?" he asked, shrugging his shoulders and turning his palms up.

"I don't know." Katcha sank down on a nearby bench to think. She pulled her luggage close.

"It's the one thing I didn't plan on," he said as he sat down next to her. "Any hotel, even the smallest or tackiest one would be risky."

"Wait, I have a better idea," offered Katcha. "Do you remember my Uncle Yakim Kondreatyev? You saw him the first day in our little café."

"You mean the uniformed bus driver—your father's brother? What about him?"

"Half-brother," she corrected. "Yakim has a married daughter living somewhere in St. Petersburg. My cousin Lyudmilla and I were the best of friends growing up. We were always together. Now, if I can only remember her married last name, I could call her. Maybe we could stay with them. But all I seem to remember is Boris, her husband's first name."

"Keep thinking, it'll come to you," he encouraged.

Katcha placed her right hand on her forehead, closed her eyes, and after several lingering minutes of silent lip motions said, "I'm pretty sure it ends with chenko. Ignachenko, Kroschenko, Ilyachenko. Ilyachenko! That's it! Lyudmilla and Boris Ilyachenko! Let me try the phone book." She left him to find a public phone.

Left alone on the bench, Kent became more aware of his surroundings. He noticed two well-dressed "suits" circulating through the immense waiting room, apparently looking for someone by the way they were scrutinizing faces, but it was impossible to determine whether they were specifically looking for him. He pulled Papa's hat down tighter and managed to keep his hands in front of his face each time one of them passed by. *Good thing the newspaper sketch is so poorly done,* he thought. While he successfully avoided the attention of both men, he did notice that one of them looked an awful lot like Dmitri Federov's companion at the last café. Now he felt antsy and wanted them to be on their way. *What's taking Katcha so long?*

She returned shortly, excited with news: "The Ilyachenkos are more than willing to have us as family visitors for the next few days. In fact, Lyudmilla screamed with delight when she found out I was calling. I had trouble ending the call, because she wanted to keep talking. I've got their address on this slip of paper I tore from the phone book—2033 Kamshina Ulitsa. It's in the Kalininski District. All we need to do is show it to a cab driver and he'll take us there. They're expecting us for supper at any time before 9:30. She looked at her watch—it's almost eight now."

"So we'd better get going," he said.

They grabbed their luggage and headed out to the street. The cool evening breeze, coupled with the knowledge that they had a place to stay, put a new bounce in their steps. Up the street to their right a taxi stand had three waiting cabs. But down the street loomed a worrisome sight: a shiny black Mercedes with the driver's face buried in a newspaper as though an arrival was expected.

"Oh no! That Mercedes looks an awful lot like the car Dmitri Federov got into in Cherepovets," said Katcha.

Kent thought, *Damn! We're still under the surveillance of the authorities when we're so close to our goal. It must be pretty unnerving for Katcha. We can't lead the sonofabitches right to her cousin's door. Maybe we can lose them on the way.*

Kent waved to the first cab driver, and the vehicle pulled up in front of them. He opened the rear door for Katcha and she ducked in and slid to the opposite side. He tossed their bags inside next to her and stood on the curb an extra moment scanning the sidewalks for Dmitri Not seeing him, nor anything more out of line, he took a deep breath and stooped down into the back seat.

As the cab labored for a chance to move away from the curb into heavy rush-hour traffic, one of the suspicious suits who was circulating through the waiting room suddenly burst through the terminal's exit, running toward their cab. Just as it started to move out, he bolted forward and slammed his hand down on the trunk lid. The sound it made was metallic. Kent shivered. Katcha cried out, "Kent, that's one of those creepy guys checking out people in the waiting room. What did he do?"

"It's not good. I think he placed a tracking bug on our trunk."

"Oh my God!" She shrank back into the seat.

Kent caught a glimpse of the man through the cab's side window. Twisting around to see more of him through the rear window, he followed the man as he changed direction and ducked into the waiting Mercedes. Kent was now certain the suit was one of Federov's henchmen.

Their cab melted into traffic before he could see if the Mercedes had become their tail. Katcha had already shown the driver the slip of paper with Lyudmilla's address. The driver acknowledged the destination and began shifting lanes and speeding up wherever he could. He turned, followed the Neva River Bank Road to the Liteniy Bridge, and sped across. A minute after turning east on the equivalent of a freeway, Kent twisted for another look back and saw it: the Mercedes starting to cross the bridge. At any moment, he expected to be pulled over for another check of their papers.

Chapter 16
Hiding Out

The Mercedes followed them at a measured distance, then began to gain on them. Kent saw it come closer and closer until it drew alongside, but he couldn't see who was in the car due to its tinted side windows. It matched their speed for a short spell, then pulled ahead and sped out of sight.

"They're toying with us, hoping we'll make a run for it," said Kent. "The tracking bug is giving them the confidence to let us have a longer leash. They won't lose us. But we sure as hell can't lead them to our host's front door. Katcha, tell the driver to turn left at the next corner and park for a minute. I need to check the outside of the cab."

She knew better than to ask why and relayed Kent's instructions to the driver. Alert and responsive, he roared around the corner at the first side street and came to a screeching halt at the curb.

Kent jumped out, ran to the rear of the cab, and yanked the magnetized device off the trunk lid. His body rigid, he waited a few moments for any traffic that might be coming from the opposite direction. A silver Volga sedan approached, cruising at a low speed. Kent reached out as it passed and slapped the tracking bug onto the sedan's trunk. Job done, he climbed into the back seat and instructed the driver to go to the address on Katcha's slip of paper. Katcha had been watching out the left window. She emitted a nervous giggle. "Darling, you're amazing!"

The driver made a quick U-turn and returned to the freeway. He drove for several more minutes, exited the freeway, and headed north. Soon the driver announced that they were on Kamshina Ulitsa at the 2000 block and would they help him find number 2033. Katcha saw it first. She held out a wad of rubles, a handsome tip, but first extracted a promise from the driver that he would forget this address and record a completely different one in his fare log book. He nodded gratefully, happy to comply.

Lyudmilla saw them pull up to the curb from a front window and sent her husband down to greet them. Boris, a large-boned man crowned with bushy, black hair and thick eyebrows, led them to his wife, a skinny woman with animated features and a mop of frizzy curls. She nearly bowled Katcha over with her exuberant embrace, topped with kisses and screeches in a loud, squeaky voice. The Ilyachenkos soon made the two travelers comfortable and seated them for dinner with the family at the kitchen table. But it didn't take long before explanations were demanded.

Lyudmilla crossed her wiry arms over her flat chest, and asked in blunt Russian, "What are you doing in St. Petersburg, of all places?"

"All I can tell you is that we are fleeing the country," replied Katcha. "But for the safety of everyone here I cannot give you any details. We don't wish to put any of you in danger. We just need a couple of days while we wait for a more opportune time to leave the country."

"Shh!" exclaimed Lyudmilla, putting an index finger to her lips. In reasonable English she whispered, "Our thin walls make good ears. Bad neighbors across the hall have reported others to the politsiya, with little or no reason at all. They think it takes them out from suspicion."

"I understand," said Katcha, responding in English. "It's only two nights, and we'll sleep on your living room floor."

"No, no," Lyudmilla said. "You and your husband take the children's bed. They can sleep in the big bed with us."

"We are not married, but maybe in the future," said Katcha, her eyes downcast. "But where are your children?"

"You will meet them soon, when dance class is done. Tatiana, seven, and Stepan, ten." Lyudmilla looked up at Kent and broke into a mischievous smile. "He's a good man, Katcha, handsome, too. You keep him, no?"

"I'm trying," replied Katcha in Russian. "Let me come in the kitchen and help you clean up. We can talk old times without the men."

The two women disappeared into the kitchen, walking arm in arm, leaving the men to get acquainted. Boris insisted that Kent sit in his large upholstered chair in the corner. He pulled a wooden rocker opposite his guest, but instead of sitting down he walked a few steps to a sideboard, broke out a bottle of vodka, and poured two water glasses half full.

"*Za tvajó zdaróvye,* to your health," declared Boris as soon as the two glasses touched in midair.

They each drank a portion of the warm smooth liquid.

"We are much indebted to you both for letting us stay with you," returned Kent in his best Russian.

"It is nothing," said Boris, responding in stilted but respectable English. "Katcha's friends are my friends. You are welcome."

They clinked glasses a second time and drank a bit more. For two strangers having little in common, meeting for the first time, the conversation proved awkward yet plausible, as the two wanted to be friends. Boris sat down in the rocker and eased back and forth a few times before breaking the inevitable silence.

"Where did the two of you meet?"

"I walked into their café, and Katcha was my waitress and we hit it off right away. We've been together ever since."

"Do you plan to marry?" asked Boris, now rocking more vigorously.

"There's a good chance we will, but we have a few things to

take care of first. We're not quite sure it's the real thing yet."

"I think I understand," offered Boris. "Love is a hard thing to recognize until you find you can't live without it."

"What do you do for a living, Boris, if you don't mind my asking?" asked Kent in his best Russian.

"I am now manager of a bottle factory," replied Boris in Russian with a great deal of pride. "I was promoted from leading foreman six months ago. That's how we can live in this fine apartment now."

"*Pozdravleniya*, Congratulations, I'm sure you deserved it," offered Kent.

"*Blagodaryu vas*, thank you!" said Boris. "And what do you do for a living?"

"Um…er…ah. I graduated with a degree in mechanical engineering, but mostly I travel, sell, and service farm machinery now. That's how I wound up in Russia."

Kent had hesitated long enough that Boris became suspicious. "And now you're running from the authorities—and the whole country, no?" he whispered. "What did you do to upset them?"

"Let's just say I pissed off the wrong person," Kent lied. "I can't give you any more details."

A thudding sound just outside the door announced the arrival of the evening paper. Boris picked up his copy of *Izvestia* off the mat in the hall. A he stepped inside and shut the door, he scanned the front page—and discovered a two-column sketch of the recent escapee—his visitor.

He walked slowly into the parlor and lowered himself into the rocker. "You are American, an American spy, no?" deduced Boris aloud and again in English.

"Yes," Kent answered in English. "And I could say the authorities aren't looking for me, but I don't want to lie to you."

"Then you place my precious family in grave danger and my mother country in peril," Boris blurted out in loud Russian.

Kent was shocked at his outburst and hoped no one else,

Lyudmilla or the neighbors, had heard it. "Please," he begged, "I wish no harm to either your family or your country. The authorities have no photograph of me, only that pencil sketch. Without my mustache, it isn't too good a likeness, but it's been printed repeatedly in the local papers across the country for nearly a month. As it became older news, the sketch became smaller and moved to interior pages. I had no idea it would still be on the front page of *Izvestia*. My papers and passport—they belong to Katcha's papa. I started alone, three thousand miles from here, and just happened to meet Katcha at her family's café. She's an important part of my life now. If we make it out of Russia I plan to retire from the profession and settle down." Kent stopped. His heart was pounding. He couldn't believe he'd said that last sentence. It was as though he had already made up his mind. But he hadn't.

Boris's dark eyes bore into Kent's. "Then, for Lyudmilla's sake and her childhood bond with Katcha, I will not report you. But if I'm interrogated, I must tell the truth. I'll have to say you forced yourselves on us."

"I understand and respect your decision," said Kent. "But please know that I am grateful for your hospitality, such as it is." The ladies finished up in the kitchen, entered the parlor exchanging anecdotes, and remained chatting until near midnight, while the men remained silent. The obvious strain wasn't mentioned until they were in bed in the children's room that night. Katcha's stilted expression gave her a troubled look. "Why were you both so quiet? What happened between the two of you?"

"Boris guessed everything and would have reported us except for the friendship you share with Lyudmilla. But if he's interrogated, he'll report us. I worry about him when he goes off to work tomorrow morning."

Brooding about Boris's conscience led to an uneasy night's sleep for both of them. In the morning of the twentieth, their first showers in many days helped to put a fresh outlook on their prospects. Boris had left for work by the time they made it to the kitchen. Lyudmilla had spoken with her husband, and reassured

Katcha that he would not turn them in. She fixed them a hot cereal breakfast and drove them, in their late-model Kamaz sedan, to the famed Hermitage Museum. Katcha's breath caught in her throat at the sight of the seemingly miles-long building, the former Winter Palace, with its white columns topped by gold capitals. The three of them spent the entire day touring the thrilling art exhibits. They had lunch in the café. Over a pudding dessert, while the women continued to catch up on their missing histories, Kent disappeared for nearly an hour.

That evening, Lyudmilla coaxed out Boris's better nature and he warmed up to his guests once more. She had prepared a festive meal of cold borscht and beef stroganoff with boiled creamy noodles, topped off with a Kagor dessert wine. Boris cheerfully broke out a Russian board game and taught everyone how to play. They played until it was time to retire. The second night's sleep came easier.

The next morning was Friday, the twenty-first. While still lounging in the luxury of a bed, Katcha asked, "Where did you go during the end of lunch yesterday? You were gone almost an hour."

"I went out to get these," he replied. On the bedcovers he fanned out a map, bus and train schedules, and a brochure on the ferry itineraries going directly to Helsinki.

They studied the map. Estonia and Latvia were closer than Finland and would be warmer, but they were NATO pact nations and the crossing scrutiny might be a good deal more stringent. So they decided on Finland, which had no NATO affiliation. Now they needed to select their final route.

Kent felt that the ferry was the most direct route, thirteen hours across the Gulf of Finland all the way to Helsinki. But with the *Princess Anastasia* running only twice a week, they'd have to remain in St. Petersburg for another two days. That meant spending another two nights with the Ilyachenkos. Still, he saw three advantages. The ferry price was right. There would probably be only one inspection of their papers by Russian authorities. And they wouldn't have to travel across many more miles of unknown

Russian territory.

The bus had its own advantages. The travel time would be cut in half and the cost was a third less. But they would have to travel across another 150 miles of unknown Russian territory and be subjected to multiple challenges of their passports and identification papers. The train created the same risk.

Kent and Katcha debated. They ruled out cost as a factor right away. Crossing Russian territory presented the greatest hazard because the artist sketch of him was still in the papers across the country. The ferry appeared to be the best way to go. They hugged, relieved that the major part of their planning was now complete. At breakfast. they joined Lyudmilla, Tatiana, and Stepan at the table, but Boris was missing. Lyudmilla served the five of them salted herring and milk-soaked bread.

"Where's your husband this morning?" asked Kent.

"He's out jogging," she replied. "Whenever Boris finds a pound or two more on the scale, he wants to get rid of it. He jogs for a whole hour several days a week. He should come back any minute now."

They heard the door swing open and scratching sounds. Boris appeared, wiping his shoes on the rubber floor mat. Kent, sitting on the opposite side of the table from the door, was able to see across the hall. The neighbor's door was open just far enough to get a good look at them all.

One more thing to worry about, Kent thought. *Did this freakin' neighbor overhear us speaking in English? Or for that matter, overhear us talking in bed about leaving the country—all the details of our planning? Just how thin are those bedroom walls?* The two house guests understood, without saying it aloud, that the threat of the prying neighbors would hang over them for the rest of their stay with the Ilyachenkos.

Chapter 17
Nosy Neighbors

Boris stepped inside and kicked the door shut behind him. "Damn Mikhail and crazy wife, too! I want to slam his long nose in his door."

"Shhh! He'll hear you," said Lyudmilla.

"I don't care!" ranted Boris. "He should mind his own business."

Lyudmilla explained. "Mikhail and Natasha Kamynina are a rather strange and reclusive couple. They moved in about a year ago."

"Do you think they'd actually report us to the authorities?" asked Kent.

"What are they like?" asked Katcha.

"I've tried to make friends with them many times," replied Lyudmilla, "but they are cold like herring. They do lots of whispering among themselves. But being nosy and secretive not a crime, I say. No, I think they are strange and harmless maybe."

"I disagree," argued Boris. "They're more like poor sardines in great tank with a hungry sturgeon. Mikhail is a small clerk in the city water management office, and Natasha is a telephone operator for government. No. I think they both have big ambitions and little talents to go with—a most dangerous mixture, I say. I'm not so sure they won't call politsiya on all of us to gain favor with authorities. Yes, my dear Lyudmilla, on you, me, and our children, too. We can't ignore their nosy interference. We must find a safe place for Katcha and Kent and quickly, too."

"But she is my cousin, and they are my friends—our guests—please, Boris. Just for another two days."

Boris mumbled a string of Russian expletives under his breath, and then nodded his approval. He looked at Kent. "I cannot deny my love anything." He held out his arms and Lyudmilla ran into them for a long embrace.

From their seats at the table, the children jeered at them in fun, banging their spoons on their plates. Lyudmilla sent them to get dressed for their activities.

"Perhaps it *would* be safer for you to be out of the house today," suggested Lyudmilla.

"But where would we go to pass so much time?" asked Katcha.

"We could all go to the zoopark," piped up Stepan.

"No, no, my dear," answered his mother. "You are going to soccer practice as usual, and Tatiana is going to her dance class. But the zoopark is a good idea for our friends. Perhaps Papa will drive them there."

Lyudmilla looked over at her sweaty husband, still in his running clothes, but Boris remained silent, still fuming over his next-door neighbors. A sterner look at her husband brought about an eventual agreement to drive them to St. Petersburg's grand Leningradskiy Zoopark.

The three left the apartment and descended the staircase. Kent looked back over his shoulder and noted the neighbors' door ajar once again and perceived a male face glaring at them through the crack. *That face appears meek and almost passive to me,* thought Kent, possibly a peeking obsession less threatening than everyone imagines. Out on the sidewalk, they continued to the late-model, forest-green Lada compact sedan parked on the street. Settled inside, Boris drove them twenty minutes across town to the Leningradskiy

Zoopark. Letting them out in front of the arched wrought-iron gate, Boris promised to pick them up at the same spot at precisely 4:30 that afternoon.

A ticket window was located in the center of a wide, white concrete building. Katcha laid out twice the 150-ruble admission fee in exchange for two entrance passes. A paved path led them to the first of the outdoor exhibits, two polar bears in a concrete habitat that included a large pool. Just as the two visitors arrived at the barrier, one polar bear sauntered into a cave, and the other lumbered to a sunny spot beside the pool and laid his massive body down for an extended nap. Disappointed, Kent and Katcha sauntered over to the Large Predators House, where caged lions, tigers, leopards, and jaguars paced the extent of their cages, parading their beauty, grace, and nonchalance. Nearby, a frightened child shrieked loudly when her stroller came too close to a tiger's cage. The embarrassed mother beat a hasty retreat, but the child continued her tirade.

Kent and Katcha wandered across the way to see giraffes, kangaroos, emus, and grizzly bears. A short zigzag up the center of the park brought them to the Deer Circle with deer, elk, alpacas, and llamas. Moving out to the perimeter, they visited the Exotarium, for all sorts of marine and amphibious life. Continuing in a counterclockwise manner, they encountered elephants and camels. A stop at the Small Predators House revealed a wolverine viciously, yet noiselessly, tearing apart a chunk of meat, while two martens slept soundly in an adjacent cage. They found all sorts of smaller animals in the Tropical House, but it was the monkeys that entertained Katcha the most.

Many shoulder-to-shoulder visitors rushed about full of excitement, while others appeared to float through the exhibits. Kent and Katcha moved slowly—surely interested in everything they saw and heard, but more attuned to slow pacing their journey to their 4:30 pickup time. Relishing these rare moments of being alone together, they also shared a people-watching pastime. Katcha liked to note the striking physical differences and similarities in couples passing by; Kent tended to analyze each new face, looking for the potential danger it might possess.

As they approached the next exhibit, the children's petting zoo, Katcha noted a father holding the hand of one son, who looked about six, and carrying his toddler son in the other arm. He walked just in front of them and Katcha ran ahead to open the gate for them. The father thanked her and set his two sons down among the goats, lambs, and ducks. As Kent came closer, she whispered to him, "Maybe we'll have sons like that someday and we can take them to the zoo, too."

"Maybe." Kent smiled and squeezed her shoulder. He had also given the father the once-over. He noticed that the man wore a gray business suit with an open white shirt collar and no tie, but more important, the father stood militarily straight with polished tan shoes. An oddly formal attire for the zoo.

"Where to next?" Katcha asked.

"I think we can skip the children's petting zoo," he replied as they stood in front of the gate. "We're a little too old for that," all the while thinking about the real reason for skipping the exhibit: *I don't want to risk him having seen my picture.*

"Oh no," she insisted. "I do want to feed the animals— please!"

Without waiting for Kent's response, she headed straight for the kiosk and purchased a paper bucket with a measure of pebble-sized food bits and leafy greens for the goats, lambs, chickens, duck, swans, and geese. At the two-foot-high fence, she began to dole out the food to the eager ones. She stood next to the father watching his two sons, who were both cautious and excited with each new feeding prospect, even dropping bits when the recipient got too eager and pushy.

"They're loving it," she said to the father, as a goat filched a lettuce leaf from her fingers.

"The boys love animals," he replied. "And this is a new experience for them."

As the smiling father turned his face toward Katcha, Kent

immediately recognized him. "It's time for us to move on now," he murmured to Katcha, in his most casual manner. Too late. The father took a keener look at Kent and said, "Don't I know you from somewhere? You look very familiar."

"Not likely, sir," replied Kent. "We're visiting from Cherepovits, celebrating our second wedding anniversary." *I don't know where I got that from,* he thought.

"Are you Army or a veteran?"

"No, sir."

"What is your name? I never forget a face." The man stared at him intently.

"Babinkin, Oleksander Babinkin, sir." Kent replied after stealing a professor's name from a nearby poster advertising an educational lecture on predators. Tossing a carrot stick to a prodding, floppy-eared goat, he nodded to the all-too-inquisitive dad, counted to ten, and slowly inched away. The man persisted in staring at him, racking his brain for the missing recognition. Kent grabbed Katcha's arm and literally tugged her out to the main walking path.

"Stop, you're hurting my arm," she complained.

"Sorry," he whispered as soon as they were out of earshot, "This man is dangerous. We must get as far away from him as possible before he remembers who I am."

"But he seems such a harmless father," she whispered back. "Who is he, anyway?"

"He's the man who got me arrested in the first place. Formally, he is Colonel Ivanov Polkóvnik, but his underlings call him Colonel Polkó. My new mustache must have thrown him off. He won't be able to chase us because he's responsible for the safety of his two sons. But he certainly could raise a major hue and cry if he suddenly fits my face to my name and remembers my crime."

"If or when he remembers you, then what?" she whispered.

"Remembering means he'll notify the police and order them to seal off all the entrances before we get out of the park. We need to be out the main gate and out of sight as soon as possible, but not so fast as to create suspicion."

"I think the main gate is this way," she whispered, now tugging him in that direction.

While the man's eyes followed their departure, they strolled down the main path nonchalantly, as though they were seeking the next exhibit. As soon as they were out of sight and certain that he could no longer see them, they hurried, without running or looking back, through the exit gate. Kent spotted an Italian café several doors down from the gate on the opposite side of the street. He figured the café would be secluded enough to provide cover, yet close enough to the gate to allow them to monitor Boris's arrival at the pickup spot. The two trotted to the café, slipped inside, and requested a table by the window. The view allowed them to see the zoopark entrance without being seen.

As they sat down, Kent concentrated hard on looking casual, even though he was overheated and wanted to remove Papa's jacket. But he didn't dare. The cold sweat in his armpits had made his shirt clammy and could betray his tension to any of the other customers. He had just ordered two glasses of Lambrusco wine when they heard the two-toned screech of police sirens. In a matter of minutes, two blue and white utility vans squealed to a stop in front of the zoopark entrance. At least a dozen uniforms poured out of the two vans and flowed, one by one, through the narrow wrought-iron gate. Two uniforms remained just inside the gate to prevent any fugitives from leaving.

"The rest must be conducting a thorough search for us inside," said Kent. "That could take hours and totally frustrate Colonel Polkó."

"Apparently your colonel did have a memory of you and phoned in an alarm," said Katcha, her round face flushed. "So what do we do now?"

"Absolutely nothing," he replied. "We wait here until they give up their search. It's only 1:30 now. We wait for Boris to pick us up at 4:30."

"What if the police decide to check in here?" she asked.

"It's not likely and even if they do, I highly doubt whether the colonel has the capacity to describe either one of us any better than that prison sketch."

"What if you're wrong?"

"I guess we'll be a real hot commodity then." To calm his voice, he took a long sip on his wine. "We'll have to be a lot cleverer to talk our way out of that."

The café owner, who was also their waitress, had been standing near the glass-paned front door, watching the activity across the street. Shaking her head, the owner grumbled, "Always something going on over there." She approached their table. "Are you ready to order now?"

Kent and Katcha looked at each other as the light dawned. They hadn't considered eating, but reality was—they couldn't just nurse their wine for three more hours. Katcha brightened, picked up one of the menus resting against the carafe of wine vinegar, and held out the other one to Kent. "In just a minute, thank you," she said in a sing-song voice. She ordered the veal parmesan with vermicelli. Kent ordered the manicotti and picked out another wine. A few minutes later, two house salads and a basket of warm bread arrived, followed by a bottle of Chianti encased in the traditional rattan. The waitress uncorked the bottle, allowed Kent a sample taste, and poured two glasses full. Thirty minutes later, their steaming pasta entrées arrived on nearly overflowing platters. The food proved to be delicious and filling. They passed on dessert and sat sipping the remainder of their wine.

Kent's apparently relaxed demeanor fooled even Katcha. He'd been keeping a sharp eye out across the street. At 3:25 his body froze. He grabbed her hand, and cocked his head slightly toward the street as he witnessed the colonel and his two sons exit the zoopark with a uniformed officer. They appeared to be arguing and it ended with the officer tossing his hands outward, palms up, signaling a helpless gesture: What more can I do? Additional uniforms trickled out of the gate and disappeared in the back of the parked police vans. The colonel and his two sons walked away, presumably toward the parking lot on the far side of the entrance.

Eventually, the two police vans retreated without leaving anyone behind.

"Now *that* was a show worth watching," said Kent. "See! You worried for nothing."

"Now don't you go getting cocky on me," said Katcha. "We're still in Russia."

"You know me better than that," he answered. "It's just that every so often I need an ego boost. By the way, don't mention our little encounter with the colonel to either Boris or Lyudmilla. They're already on edge, so there's no need to upend their life any further. The less they know, the better off they'll be."

"I agree," she responded, nodding vigorously, her palms down gesture answering her agreement as well. "They have been so nice to take us in like this. I wouldn't want them to get in any trouble on our account."

The two sipped and talked until the Chianti bottle ran dry and their heads tingled with a pleasant buzz. Kent paid their bill and left a generous tip. At 4:37 the green Lada sedan slowed to a stop in front of the park entrance, but on their side of the street. They slipped out of the café and ran toward the Lada, waving their hands, but Boris had his eyes on the exit gate across the street. He was indeed surprised when the rear door on the curb side of the car opened, and his expected passengers piled into the back seat.

After a short greeting, Boris pulled away from the curb and joined the late-afternoon traffic. Forty minutes later, he drove down the Kamshina Ulitsa, but slowly—right past his own apartment building, despite the plentiful parking spaces out front. At the corner he turned right.

"Why didn't you stop in front of your own building?" asked Katcha.

"Two men are sitting in a black car parked across the street from my building," said Boris. He turned into an alley halfway down their block. "Police, no?"

"Man, you are one sharp cookie, Boris," declared Kent. "You just saved our asses."

Boris ignored all the American slang. He had important news. "You cannot stay in our apartment tonight." He continued driving through the alley to the open area in the middle of the block. "Our bastard neighbors called authorities—already."

Chapter 18
Under Wraps

Boris backed the little green sedan into one of a dozen sheltered parking stalls in the middle of that block. He killed the engine and turned around to face his passengers. "I don't know where to take you now." His normally careful English turned broken in the tension of the moment. "If I stop by my front door, police see you and if I bring you by back door, nasty neighbors see you and call police again! Each way, you are in trouble."

"Are the police likely to search back here?" asked Kent.

Boris shook his head. "I think not so much likely."

Kent persisted. "Do your neighbors know about this parking place?"

"No. They don't have a car, so they not know this place."

"We could sleep in the car overnight," suggested Katcha. "It's a tight fit, but I think we can manage it."

"Yeah. Okay," said Kent. "We can spend the night in here. But Boris, what happens in the morning? You need your car to go to work. And we sure as hell don't want to put your family in any more danger than we already have. We do need to be on the *Princess Anastasia* at seven tomorrow evening when she leaves St. Petersburg for Helsinki."

"No worry, I will take you tomorrow," said Boris. "Tomorrow is Saturday, I not working. I'll drive you to see sights in the daytime, then get you to the ferry."

"What about Lyudmilla?" Katcha burst out, a sob catching in her throat.

"Lyudmilla stays home with the children," replied Boris. "The car takes only four."

"We need to tell her goodbye," Katcha said. "I might never see her again."

"Wait for morning," said Boris, as he opened the car door and climbed out. "Goodnight, my friends."

Kent and Katcha watched as Boris left the car and disappeared through a gate in a seven-foot wood fence. He had let them know that a path on the other side led to the rear door of their apartment building.

Katcha moved to the front seat, leaving the more spacious back seat to Kent. But normal traffic noise and not being able to stretch their legs in the cramped interior led to a fitful night's sleep.

Sunrise found the couple cuddling in the back seat, sharing body warmth and mulling over plans for facing the unknown ahead. Saturday morning at 9:30, Lyudmilla came through the gate in the fence, bearing a box of warm pastries and a thermos of hot coffee. A few steps behind her, Boris closed the gate and they slid into the front seat. The four of them chatted for nearly an hour.

"I really must get back to the children," said Lyudmilla. "It's time for goodbyes, I think."

Kent and the two ladies got out of the car and stood alongside, embracing and kissing. Kent returned to the back seat while the cousins stole one last hug. Katcha returned to her seat, wiping tears from her eyes. They waved to a sad-faced Lyudmilla as Boris backed out of the sheltered parking stall and drove down the narrow alley to the busy street.

He drove them first to the Peter and Paul Fortress, and from there, they had a tour of downtown St. Petersburg. Crossing the Liteynity Bridge, they motored along the banks of the Neva River, then inland to the Marinsky Theater, the premier ballet and opera house. Next, they rode by the Yusupov Palace, the Kazan Cathedral, the Bronze Horseman Statue of Peter the Great, the Fabergé Museum, St Isaac's Cathedral, and a myriad of other municipal and cultural buildings. As they drove past each one, Boris proudly announced the name and explanation for each.

Katcha uttered a shriek of joy at spotting the most dramatic and dominant sight of all: the Russian Orthodox Church of the Savior on Spilled Blood. They could hardly take their eyes away from the towering assemblage of graceful arched windows, russet-colored brick, and onion domes of green, blue, and gold. It was built on the site where political rebels assassinated Romanov Emperor Alexander II in 1881.

A small Chinese restaurant in a galleria mall provided their lunch—*lo mein* à la Russian style, noodles, chopped cabbage, and mushrooms plus shrimp rolls.

After a full day of touring, Boris drove them close to the port area. It was four o'clock, a good three hours before the *Princess Anastasia* was scheduled to leave St. Petersburg for Helsinki. Boris pulled over to the curb a few blocks from the terminal. He didn't want anyone in authority to make a connection between the illegal travelers and his family. All three got out of the car for final hugs, kisses, and handshakes. Boris opened the trunk and set their luggage on the sidewalk. Back in the driver's seat, as he started the ignition, he rolled down the window and turned to look out at Kent and Katcha. Lifting up a small silver flask, he took a short swig, and held it up again as if in a toast. "*Do svidaniya,* Until we meet again."

He put the car in gear and drove off. Kent and Katcha watched the little green sedan get smaller and smaller until it turned off at an intersection. Each of them sighed, experiencing that deep pit in your stomach when you realize you'll never see that precious person again. They picked up their suitcases and trudged the last few blocks to the port.

Arriving at the terminal, they found that all walk-on passengers had been ushered into one of three queues to purchase passage aboard the *Princess Anastasia* ferry. The first queue included tourists already possessing visas and wanting return-trip tickets. The second queue included already-ticketed, round-trip passengers originating in St. Petersburg. Kent and Katcha joined the third queue, the unticketed passengers planning to purchase tickets and board now. The drive-on passengers queued up in a special end-to-end parking lot across the way.

"If they ask you why we are going to Helsinki, tell them we are accepting the invitation of your father's business associate. You don't know his name."

"What if they want you to call the man?" asked Katcha.

"Don't worry, I've got that covered."

At precisely five o'clock, the officials began to process the queues, with the tour groups and individual pre-certified tourists ushered straight to the ship's gangway, literally a bridge from the pier to a door in the hull of the ship. It was more complex for the other queues; passports, visas, and identification papers were necessary. Some passengers were asked a few pertinent and leading questions. Most of those were approved and motioned to the gangway as well. A small number were diverted under escort to an adjacent building for further interrogation. An even smaller number left that building for the gangway. What happened to the diverted group wasn't clear. After thirty minutes, Kent and Katcha had advanced to first in line. The security agent at the gate perused Katcha's papers for several minutes before looking up.

"Oleksander Kroschenko!" he called out.

"Da," Kent answered, stepping closer to show off his pretended confidence.

"You are together?" asked the agent in Russian.

"Da."

"You look much younger than forty-seven, and your face is thinner," the agent remarked after studying Kent's face and Papa's photo.

Kent pumped up his biceps and claimed in his best Russian, "No doubt my daily exercise and clean living." He added a broad smile to further convince his doubter.

"Do you intend returning to St. Petersburg?" asked the agent.

"Da."

"Within seventy-two hours?"

"Da. We have only overnight baggage."

"Is your purpose in Helsinki business or pleasure?"

"A little of both," Kent replied. "It's the way business is done."

The security agent scrutinized their papers for another few minutes, then pointed for them to detour through the adjacent concrete, one-story building. An armed guard stood in the way of going anywhere but that building. Inside, they were told to sit until called. A few minutes later, the door to the next room opened. This time, a uniformed officer called Kent into the interview room to sit several feet in front of a desk. The chair had one short leg designed to make it wobble back and forth, to the chagrin of anyone who had to sit there.

"I'm Captain Ilitskova." He began with the same questions asked outside at the end of the queue. He seemed satisfied and was about to put an exit stamp in Kent's passport when the door opened and in walked Dmitri Federov in full uniform. The long brown birthmark on his cheek looked even more prominent than Kent remembered.

"Do you mind if I sit in?" asked Dmitri in English, flashing his official credentials. His tone spoke more of an order than a question. "We have some interest in this case."

Kent rolled his eyes. *This guy keeps turning up like a bad penny, or worse yet, a bad ruble. What else can happen?*

"I was about to approve these two," responded the captain in Russian. "What do you have to contribute, Comrade?"

"Are you aware that Oleksander Kroschenko is presently serving time in jail for speaking out against the state?" asked Dmitri in English for Kent's benefit. He expressed a sour, superior grin.

"Is this true?" asked the captain.

"Yes, and two Oleksander Kroschenkos is not believable. Nor can he be in two places at the same time," assured Dmitri. "Have the girl brought in."

The captain turned to Kent looking for an explanation. The uniformed agent stepped out and returned with Katcha. She had to stand next to her "father's" chair, the only chair in the room.

"It's the same mistake over and over again," said Kent in his best Russian. "The names are mixed up again. Do I have to be punished for his foul mouth?"

"What mistake is that?" asked Dmitri in Russian.

"You're talking about my big-mouthed cousin, Alexander Kroschenko," lied a desperate Kent. "We are always getting mixed up with each other."

"Why the similar names?" Dmitri demanded.

"I don't know. His mother is British. You know how dizzy the British are. They want to anglicize everything," Kent continued, smoothly.

Dmitri quickly turned to Katcha and asked, "Young lady, why are you and your father going to Helsinki?"

"We accepted the invitation of one of my father's business associates," she replied with her father's prepared answer.

Dmitri frowned and twisted his lips in a gesture of disbelief. "What is the name of this so-called business associate?"

Kent started to answer but Dmitri motioned for him to remain silent. He turned to Katcha, wanting the answer from her. "The name, please?"

"I don't know his name. I've never met the man. He's my father's associate."

"Was the invitation written or verbal?" demanded Dmitri.

"Written," interrupted Kent. "I have it right here." He reached inside his pocket and retrieved a folded piece of stationery conveying the invitation, including name and a Helsinki address.

Dmitri read the note and declared, "There's a telephone number, too."

"Let me have that," snapped the irritated captain, holding

out his hand. "Ah, Victor Volkov." He read the name aloud. The captain pulled his phone closer and dialed the number he believed to belong to Victor Volkov, a businessman living in Helsinki. What he didn't know was that he'd dialed one of a group of special numbers inside the U.S. Embassy in Helsinki.

"Volkov residence," the man answered in perfect Finnish.

"Victor Volkov?" the captain asked.

"Yes, I'm Volkov. Who's calling?" The man switched to Russian after detecting an accent.

"I am Captain Ivan Ilitskova of the Russian Border Police, the Federal Security Service, PS FSB Rossii. Are you expecting visitors this weekend?"

"Oh yes, I'm expecting a large group of business associates for the weekend," answered Volkov with a prepared and rehearsed stock answer for this special line.

"Could you give me their names?" asked the captain.

"Not without going to my office in the city," Victor answered.

"Do you recognize the name Oleksander Kroschenko?"

"Of course, he's one of my oldest suppliers."

"Might I ask what he supplies?"

"I believe I've answered enough questions," said Volkov. "Can you tell me what your queries are all about?"

"Thank you," said the captain, replacing the receiver.

Just then the *Princess Anastasia's* whistle released a long, thunderous blast, indicating that the end of the boarding process was near.

"Well?" said Dmitri with his arms folded across his chest. "What did the man say?"

"He is expecting Kroschenko to attend some suppliers' meeting tomorrow afternoon," said the captain, speaking slowly in thoughtful tones. "I believe we have no reason to hold them now. Do we?"

It was ten minutes to seven. The *Princess Anastasia* released another warning blast.

"I disagree, Captain," said Dmitri, his jowly face a storm cloud of anger, the birthmark throbbing. "I believe we do."

The captain's face turned a contorted red. "I am the captain here, and I am the authority here! No?"

"But there is something very odd here," insisted Dmitri. "I just can't quite put my finger on it."

Chapter 19
The Ship to Helsinki

Captain Ilitskova picked up his rubber approval stamp and slammed it down, first on the inkpad and then on both sets of papers and passports. "But nothing!" said Captain Ilitskova. "Facts only. 'Odd' is no way to run this office." He handed both sets of papers and passports to Kent. "Have a pleasant trip."

Dmitri stood there fuming, but helpless to stop them. The guard opened the side door, an access to the pier. Kent thanked the captain, and the two travelers hurried out. The huge, multi-storied *Princess Anastasia* loomed alongside the pier. Seeing crew members preparing to remove the ship's gangway, they dashed to it, luggage in hand, without looking back. Somehow, looking back would have been a bad omen. As they climbed the gangway into the ship's hull, Kent did chance a compulsive glance back toward the terminal where they'd been held. He could barely make out Dmitri Federov standing outside the door with his hands on his hips.

"Why are you smiling?" asked Katcha, as they stepped into the main salon. Rows on rows of wooden benches were already occupied by passengers sitting hip to hip.

"I do believe we outwitted and frustrated our favorite policeman," Kent replied. "I looked back at the man and I didn't turn into a pillar of salt like Lot's wife in *Genesis*."

"Shussh! Don't jinx us," she said. "We haven't even left the pier yet."

The last vehicle had been parked aboard, and the massive forward doors cranked closed with a grinding complaint. At precisely seven o'clock that evening the car ferry blasted its ship's horn one more time, released all of its hemp lines—and all of its connections to the Russian mainland. The *Princess Anastasia* sailed out of St. Petersburg harbor into the Gulf of Finland, a tributary of the Baltic Sea.

They stood at the rail as the harbor and then the landfall shrank, finally slipping away from view. When the sun disappeared across the bow, Kent and Katcha retired to the second-deck sitting salon. It wasn't even half-full, so Katcha stretched out on their bench with her head in his lap. But sleep was hard in coming.

"It's too bad we couldn't afford a cabin, even one of the cheaper ones," she said.

"If you hadn't been such a spendthrift, maybe we could have," he kidded.

She pinched his arm.

"Ouch, that hurts," he complained. "We're down to our last fifty rubles. Do you ever wonder if your mother can handle the café all by herself?"

"We talked about it," Katcha said. "Mama reminded me that Uncle Yakim's wife, Nelva, helped out as a waitress when I was away at school. I think she actually loved working in the café, so I don't think that will be a problem."

"Why were you and your mama so willing to have me take you away?" he asked. "You seemed so close. What more did she imagine for you elsewhere?"

Katcha hesitated, swung her legs on the floor and sat bolt upright. Her face turned pale when she spoke. "Mama is very sick with liver cancer. The doctors give her no more than a year to live."

"Oh no! I'm so very sorry," said Kent.

"I wanted to stay and help her. But she didn't want me to

get stuck being her caregiver. She didn't want my memories of her to be of a sick old lady. You were her last hope for me."

"Oh, man, I never thought I'd be anyone's last hope," said Kent. "Especially under such terrible circumstances. I guess that's why your mama took to me so quickly and didn't object to our hanky-panky." He saw Katcha's puzzled look. "Sex, hon."

Katcha gasped. "Oh my! I was so wrapped up in you I didn't think about that. It's true. Mama knows the end is coming. She doesn't know when, of course, but she wants to be assured that I have a real future. She wants to know that her only child is married happily, that I have more opportunities than she had, and that maybe I can finish my education abroad. There's no way I can help her and, if she hadn't pushed me away now, I would be stuck running the Malen'koye Kafe with no chance of finding a romantic match in our little village. Nelva will take over the café and be her caregiver, too. And, of course Papa will be home in another two months, earning money. That is, if he can get his old job back."

"I'm curious," asked Kent. "Just how are your father and Uncle Yakim related again?"

"They are half-brothers. They share the same mother. Nelva is his second wife. She is the sister of Sasha, who was his first wife. It is a common custom for widowed husbands to marry younger sisters. Nelva is a kind woman. She will take good care of Mama." Katcha frowned, and hugged her wool sweater around her. Thoughts scrambled through her head, triggered by memories of her mother's hopes for her. She suddenly realized that they had never finished their conversation on the bus to St. Petersburg—an argument, actually, about their future. Kent was right that it was too private to be held among a full busload of passengers. But he had carefully avoided bringing it up again during their entire stay in St. Petersburg.

The ferry churned through the darkness. Katcha glanced around the deck and noticed that most of the other passengers had drifted elsewhere. The few who had stayed were at the other end, engaged in their own conversations or dozing. She and Kent were alone. It was now or never.

"Kent? We never finished our talk on the bus. I still have so many things to ask you. All about your future—our future. And by the way, even more important, I need to know things you've never told me. I know you're a spy, but…" Katcha's breath caught in her throat. "I have to ask you. Are you also a professional criminal? What did you do that made the authorities arrest you? Why were you in that prison camp in the first place?"

Kent knew this bombardment was coming and he had steeled himself for it. "Dear, I'm not a professional criminal. All I can tell you is that I was on my first mission—in the wrong place at the wrong time in a military building in Moscow. I got caught and was arrested. That's why I was sent to prison, to Camp Obuchat. Right now, as far as the Russian government is concerned, I'm an escaped criminal. Katcha, you knew that risk when you chose to come with me. Are you sorry you came?"

"No, of course not," she burst out. "And I'm not afraid to say that I love you and want to be with you. I will be your mistress, but not for long. It would be too degrading. I want to be your wife."

"I suppose there *will* come a time when I'll have to settle down and live a more domesticated life," he grumbled.

"I see. So, until that time, there's no room for a woman, a wife, not even me, in your life?"

"I didn't say that," he replied. "If you're still willing, we can stay together for a trial period and see how well you and I adapt to my here-again, gone-again living style. I do love you, so be patient with me. In time, anything's possible, even total domestication. Oh boy, did I just say that?"

Katcha leaned back on the bench, her thumping heart easing, reconciled to the end of their talk, whether she liked the result of it or not. At least it did offer her a glimmer of hope.

Three hours later, the lights dimmed. Passengers quieted and settled in for the night. The rumbling sounds of diesel engines turning over, churning screws propelling and cavitating through the water, and the hull meeting and pounding the oncoming waves—all creating a calming, rhythmic inducement to sleep.

But not for long. Three hours later, a nasty squall whipped up. It tossed the 580-foot ship against raging waves, rolled it broadside with buffering surges, and tossed quite a few stomachs as well. As vicious as the squall was, it passed in the next forty minutes, and calm presided for the remainder of the crossing as the loaded car ferry tacked its way across the Gulf of Finland. Several times in that crossing, they passed a number of buoys demarking the watery border between Russia and Finland. The thirteen-hour ferry trip covered just over two hundred miles at sea.

Kent and Katcha awoke at daybreak and decided to move to a bench with a better view. As the brightening sun rose behind them, they could just make out land, the distant shoreline of Helsinki. They found a new excitement as the ferry churned into the harbor, approaching Market Square—a bustling plaza bordered by three-story buildings in colors of yellow, pink, and brown. Vendors' small pointed tents crowded the plaza with early shoppers already squeezing together for tempting deals.

For Kent and Katcha, the view miles beyond Market Square took their breath away. Rising majestically against an azure-blue sky, they saw Helsinki Cathedral. Gleaming, pristine white, its green dome was surrounded by four smaller green domes and elegant columns on all sides. The couple clasped hands and gazed in silence, feeling a rare moment of freedom and gratitude.

Their rapture was disrupted when the ferry collided hard with the head-on wooden landing, followed by gentler bumps until its squarish bow plugged into its shore socket. The bow doors opened, vehicles began to roll out of the hull, and passengers began to spill onto a forward gangway.

Waiting their turn, a half-hour later they pulled their bags down the gangway into the Helsinki terminal. Ahead lay the Finnish customs office in a separate terminal building. Entering, Kent began searching for a pay telephone, but the only one he could find was on the opposite side of the building, so they got in line with other arriving passengers and again awaited their turn. At last, they arrived at a Customs counter and Kent presented both their passports.

"Business or pleasure?" asked the uniformed agent on the other side of the window.

"A little of both," said Kent.

"You are together?"

"Yes, Katcha is my daughter."

"How long are you staying?"

"Two nights," he continued lying.

The agent regarded their faces for a few seconds, stamped their passports and visas, and released the gate. "Welcome to Finland. Enjoy your stay."

Kent settled Katcha in a waiting room seat and made a beeline for the pay phone he'd spotted earlier. He called a special number at the U.S. Embassy that bypassed the switchboard. It connected him with the intelligence liaison for the embassy. After identifying himself, Kent was given an appointment with the liaison person at one o'clock that afternoon for the purpose of debriefing and resettling. When he told the liaison that he didn't even have cab fare, the man replied, "I'll send a car for you. It should be out front of the terminal building in twenty minutes." Kent hesitated to tell the man about Katcha until they actually met. When he returned to her, he found her hunched over, sobbing into a large handkerchief.

"What's wrong, dear?"

"Now that we are here in Helsinki, are you going to leave me and go back to doing whatever it is that you do for your country?"

He wiped a tear from her cheek with his finger. "Katcha, you're extremely important to me, but my head is divided right now between my current profession and my devotion to you. I love being with you. I love talking to you. And, right now, I'm sure I'd miss you if you weren't a big part of my life. But I'm also duty and morally bound to my country. I'm hoping there is room for both. I also wonder if I've done enough for my country already, and maybe it's time to think about me and the rest of my life. Dear, I'm trying to fit all these things into my head. All I can promise is that I will have a better understanding of our relationship after I finish with my embassy visit."

"Can you blame me for worrying, Kent? I'm wondering whether you will take me to America, or will I have to settle in Finland or some other European nation. And will any of those places accept my immigration. I even worry they might ship me back to Russia as an illegal immigrant."

He placed a strong arm around her shoulders. "Don't worry, taking you to America is my first priority. We've been through a lot together. I understand your fears. I won't leave you, no matter what. I just couldn't. In any case, I'll stand by you until you're safely settled."

"What about marriage?" she asked in a querulous voice. "You know I love you. I've loved you from the start. I'd do anything for you. What more do you want from me?"

Here we go again, he thought. He felt a stab of impatience and tried hard, with a controlled voice, to suppress it. *I really didn't want this friggin' conversation right now.*

"Katcha, dear, we've already talked about this. I believe I'm in love with you, too, and there's a good chance of marriage ahead. But I have to say it again. It will be a lonely and worrisome life for you. My profession requires me to be gone for long and risky adventures in God-knows-where much of the time. And for me personally, call it wanderlust. I'm not sure I'm ready to give up the excitement that goes with all that. If I do give it up right now, maybe to be a stodgy lawyer, I'll always wonder what I've missed for the rest of my life."

"Thank you for telling me this," said a sniffling Katcha. "I understand, sort of. I want to be with you no matter what you decide. I would hope that your marriage to me can fill that void. I promise to always keep our love fresh and as exciting as I possibly can for as long as I can. That's what your love means to me."

Enough already, he thought. "We'd better get outside now

before our transportation to the embassy leaves without us."

Just as they passed through the automatic sliding door of the terminal, a black Nissan SUV bearing diplomatic plates pulled up to the curb. The driver remained inside and kept the engine idling. A man about forty with horn-rimmed glasses emerged from the passenger seat, approached them, then hesitated when he saw that Kent wasn't alone.

"Well, as I live and breathe, it's Kent Brukner," he began, "and with a mustache, too. I almost didn't recognize you with that hat and brush on your face."

"Ralph Ebernath, you dog you," declared Kent, addressing one of his former instructors. "What the hell are you doing in Helsinki?"

"I was assigned to the embassy here fourteen months ago, but I might ask you the same thing."

Ralph had excessively ordinary looks. Slender, about five-foot-ten, an oval face and close-clipped dark-brown hair. The tops of his ears poked slightly away from his head. He had an unaggressive but confident stance and looked fit in his black suit, white shirt, and black tie. "And, I might I ask, who is this lovely young woman?"

"This is Katcha Kroschenko. She and her family were quite instrumental in enabling my escape from Russia. We've been through a lot together. I'd like to bring her to America with me."

Just the few steps outside the terminal Kent felt the warmer, moist air. He and Katcha had wisely packed away their winter jackets and wore sweaters now. Helsinki's August weather meant daytime in the mid-sixties and maybe low-fifties at night.

Ralph waited for the two new arrivals to climb into the SUV, then returned to the front passenger seat. As soon as the doors were closed, the SUV cruised through the heart of Helsinki to Itäinen Puisttotie, its equivalent to Embassy Row in Washington, D.C.

"Are you two married?" asked Ralph, twisting his body slightly and turning his head toward them.

"No," Kent answered abruptly. "But that's not off the table," he added, when he looked at Katcha's anxious face.

"The first order of business is to get you two debriefed so you can be on your way," said Ralph.

"We could use showers and decent wardrobes first," Kent admitted. "A shave, including demolishing this hedgerow under my nose, would work wonders, too. A good hotel room and a wee bit of walking money would be awfully nice, my good man."

"You know the rules—debrief, first," reiterated Ralph. The SUV was waved through the U.S. Embassy gates by the U.S. Marine guards and directed around the building to a side entrance.

"Oh, by the way, miss, you'll need some debriefing, too."

"Why would they want to debrief me?" whispered Katcha. "I'm not a professional spy."

"That is what the embassy needs to determine," said Ralph. "It's routine questioning for a foreign national. No need to worry."

Chapter 20
The U.S. Embassy, Helsinki

The SUV driver dropped Ralph and the new arrivals off at the U.S. Embassy's Annex Office Building. Kent and Katcha had assumed, by its name, that it would be a severe gray building. Far from it. The imposing structure had a façade of stunning pink stone with elegant architectural detail over the front door and tall windows. Vertically separating the windows were classical pilasters: half-columns three stories high placed flat against the building and topped by Greek Ionic capitals, curled like rams' horns.

Two U.S. Marine corporals with sidearms, a male and female, stood guard in the small vestibule just inside. Before being awarded identification badges, Kent and Katcha were meticulously questioned, wanded, and body-searched by the two guards. Next, Ralph escorted them down a seemingly endless hall lined with oil paintings of Nordic landscapes. At an open door, a solemn, thirty-ish female Marine stood waiting for them. With an extended open palm, she motioned Katcha into a private office and instructed her to wait for an interviewer. Katcha's eyelids flickered with apprehension at being separated from her lover.

Ralph and Kent continued down the hall to an elevator that lowered them to a sub-basement level. They entered an electronically protected "Screen Room," used for debriefing and lie detecting—a room replete with one-way mirrors. A massive steel desk held an array of detectors: a portable EKG recorder, blood pressure cuff, and pulse-oximeter, as well as recording devices and sensors that measured perspiration, heart rate, and other reliable indicators of anxiety and fear. Kent stopped cold. It wasn't his first time under microscopic probing, but it always took its psychological toll.

"Do I have to go through all that rigamarole again?" he asked.

"It's routine for those who have been in deep penetration for any period of time," replied Ralph. "You've been out of touch for some time. And…" His pause seemed almost accusatory. "You've acquired an unknown and unauthorized colleague during that period as well."

"What I want to do is tell my story and soak up the luxuries of a decent hotel room."

"Is that all?" asked Ralph, in a sarcastic tone.

"No. I'm anxious to get the machinery rolling to get the two of us to America—and Iowa in particular."

"That's not my department," said an impatient Ralph. "The debriefing is."

"Before we go any further," intervened Kent, "there are a couple of things I'd like to know. Did the bug I planted go active in General Molitkov's office? And if it did, is it still a viable intel source? I need to know if all my efforts actually paid off."

"I'm supposed to be asking the questions here," answered Ralph. "But yes, the bug you planted went active and turned out to be a rich source of reliable and useful information. Now have a seat here. Are you comfortable?"

Kent lowered himself into a leather swivel chair. "Yeah, I suppose so."

Ralph finished connecting the various polygraph devices to his arm and hands and picked up the desk microphone. "It is Sunday, August 23rd, 1992 at 10:53 a.m. local Helsinki time. This is Ralph Ebernath debriefing the mission of Agent Kent Brukner."

Addressing him, Ralph suggested, "Perhaps you should start your account when you crossed into Russia as George Thermon, a senior buyer for Ingleman's Department Stores."

"I arrived in Moscow at near midnight on May 20th, 1992...."

Two hours later, an exhausted Kent paused his narrative, completely drained. Ralph had constantly interrupted him for more details whenever he thought his story needed additional clarity.

"Why don't we break for lunch now?" said Ralph. "We can pick up where you left off this afternoon."

"What about Katcha?" asked Kent.

"Are you asking about taking her to lunch? Or your crazy idea of bringing her to the States with you?" asked Ralph.

"What do you mean crazy?" asked Kent. "I'm not going to lose her after all we've been through together."

Chapter 21
Dmitri's Epiphany

Back in St. Petersburg, Major Dmitri Federov sat scrunched down in the swivel chair behind his desk in the local office of the *Federalnaya Sluzhba Bezopasnosti*, the FSB. The federal security officer was still upset with the port captain who overrode his authority, allowing the Kroschenko pair to board the *Princess Anastasia* and leave the country. Dmitri was certain that the couple was up to something illegal, but he couldn't quite put his finger on what that something was. His detective's intuition, which rarely failed him, bristled whenever the couple came to mind. *That blathering idiot of a port captain robbed me of the time I needed to properly investigate them.* Dmitri's pride had been wounded and he bled fuming regrets over and over again. *Why hadn't I pulled rank on that incompetent sonofabitch?* Dmitri took one last puff on the Turkish cigarette dangling from his lips and stabbed it into the glass ashtray at the corner of his cluttered desk as if it were a dagger in the heart of Captain Ilitskova.

The chaos on the major's desk consisted of outdated "Wanted" posters, unanswered mail, and assorted pointless paperwork. He gave all of it a shove with his right elbow and bent down to open the left-hand bottom drawer—to retrieve a bottle of vodka. Unscrewing the cap, he brought it to his lips, threw his head back, and imbibed a long swig of the liquid fire. It wasn't the first time that morning. *Maybe three or four, but who's counting?* he reassured himself. He replaced the cap and returned the bottle to the drawer.

As he straightened up, something odd caught his eye. It was a "Wanted" poster with the flap of an interoffice envelope attached, covering the forehead as a hat would. He stared at the artist's sketch for several seconds, picked up a pencil, and with a gleeful grin, drew a mustache beneath the nose on the sketch's face.

"Yes! Yes! I know that face!" he shouted and slammed his fist down on the desk. "It's Oleksander Kroschenko! I just knew it!"

He slid the poster out from the envelope and read the description. "George Thermon, U.S.A, possibly an alias, an escapee from Obuchat Prison Camp." Height and weight followed. There was no other information except the contact number for the prison camp. That was enough for Dmitri. He dialed and reached a corporal in the security guard office. Identifying himself, he asked to speak to the camp's commanding officer about the escapee.

"Yes, sir," the corporal said. "There will be a short wait, possibly ten minutes, while I fetch Captain Veloboro from his quarters." Dmitri fumed. *A captain doesn't have a phone in his own quarters?* While he waited, he started to organize his desk clutter and came across an Incident Report concerning a suspicious man and woman at the St. Petersburg Zoopark. He set it aside.

"Yes, what is this all about?" asked the deep voice on the phone.

"Captain Veloboro?

"Yes."

"I am Major Dmitri Federov of the Federal Security police. I have in my hands the Wanted poster of George Thermon, your recent escapee. I might have a suspect in mind, but I require more information to work with. Would you mind answering a few questions?"

"Be glad to, Major, but there is little to be said about the man. He arrived without paperwork. He used the name George Thermon while he was here, but we are quite sure that was an alias, as the poster says."

"Why wasn't his real name determined? Didn't you interrogate the man thoroughly?"

"As I said, Major, Thermon arrived here with no paperwork. We had no basis to interrogate him. He was a model prisoner right up to the night he broke out."

"Model prisoner, hah! What was his crime?" asked Dmitri. "What did he do that got him sent to your prison? Who was the arresting officer?"

"Sorry, Major. The only thing I can tell you is that a Colonel P. Korashnev at the Army annex in Moscow signed the warrant. He wrote the words 'spy' and 'later' in the 'Details' spaces of the warrant."

"Might I also ask how the man escaped?" Dmitri asked in a voice tinged with impatience.

"He squeezed through the barbed wires at night," replied the captain in a hesitant voice, uncertain whether he should have revealed quite so much to some outsider.

The birthmark on Dmitri's face throbbed a deeper brown bordering on dark red with his frustration. "What kind of a camp are you running, Captain, that a prisoner can leave when he pleases?"

"Major, I run a very large and undermanned camp for political and demented prisoners. We are labeled a minimum-security facility."

"I see. Thank you, Captain," offered Dmitri, while he was really thinking: *Another incompetent officer.*

Dmitri hung up the phone and repeated aloud, "Korashnev, Colonel P. Korashnev. Where have I just seen that name?"

He picked up the zoopark Incident Report once again. The heading read: "From Colonel Polkóvnik Korashnev, Russian Federation Army, Deployment Planning Section." The major found some of the answers he was looking for, including physical descriptions of the couple. Ah! Oleksander and Katcha—the couple being interrogated by security at the ferry.

Dmitri straightened up in his chair and reflected. About a month ago, a memo marked Urgent had crossed his desk about an unnamed man—an American spy posing as a Russian major—who had attempted to break into General Uri Molitkov's office at Army headquarters. The colonel was the officer who arrested the perpetrator in the act.

Dmitri set the Incident Report down and leaned way back in his chair. He held his chin between a thumb and forefinger to help organize his thoughts. *I will need to speak with this Korashnev fellow. So Oleksander is an American spy after all. Is George Thermon his real name or an alias? I'll have someone check to see if the name is in our files. Maybe immigration's files also. And who is the woman Katcha? What role does she play in this farce? Is she an American spy as well, or is she merely some perverted Russian peasant soul he picked up along the way? Her crime: Aiding and Abetting an Enemy of the State. I've got to get those two back to St. Petersburg where they will be accessible again. Perhaps the woman can prove useful to me. Let me think. Ah, I believe I have an idea how to bring them back.*

Dmitri rifled through the pile on his desk for the latest schedule of the *Princess Anastasia. When will the ferry be making its next run to Helsinki?*

* * * *

At the approximate time of Kent's debriefing, Laura Tipton, an embassy interviewer, entered her office to question the waiting Katcha. Fortyish Laura had a buttoned-up look in her severe beige suit and a single chestnut-colored braid going down her back. She had risen to a GS-12 in her eighteen years in the diplomatic service, but with her skills in interrogation, secretly felt she deserved higher.

Katcha sat stiff and alert and declined Laura's offer of coffee, tea, or water. *I wonder what this lady wants from me. It can't be good.* She anxiously waited for the woman to take her chair behind the large oak desk and begin the questioning she knew was coming. On the wall behind the desk, Katcha saw a framed picture she assumed was the American President. Sadly, she did not know his name. She could almost hear her own heart beating.

134

Laura's eyes flicked over the young woman, assessing the fresh, honest look, the simple outfit—black slacks, white blouse, and gray sweater. But she decided to hold her first impression at bay and remain objective.

"Your full name, please?" asked Laura, ready with a pen to capture her responses.

"Katcha Nadia Kroschenko."

"Katcha, were you born in Russia? That is, are you a Russian citizen?"

"Yes, to both questions."

"How long have you known Kent Brukner?"

"About two months."

"How did you two meet?"

"Kent was a customer in our café. I waited on his table."

"You own a café?"

"No, my mother does. She does the cooking, too. I just worked there as a waitress."

"What is your mother's name?"

"Mavis Anne Dowd Kroschenko. She is a British citizen."

"Really? Where was she born?"

"Sussex, England."

"And your father's name?"

"Oleksander Kroschenko. He is from the Ukraine."

"His occupation?"

"He's a salesman for an agricultural machinery factory—when he's working. Right now, he's finishing up a prison sentence that will be completed next month."

"What was he sent to prison for?"

"He spoke out for the opposition, and a neighbor reported him."

"Is he active in Russian politics?"

"Not really. It was just that one rally. Kent used Papa's papers and identity to get out of the country."

"Didn't your father need those papers? Won't he get in trouble without them?"

"Not while he's in prison. I plan to send them back to him first chance I get."

"I see. Tell me about Kent. What is the nature of your relationship with him?"

"We are very close."

"Are you intimate with him?"

"Yesss," Katcha stammered as she blushed. "That's a very personal question, but *yes*, we are intimate."

"Are you engaged to be married?"

"Not formally, but we've talked about it."

"Do you love him, or do you consider him to be merely a ticket to the United States?"

"I love Kent very much. Going to his country is my dream, but to say that I am using him is insulting. I would live anywhere with him."

Laura was beginning to like this woman. Still maintaining her professional demeanor, she nevertheless felt a wave of sympathy—and a first impression that Katcha was not any kind of security risk. "Sorry, Katcha, but I have to know these things. "Do you believe he loves *you* as well?"

"I know he loves me, too," Katcha burst out, feeling more and more defensive. "But he hesitates with marriage because he believes it will interfere with his profession. He's told me so. He thinks it's unfair to me—he'll be away so much, but I would marry him anyway. I love him that much."

"Then you two have openly discussed how he makes his living?"

"Only that he's an American secret agent. He won't—and says he can't—tell me anything else. But I understand. I will be a good wife and not ask for any more."

"Your English is good," admitted Laura. "Did you learn it from your mother?"

"Oh yes. We've been having conversations in English almost since I was able to talk. She grew up in England until she married, but she wanted to keep up her English language skills."

"I see," said Laura. "Where will you be staying in Helsinki?"

"I don't really know. I suppose in some hotel room with Kent. He hasn't had a chance to make any reservations. Maybe you should speak with him about this."

"I'm sure Ralph Ebernath intends to make some reservations for you both at a nearby hotel, if you wish," offered Laura.

"That would be very nice," said Katcha.

"One room or two?" asked Laura.

"One room, please. But he needs to check with Kent first."

"I'm sure Ralph will. Let's say for a week," said Laura. "We should learn more of your status by then."

"My status?" Katcha's voice quavered. "You mean they could send me back?"

"It is possible," said Laura. "But you're an unusual case, so there is hope."

"I can't go back there," Katcha burst out. "I'll be arrested for helping an American prisoner escape from my country. Kent even used my father's identity and papers for that escape. They'll arrest me and send me to prison. That is one serious crime in Russia."

"You may be worrying for nothing," offered Laura. "There's also the possibility that the Finnish government would allow you to immigrate here."

"But my visa to Finland is only good for a few more days," protested Katcha, dabbing at her tearing eyes. "They could decide to send me back as well."

"Wait! You said your mother was born in Sussex, England. Did she grow up there?"

"Oh yes."

"Does she have any family still living in Sussex?"

"There should be at least my Aunt Emily, my mother's sister, and a couple of cousins. I don't know their names. Mama did all the corresponding, so I never paid any attention to their names. They were mostly people I never met. I knew my maternal grandparents, Edyth and William Dowd, but they are long gone."

"What's your mother's maiden name again?"

"Mavis Dowd."

"Did she ever renounce her British citizenship?"

"Of course not. She's proud of it."

"That means you're the daughter of a British citizen. Not just a random applicant."

"But I was born in Russia. Doesn't that make me a Russian citizen?"

"You might have dual citizenship," said Laura. "I'll have to look into that."

"Do you think this additional information will help my cause?"

"I can't make any promises, but it just might." Laura heard a knock at the door and called, "Come in."

Ralph stuck his head in and asked, "We're taking a little break. If you're finished, would you like to join us for a bite of lunch?"

"We're all done except for the fallout," said Laura. "Yes, we'd love to join you."

"Fallout?" queried Ralph.

"Yes. We were having an extended discussion of possible immigration status rulings and Katcha's available options."

The four headed to the embassy dining room. Ralph led the way with Kent close behind. He was only a few feet ahead of Katcha, but to her it seemed like a mile. She yearned to catch up with him, to tuck her hand in the crook of his arm. She missed his strong, warm body. The interrogation gap of several hours, and the few feet physically between them right now, made her feel as if she'd entered a cloud of cold isolation. *Was this to be her future?*

Chapter 22
Debriefing, Day Two

Ralph had booked them into a hotel, the Villa Keirkner. Two sharp knocks and "Room Service" in English announced the breakfast they'd ordered the night before, interrupting Kent's final moments of sleep. Katcha, already awake, stood naked at the window overlooking the city and the coastal waters beyond. She wrapped herself in one of the hotel's terry robes and hurried to answer the door. A uniformed waiter pushed a tea trolley into the room right up to the small table opposite the bed. Katcha penned a tip to the bill and signed it with their room number, 512. The young man smiled and left.

"Hey, Mr. Lazy, the new day's sun is being wasted," announced Katcha. "Come on, get up and out. Breakfast has arrived." She arranged all the food and silverware on the little table.

Kent sat up and emitted a long, loud yawn in response. He threw his legs over the side of the king-size bed, pulled on a pair of briefs and the other terry robe, and padded off to the bathroom. Some minutes later he emerged refreshed and sat down at the little breakfast table next to Katcha.

"Wow. Bacon, sausage, eggs, hash-browns, and toast plus real coffee," exclaimed Kent. "I must be in heaven."

"It's exactly what you ordered last night," she reminded him.

"How'd you sleep?" asked Kent, when he set his half-emptied coffee cup down on the table.

"Oh my," she giggled. "After we *played*, I was exhausted. I slept like a baby until around four, and then my mind went to work. I reran all those scary, undecided outcomes that Laura told me about. I don't want to go back to Russia. I would be a criminal there and I fear what would happen to me."

"Don't be afraid, sweetheart," he reassured her. "I won't abandon you. And yes, I was exhausted too. We hadn't had the privacy to *play* in such a long time. It was so satisfying." He leaned over and kissed her on the cheek.

"It was nice of the embassy people to provide a debit card and some ready cash," she commented. "The hotel is very nice, too."

"Nice? Hell, no! They owe me over four months hazardous-duty pay and a bunch of vacation days, and a few delicate favors after what I accomplished for my country."

"What did you do for your country?"

"That's just it, I can never tell anyone except my debriefer, and that is the business for my second day at the embassy. Speaking of which, I'd better get dressed and down there before the whole morning is shot."

"What about me?" she asked. "Will they need me at all today?"

"No, I don't believe so, sweetie."

"But what will I do with myself alone all day?"

"I'm sorry, hon, but the embassy wants you to stick around here for another couple days. They need to work on getting an extension to your visa so you have more freedom here. And anyway, there's all kind of good stuff you can do here in the hotel. By Wednesday you'll be free to go shopping. I'll give you my debit card. There's 500 bucks American on the card now and I'm sure I'll get more later. The hotel people should be able to direct you to some first-class stores. You'll be able to shop your heart out and have some fun."

He spent the next twenty minutes showering, shaving and dressing. Katcha hugged him as he left for the embassy for his second debriefing.

* * * *

Kent left the Villa Keirkner lobby, turned right, and walked to the corner of Itäinen Puistotie. Then a right again for a block to Siltotie and finally into the embassy grounds. Using the temporary photo-pass provided the previous day, he entered via the main entrance and proceeded directly to the basement and Ebernath's office. Ralph was waiting for him. After an exchange of pleasantries and a cup of coffee they were ready to continue with Kent's debriefing.

As Kent slipped into the monitoring devices, he asked, "How much longer is this gonna go on?"

"As long as it takes," snapped Ralph.

"Let's see, yesterday I told you about slipping through the camp perimeter. I made my way through the surrounding woods to a wealthy horse farm, hid throughout the daytime in the stable loft, stole some civilian clothes from the wash line, and buried my prison garb. I took any roads heading westerly. I managed to stay clear of the pursuing guards that night and for most of the next day. By then hunger and weariness caught up with me, so I tried a nearby café for food. My waitress was friendly. She figured out who I was and decided to help me."

"Was this waitress your young lady, Katcha Kroschenko?" asked Ralph.

"Yes, of course. And she introduced me to her mother, Mavis Dowd Kroschenko. It was through their kindness that I wound up with a place to stay for several weeks until the hue and cry for me had died down."

"Wasn't there a father in the picture?" questioned Ralph.

"Not exactly. Katcha's father, Olexsander Kroschenko, was serving the last months of a prison sentence for speaking out against the local government. During this period of closeness with the family, Katcha and I developed a strong attraction for one an-other."

"Be honest, you two were intimate, weren't you?" corrected Ralph.

Kent scowled. *What a dumb-ass question.* "Of course we were sleeping together, but to earn my keep I helped out in the kitchen alongside her mother. When Mavis fell and sprained her ankle, she was confined to her bed for a few days. Katcha and I managed the cafe. I even did the cooking. Mavis really appreci-ated my pitching in. She and I developed a fondness and trust for each other. Eventually, she made me an offer I couldn't refuse. She would furnish her husband's passport and identity papers and additional means for us to travel by rail and bus and ferry across one-third of Russia."

"Meaning you and Katcha?" Ralph asked.

"You bet. Right from the beginning she was part of the deal."

"Deal? What kind of a deal?"

"Mavis wanted me to take Katcha to the Free World to experience the kind of life she knew growing up in England. She never regretted her marriage to Olexi, but she wanted something more for her daughter. Katcha never went past high school. Yes, we discussed both the risks and advantages of traveling as a couple. She knew how we felt about each other. I told her the truth, that I didn't know whether marriage was possible, but I would never abandon her. In return, Mavis would finance the travel, and drive us to the nearest rail head at the town of Pechora."

"Do you love her? Do you actually mean to marry her?" asked Ralph.

"Right now, I'd have to say yes. At least I'm ninety-five percent certain of it."

"What about the other five percent?"

"I'm reserving that for figuring out how I'm going to man-age the rest of my professional life as a married man. We've dis-cussed marriage, but I haven't proposed yet. I don't know what parts of my professional life I'm going to have to give up, but I'm definitely not going to give *her* up. It so happens I'm thinking of proposing this very evening and taking her to America with me. We can be married in Cedar Rapids, Iowa, where my family is."

Ralph raised an eyebrow. "When you're back in the States, suppose you decide not to marry. What happens to the little lady then?"

"I'll do my best to see that she's properly settled, happy, and self-sufficient."

"Happy and self-sufficient without you? In Iowa?" Ralph sneered. "That sounds like bullshit, Kent. Do you realize what you've gotten yourself into? Your whole career could be jeopardized by this woman. It could severely affect your judgment when you're out in the field."

Kent's eyes narrowed. "I think that's my business. Maybe you should have a little more faith in me that I can do my job."

Ralph raised his hands in a gesture of frustration. "And I'm just doing my job by playing devil's advocate. Besides, I think you've been warned about the difficulties of immigration into the U.S. She could be rejected. Did you ever think of that?"

Kent pressed his lips together in sullen silence.

"Enough on that subject for now. Tell me about the rest of the trip."

The debriefing continued for another hour. By then Kent was getting anxious. He'd had enough of debriefing. He wanted to put it all behind him and start looking forward to the promised leave he'd accumulated. "Glad we're done," he said.

Ralph leaned back in his chair with a smug smile. "Dream on, friend. We're not done. We have two more days of debriefing. But also on Wednesday we'll be discussing potential new assignments for you."

Chapter 23
Missing

On the fourth day of Kent's mission debriefing, Ralph was still extracting every last detail from him. Kent's patience was beginning to wane. Katcha had been cooling her heals at the hotel for two days—the exercise room, the pool, and the six boutiques within its walls. With her visa extention, she was ready for something more.

* * * *

Meanwhile the *Princess Anastasia* was approaching Helsinki's South Harbour—after another Wednesday/Sunday arrival from St. Petersburg. The ferry fitted its bow into the pier and lowered the ramp connecting its vehicle deck to land. A late-model shiny black Mercedes, the third vehicle in line, exited from the vessel and drove to the port's gate. The driver and passengers presented appropriate diplomatic identifications, allowing them into the city of Helsinki. The car sped six blocks parallel to the water and pulled up in front of an unmarked red-brick warehouse. Its huge steel door unfolded vertically, and the Mercedes drove through an entrance large enough to accommodate a tractor-trailer. The door rattled closed behind them.

The midmorning sun cast harsh rays on a tramp freighter

docked across the street from the warehouse. The freighter, the *MVC Maersk II*, had seen better times. Yellow primer failed to cover roaming rust in large patches over the ship's decks and hull. Still, the Russian-owned, coal-fired, tramp freighter conveyed goods on a weekly basis in both directions across the Gulf of Finland.

Three men exited the parked Mercedes. The first man out was the bald, jowly Dmitri Federov. A second passenger, a lanky man in a black suit, had slicked-down black hair atop an inverted-triangular face with bony cheeks and a satanic expression. A short stocky, broad-shouldered man with unkempt red hair tagged along behind the other two.

A straw-blonde woman approached the car to greet them. In a white tank top and black chinos, she had a lithe, flat-chested build with surprisingly muscular arms.

"Ah, Sasha, my dear," said Dmitri. "It's good to be working with you again."

"Yes, Dmitri," said the local agent. "It's been quite a while since we created havoc in Istanbul."

Sasha wore her chopped, chin-length hair without a curl and possessed a repertoire of mature facial expressions that betrayed her youthful, athletic frame. She moved with the grace and confidence of a professional dancer or gymnast.

"Sasha, we will be working with these two," said Dmitri. He pointed with his thumb at the black suit, "Vadim," and nodded to the redhead, "Adrik." I believe they will prove most useful in the next few days."

"Just what do you have in mind?" she asked.

"Come. We will go across the street and meet one more member of our little cabal. I'll explain more there."

Leaving from a pedestrian door near the front of the warehouse, the four crossed the road to the freighter's gangway and climbed up to the main deck. The ship's third mate met them there and led them up two flights to the captain's cabin. It comprised two compartments: his living quarters tucked in the back, and, most important, the large room just behind the bridge that served as a charthouse and radio room as well as a conference room. They took seats around the table.

"So, Dmitri, what nefarious purpose do you intend for my ship this time?" asked Captain Vyachesslav, a stocky man with grizzled gray hair and full beard.

"I'll get right to the point," said Dmitri. "We need two of your passenger cabins for approximately one week, meals included. We will bring you a guest for safe-keeping to occupy the first cabin. Sasha here will occupy the second cabin when she is aboard. She will ensure that the guest does not leave the cabin until we come for her."

"A prisoner, eh?" taunted the captain. "I might have known. You do realize we are scheduled to make a round-trip crossing in a few days' time."

"I understand. Just remind me of your departure date. We'll make sure to remove her before you depart."

"What if the authorities decide to inspect?" asked the captain.

"The authorities are more interested in cargo than passengers, are they not?" replied Dmitri. "Don't forget, you will receive your usual fee for assisting the Federation police."

"Then of course I will accommodate your guests," said the captain in a tone of mock respect. "I am now running a damned hotel as well as a ship. Or should I call it a jail? Hah!"

Dmitri began explaining what he expected of each participant. Their meeting lasted another twenty minutes, then his two henchmen left and returned to the second level of the warehouse, where cots, hot plate, and a refrigerator would accommodate their needs for the coming week. The captain and Sasha remained aboard and he showed her to her cabin.

* * * *

After Kent had left for his final briefing on their fourth day in Helsinki, Katcha pranced around their hotel room. She was finally allowed to go out. Feeling both light-hearted and liberated, especially with Kent's debit card, she called the concierge desk and learned the location of the nearest shopping mall. It would only be a short taxi ride and all the stores had already opened. Happy to abandon the clothes she'd traveled in, she donned an outfit she had purchased in one of the hotel boutiques the night before: a flared skirt patterned in tiny blue and purple flowers, a sleeveless blue blouse, and black flats. She grabbed her purse and heavy gray sweater and took the elevator to the street level.

Katcha asked the doorman to get her a taxi. Pulling out his whistle, he tweeted for one of the Helsinki *Taksi* cabs at the stand down the street. The first one in line started toward the hotel. But across the street, another cab from the same company performed a U-turn and screeched to a stop in front of the hotel before the first one could arrive. The driver got out and held the door for her. She climbed in. After all, she saw no difference between the two cabs. Returning to his seat, the driver turned to his passenger, and asked, "Where to, ma'am?"

"Kämp Galleria, please," she replied.

He drove a few blocks, turned a corner, and stopped at the curb.

"Why are we stopping here?" she asked, but did not receive an answer.

A black-suited man stepped out of a doorway and pulled open the curbside back door.

Suddenly, Katcha saw a mean-looking face confronting her. His slick, slithery movements somehow reminded her of a crawling snake. She shuddered.

"Sorry," she stammered. "This cab is already taken."

"I agree," he said with a twisted grin. "We're taking it together, aren't we? Now move over and make room for me."

The stranger didn't wait for her response. Instead, he shoved her hard, pushing her to the left as he climbed in beside her. She reached for the left door handle, but found it locked from the front seat—a child-safety feature being used for a criminal purpose. The driver sped off as soon as the door was closed and locked.

Katcha immediately realized that the driver and intruder

were in cahoots. Minutes later, the stranger grabbed her right fore-arm. She struggled to get free, but he held her with an iron grip. She saw the syringe in his opposite hand coming close to her bare upper arm. With her free left hand, she struck him hard across the side of his face. The blow left a red mark, but his evil grin persisted. His grip on her right forearm tightened and half-twisted to prevent her from striking again. She wasn't one to surrender easily, but the man was incredibly strong.

She helplessly felt a sting in her right bicep, the penetration, the shivering cold fluid, and the pain of his cruel grip. *And now he's letting me go, but my arm is all back and blue and still hurts. Hurts less and less . . .*

Adrik drove on until they reached the warehouse. He pushed the hand-held remote button marked LIFT, and the truck entrance door rattled upward and out of their way. The cab rolled inside. Opening the right-side back door, the two men dragged the unconscious Katcha out and upstairs to a storage room. They laid her down roughly on a tattered couch amid stacks of cartons and crates.

Vadim, the snake-like stranger, said, "We'll wait 'til it's dark, then transfer her across the street to the ship's cabin accommoda-tion."

After four hours, Katcha began to stir. She swung her legs onto the floor and sat up on the edge of the ratty couch. Her brain didn't seem to be available yet. Vadim, keeping watch, saw these movements. He instantly gave her another shot. This one lasted until dark. When she finally awoke, all alone in the room, she struggled to sit up and place her feet on the floor. She screamed, "Help! Somebody help me!"

The two men burst into the room. She struggled and screamed as they blindfolded her and tie-wrapped her wrists be-hind her so they would be able to force her onto her feet. Kat-cha flexed her feet and kicked hard, heels first, aiming for Vadim's groin, but she was powerless against the two of them.

"Want another needle?" he sneered. Still blindfolded, only

then did she begin to cooperate. With each man holding her by an arm, they dragged her out of the room.

She screamed. "Where are you taking me? Let me go! I haven't done anything to you. Let me go!" She tried to plant her feet on the ground but to no avail. Her eyes, behind the blindfold, could tell they were outside and it was nighttime. Hands with steel grips tightened around her arms as they hauled her across the street and onto the gangway.

She stumbled, still dragging her feet as much as she could, up two staircase levels. She heard a door squeak open and felt herself being thrust inside. "Where am I?" she begged. No one answered. As the two men started to remove her restraints, she heard a woman's voice, loud and mean.

"You're in a cabin on a Russian ship, my dear. Cooperate, and there will be no pain. You may call me Sasha. I will be your close companion for the next few days."

When the blindfold was removed, Katcha didn't believe the powerful voice belonged to such a petite creature. She watched the two men stomp out of the cabin. Katcha's immediate thought was, *Now that those bozos are gone, I can handle this woman easily.* She jerked her head around. "Why am I on a ship? You can't keep me here!"

"You're wrong, my dear. We can keep you anywhere we want," replied Sasha.

When Katcha eyed the cabin door, Sasha darted to it, and stood ramrod straight with arms outspread and her back against it. "Hey, girl," she taunted, "the only way you'll get free is by getting past me."

Katcha studied the young woman. No more than five feet tall, in her early twenties. Tiny breasts in a white tank top tucked into black chino pants. Petite as she appeared, the bare arms were sinewy and muscled, and the heavy-soled black boots looked like they were meant for kicking.

Katcha got the message and understood the challenge all right, but she was still a little groggy from the drugs. *Later is better,* she thought. But then she witnessed Sasha doing the unexpected—showing her a padlock, then quickly slipping out the door. Next came the loud clang of the heavy metal door slamming, the sound of a hasp slapping home outside and the click of the padlock shutting her in the cabin She could only imagine where the key to the padlock would wind up. *Damn,* Katcha thought. *An opportunity lost. This is no time for desperation,* she told herself. She plopped down on the bed to reason out her situation. *Kent or even the police will never find me here. I'll have to escape by overcoming Sasha. It's my only chance. I need a weapon of some sort so I can strike quickly and soundly.* Katcha looked about the cabin. *Damn! Everything is either welded or screwed in place, even in the tiny bathroom.* She stretched out on the bed, laid her head back, and stared at the ceiling to think. It was then that she saw her sweater bunched up on the end of the bed. But not her purse. Her captors had taken it.

* * * *

Outside the cabin, Sasha scowled. Her prisoner had remained seated on the edge of the bed, refusing to answer the challenge. The gatekeeper felt a crushing disappointment that Katcha hadn't picked up the gauntlet she'd thrown down. She lived for chances to show off her physical prowess. A few minutes' wait hadn't changed her prisoner's mind, so she had quickly slipped out of the cabin and loudly slapped the hasp and lock in place—loudly enough for her prisoner to know she had been locked in.

* * * *

Late that afternoon, Kent stood on the top step in front of the embassy entrance, the fading sun casting long shadows. He felt exhilarated. *It's been a good day so far. I'm finished with the debriefing and I can put off any major decisions. I can't wait for my next assignment. On the other hand, should I give it all up to marry the woman I love? All I have to do is go to the hotel and propose to her. Even though she says she'll tolerate my unpredictable job as a spy, I know she'll tire of it. She'll expect me to settle down, especially if she gets pregnant. Will I end up with a stifling desk job pushing paper? Even if I still want to become a lawyer, am I ready to reenter law school, slog through to graduation, and face a grueling bar exam? I shudder to think of what'll become of me. I cringe at the idea of abandoning my dangerous, far-flung field work. It's friggin' exciting.*

The walk back to the hotel took only ten minutes. He stopped at the desk in the lobby to ask if there were any messages for him and the answer was negative. He took the elevator to the fifth floor and walked down the hall to room 512. Drained from his intense day at the embassy, he fumbled for his key, and then had trouble finding the keyhole. Finally, he swung the door away and stepped inside.

"Sweetheart?" he yelled when first he didn't see her in the room. "Where are you?"

When Kent received no response, he concluded that she was still shopping. He looked at his watch. Four-twenty. The afternoon wasn't over yet. *With a full debit card in hand, she's probably enjoying every last minute of it.* His wait began at the writing table where he wrote a few reminder notes. Then he shifted to the easy chair and the television. By eight-thirty that evening, he'd been pacing the room for the last half-hour.

At nine o'clock he called Ralph at home and yelled into the phone, "Katcha's missing."

Kent's shout proved so loud and panicky that Ralph had to pull the phone away from his ear. He filled the silence that followed with "Are you sure?"

"Yes!" snapped Kent. "I called the reception desk and they referred me to the concierge desk. The concierge on duty told me there was a note in the log at ten o'clock this morning saying that room 512 had asked for information pertaining to a day of shopping. She was advised to take a taxi to Kämp Galleria and the adjacent Kluuvi Shopping Centre. The stores closed at nine. She should be here by my side by now."

"Calm down, Kent," said Ralph. "Some of the stores here stay open 'til ten or even eleven. She's probably having a ball and lost track of the time. You know the shopping gene and all that."

"Katcha knew I would be home by about four. She was just

killing time with the shopping. I think something terrible has happened to her."

"Have you checked with the doorman?" asked Ralph.

"Yes, but the current doorman is two shifts removed. The desk wouldn't give me the man's contact information."

"Have you contacted the police yet?"

"No. I was afraid I would draw attention to the fact that her visa to be in Helsinki is for only a few days. I'm also afraid the Russian Federation police, the FSD, and Dmitri Federov, in particular, has a hand in this. He was pissed that we outsmarted him at the St. Petersburg pier. But I know it's really me he wants, and he may be holding her hostage to bag me."

"I think she'll still turn up tonight," said Ralph in a soothing voice. "But even if she doesn't, there's really nothing we can do tonight unless you want to bring the Helsinki police into this. I can come over there now if you think it will do any good."

"No, no, that won't be necessary. I'll see you at the embassy first thing tomorrow."

Kent hung up. While he had the phone in hand, he called two or three hospitals in case she'd had an accident, but there was no Katcha listed as a patient in the ones he tried. He knew it was a hopeless pursuit; there were more than ten hospitals in Helsinki. He settled into the sole easy chair, lights on, fully dressed, determined to remain alert for any news of her. Two hours later, sheer exhaustion took hold of him, He slept in the chair until seven the next morning.

Chapter 24
Searching

Aboard the *MVC Maersk II*, Katcha spent an uneasy night racking her brain for a way out of her captivity. Toward morning of the new day, sleep caught up with her. After only two hours of sleep, she rolled over on her back awake again.

Minutes later, Katcha realized her eyes were fixated on a ceiling light fixture directly above the bed. A small steel cage surrounded the single lightbulb with a thumbscrew to hold it in place. Nothing decorative, strictly utilitarian. *Hah, it'll do. After all, they do have to change a lightbulb once in a while.* She bolted upright. With a new determination, balancing carefully, she stood up on the thin mattress. Anchoring her feet to steady herself, she stretched high with her right hand, reached for the thumbscrew, and turned it counterclockwise several turns to release the cage from the bulb. *Yes!*

Katcha lowered herself back down to a sitting position with the cage in hand. She studied it. *Not really heavy enough to be a blunt instrument, but it does have a few jagged edges that might do some serious damage. I'll wait. When I hear her working at the lock outside I'll run to get behind the door before she opens it inward. It has to be almost noon by now and I didn't get any breakast. She'll be bringing me food sometime soon, I hope. Or are they planning to starve me so I'll spill crucial information about Kent?* She shuddered at the thought.

That sometime arrived an hour later when Katcha heard the lock and hasp clatter. She sprang into position behind the door and waited. A keenly alert Sasha swung it open, but did not enter.

"My dear Katcha, come out where I can see you, or there will be no food for you today."

Katcha walked boldly to the center of the room with one hand behind her.

Sasha stepped inside. "Back up, lady!" she ordered.

Katcha did, all the way to the bed, thinking. *A run at the woman will give me an advantage.*

Sasha immediately detected the look in her prisoner's eyes. She set the food tray down on the writing shelf next to the door and assumed a martial arts stance. "Okay, my dear, give me all you got."

That was all Katcha needed to hear. She charged at Sasha, swinging and slashing with the lightbulb cage-turned-weapon, but always too late to make contact. Her fleet-of-foot foe darted right, left, sideways, or backward to avoid even a scratch. At one interval Sasha's open palm slammed onto Katcha's cheek with considerable force. Katcha shook it off and resumed her relentless attack. Seconds later, Sasha's right foot rammed into her solar plexus, taking all the wind out of her.

Doubling over, Katcha thought she would never breathe again, but seconds later she had recovered enough to resume the battle. Finding it curious that her opponent waited for her to recover, Katcha struggled on and on, never able to land a single blow or scratch. The battle lasted almost five minutes with Katcha absorbing several more significant blows. In despair, she withdrew and sank down on the bed, exhausted to the bone.

Sasha, still looking quite fresh, simply smiled, removed the tray from under the plate of food, and started to leave with the tray under her arm. As soon as she turned her back, Katcha flung the metal cage at her. It grazed off her jailer's left shoulder, doing no damage at all, and fell to the floor. Sasha laughed, sailed out the door, and padlocked it.

Katcha had lost the battle. It took ten minutes to swallow her pride enough to think about the food on the writing shelf. Actually, she was famished. The writing shelf was an eighteen-by-twenty-four-inch surface that folded out from the bulkhead next to the door. A stool folded out on an arm beneath it. Katcha sat down and examined just what Sasha had brought: two ham sandwiches on buttered rye bread, each with a generous slab of meat and thick slice of cheese, and accompanied by lettuce and tomato. A pint-size carton held cool milk. Wolfing it all down, she began formulating her strategy for the next Sasha confrontation. She had to outsmart the woman in some other way.

* * * *

The Thursday morning sunlight washed over room 512 in Villa Keirkner, waking Kent from his nightmare-filled sleep. Last night's skin-crawling reality jolted him into full consciousness. Except for his tie and open collar, he'd been in this easy chair, fully dressed, the whole night.

He suddenly remembered the doorman. *I've got to talk with him first thing.* A stop in the bathroom gave him a chance to wash his face and shave. Hurriedly donning a fresh shirt and tie, Kent slipped into his suit jacket, locked the room door, and raced down the hall to the elevator. At the lobby level he rushed out the main hotel entrance in search of his quarry. The morning-shift doorman had just helped an elderly lady into a cab. As soon as he turned and walked toward him, Kent approached.

"My good man, I wonder if you can help me."

"Of course," he replied.

"I'm one of the hotel's guests, and my fiancé didn't return to our room last night, so I'm trying to retrace her steps. Yesterday she told me she was going to ask the concierge where the best shopping was. The concierge suggested that she take a cab. That would have been somewhere between nine-thirty and eleven yesterday morning. Do you remember getting a cab for a pretty, young, blonde woman, rather tall, about five-foot-eight?"

"Yes. It was sort of a strange thing."

"Strange?" asked Kent. "What do you mean, strange?"

"Two things," the doorman replied. "One, when I whistled for the first cab in line at the stand down the block, this different cab cut in crazily making a U-turn from across the street to take the fare instead."

"Is that kind of thing unusual?" asked Kent.

"Very unusual. Nobody likes a line jumper."

"What was the other thing you found strange?" asked an eager Kent.

"I recognized the cab and the company, Helsinki *Taksi*, number 2031, but I didn't recognize the driver. It should have been Tapio. After twelve years on this job, I know most of the drivers. If not by name, at least by face. I just figured this chap was new on the job."

"Can you describe him at all?" asked Kent.

"Well, he sat pretty low in the driver's seat, so I assume he was short, but he had a head of red hair and red bushy beard as well."

"Thank you," said Kent. "You have been very helpful. Is there any way I can get in touch with you if I need more information?"

The doorman took out a small pad, jotted down his telephone number, tore out the page, and handed it to Kent. Kent thanked him again and returned to the lobby to inquire after any messages.

"Yes, Mr. Brukner," replied the desk clerk. "There's a message from a Mr. Ralph Ebernath, asking for you to remain in the hotel until he arrives."

Kent thanked the clerk and sat down in one of the more comfortable divans in the lobby, facing the front of the building. He reached out to a side table and retrieved a copy of the *Helsinki Times,* a local English-language newspaper abandoned there. After reading a few pages, he looked up while he turned the page—and felt a pair of eyes bearing down on him. Quickly scanning the room, he picked out the offender and continued his scan well beyond, so as not to alert the man that he was aware of him. He pretended to read another page, then casually stared straight out the front window and picked up the reflection of the man's image in the periphery of his right eye. The tall, thin man with slicked-down black hair was staring straight at him. Each time Kent glanced in his direction the man turned away. Still, Kent avoided letting the man know he was aware of him. And with each glance he gleaned a little more about the man's appearance. That bony face seemed vaguely familiar but he could not remember where. It was a strange, but not quite ugly face, with an expressive look that came close to a sinister sneer. Kent was so engrossed that he didn't see Ralph come in the main entrance through the revolving doors, nor hear his name being called.

"Hi, Kent! Kent!" Ralph stood practically next to him. "Kent?"

"Oh! Hey, Ralph. Thanks for coming."

"Well, I'm in it for the whole affair, buddy. I know you'd do the same for me." He sat down next to Kent, turned to him, and murmured, "You seemed pretty distracted."

"I'm being surveilled right now," whispered Kent. "The man of interest is sitting at two o'clock maybe fifty feet from here. No, don't look now. It might be prudent for us to continue our conversation in whispers."

"What do you make of the man?"

"I'm pretty sure he's FSD, one of Dmitri Federov's cohorts," said Kent, close to Ralph's ear. "He's been watching me since I came down from my room this morning. I also think it's me Dmitri wants and not Katcha. I believe he intends to use her as bait to get me to cross back into Russia. I'm also sure he knows where Katcha's being held."

"Do you want to pick him up for questioning?" asked Ralph in a hushed voice.

"Short of torture, I don't think you'd get anything out of

him. But as long as he's tailing me, I'll know where he is at all times. We can pick him up whenever we want. What I can't do is let him know that I know. That could screw us big-time."

"Maybe we could put a tail on the tail," murmured Ralph. "I think I know just the person for the job. Excuse me while I go make the call."

Chapter 25
Two Better Than One

The hotel lobby crawled with visitors upon the arrival of several tour buses out front. The exuberant din made whispering an uncertain mode of communicating. When Ralph returned from the house phone, he and Kent moved into the dining room and were led to a table by the hostess. Minutes later, as of one mind, they noticed the bone-thin man taking a table some distance away. They were pleased that he had followed them, because it gave them time to get a third agent in place—the tail's tail.

"I'm hungry. How about you?" asked Ralph as they browsed through the menu.

"Starved. I rushed out to question the doorman as soon as I could," said Kent. "Then, when I got your message, I waited around in the lobby for you. I wasn't even thinking about breakfast until now. I wanted to start looking for poor Katcha before they had any chance to ship her back to Russia."

The waiter came, and Kent asked for coffee and pancakes with jam. Ralph ordered "Loose scrambled eggs, crisp bacon, whole wheat toast but only lightly toasted, and hot, hot coffee."

I didn't know he was such a priss about his food, Kent thought. *But I guess I should have known.* It had been almost mystifying to him that Ralph had so many sides to his temperament. Transitioning and compartmentalizing from being one of his instructors dur-ing his spy training; to embassy assistant station chief; to debriefer with a pit-bull mentality; and now that he had passed muster, a solid colleague and friend.

They ate in silence for a time, then Ralph surreptitiously nodded to a tiny, gray-haired woman with a cane who entered the dining room.

Kent deciphered the gesture as acknowledging the third agent. Glancing up, he decided the cane was a good prop. A second glance noted that she casually took a table next to the bone-thin man, who was still nibbling away at a Danish.

Kent took a sip of coffee and began the conversation. "I'd like to start investigating with the cab dispatcher and see what he knows."

"Not a bad idea," commented Ralph. "But I thought seal-ing off the exits to the country was far more important. Last night I copied Katcha's picture from her embassy access pass, added a full description of my own, and wired it to the border police. I figured these flyers would cover the airports, bus terminals, and the ferry. I only hope it was soon enough."

"But you knew I didn't want to go to the police," Kent replied in a tremulous voice. "She's here on a two-day visa. When they find her, they'll send her back."

"You're forgetting that we got her a couple days' extension to stay in the hotel. Don't worry," said Ralph. "I listed Katcha as a kidnap victim. It's better that we get her back out of danger and worry about the deportation thing later. The embassy might come through for her in the end."

"I hope to hell you're right," said Kent. "Do you have any more of those flyers of Katcha that you distributed? They might prove essential in our queries."

"Yeah," replied Ralph. "I've got at least a dozen out in the car."

"A car?" repeated Kent. "You're amazing, pal. And you're right, we'll need one."

"I rented an Opel Astra sedan because I thought one of the embassy vehicles would be too visible. I don't want anyone to see us coming."

"Will there be anything else, sir?" asked the waiter as he presented them with the check.

Kent signed the check to room 512, pushed his chair back, and stood, triggering a sequence of mixed agents exiting separately from the dining room, and through the lobby to the street—Ralph, then Kent, next the bone-thin man, and last, the tiny, hobbling, gray-haired woman.

Outside, Kent approached the doorman, who gave him directions to the cab company. The two agents walked to the Opel, parked curbside half a block away. Ralph drove and after a number of turns and lane changes, Kent noticed Ralph eyeing the rear-view mirror.

"Is someone there?" he asked.

"There's a black Mercedes that's been playing follow-the-leader with us."

"That's Dmitri's vehicle. Can you see who's driving?" asked Kent.

"No, the sun's glaring on its windshield." Ralph sped up and expertly evaded the Mercedes. Two miles later, they arrived at the Helsinki Taksi company. They parked close to the entrance of the wood-slatted one-story building and walked inside, looking for anything resembling a dispatch office. Across the room, they spotted the open door of a glass-paneled cubicle, where a pony-tailed woman sat with microphone and headset. She ignored them.

"With her headset on she can't hear you," volunteered the young man seated at a steel desk in a corner of the room. He turned in his swivel chair to face them. Wearing an unzipped black windbreaker, gray polo shirt, and tan slacks, he had alert dark eyes.

"I'm Lars, the manager here. My English is pretty good. What do you need?"

"Thank you, Lars," Kent said. "We're from the American

Embassy. We're looking to speak with the driver who picked up a fare at the Villa Keirkner yesterday morning between ten and eleven. I believe the cab number was 2031. According to the doorman at the hotel, the driver was supposed to be someone named Tapio, but it wasn't him."

Deep worry lines creased Lars's brow. "Tapio is in the hospital. He was hit over the head right here in our parking lot." His tenor voice rose, outraged and helpless. "His cab, the 2301, was stolen yesterday and found abandoned this morning down at the docks. There it is—over there awaiting a cleaning." He stood and pointed. Out the floor-to-ceiling window they saw a white Toyota Corolla parked in the lot next to the building.

"Just where on the docks did you find it, Lars?" asked Kent.

"Some nice guy—didn't give his name—called to let us know. Said it was left a couple blocks north of where that Russian tramp is parked. One of my drivers and I were able to retrieve it. No damage to it, luckily."

"Russian tramp?" questioned a stunned Ralph.

"That Russian tramp freighter that makes the cargo run between here and St. Petersburg twice a week."

"A Russian ship," repeated Ralph. "I hadn't thought of that."

"What do you mean?" asked Kent.

"It's another way to get Katcha out of the country that I didn't count on," explained Ralph.

"Lars, did you call the police?" asked Kent.

"No. Nothing ever comes of it," he said, bitterly. "The interview takes more time than it's worth. Probably some joy-rider teen, anyway. It's not the first time it's happened."

Ralph frowned, thinking, *Unlikely that a joy-riding teen would brutally assault a driver.* "Would you mind if the two of us took a good look inside cab 2301?" he asked.

"Go right ahead, but all you'll find is tissues, chewing gum, and if you're lucky, a coin or two."

"You've been very helpful." They left to examine cab 2301 for any residual signs that Katcha might have left behind and any clue to where the cab had been previously. Ralph chose the front seat, Kent took the rear, and together they pored over every pocket, crease, and cranny. Kent's result was, as Lars had predicted, tissues, gum wrappers, and a couple of coins, a 1-FIM and a 5-FIM Finnish markka. The one exception was a handkerchief in full view on the back floor. Kent picked it up and sniffed it. "It's Katcha's!" he said, holding it up for Ralph to see. "She's trying to leave us a trail." He tucked it in his pocket.

"Great! That's evidence!" Ralph replied.

"What're you doing now?" asked Kent.

"I'm going back inside to ask Lars to turn on the engine so I can check the odometer *métrage*—the mileage measurements," replied Ralph. "It's in kilometers, of course. I found Tapio's log in the glove compartment and I'm taking it with us. It might set some boundaries for our search." He tucked the log book in his belt and buttoned his sport jacket around it. "Tapio doesn't need it while he's in the hospital, and I'll return it before he knows it's missing."

Lars was happy to comply. Ralph thanked him and recorded the mileage. He also raised his palms up to indicate they had found nothing of interest. Lars nodded that he understood.

The two agents climbed into the Opel. Ralph turned on the ignition and recorded the odometer reading. Turning the ignition off, he launched into his process. "We'll need to subtract the distance to the hotel from here in the final equation. The odometer difference between Tapio's last fare and the reading we just took from the cab tells us how far the cab has traveled since he was hit over the head. Subtracting the distance from here to the hotel and the distance from here to the docks where the cab was found tells us how far the cab traveled after they nabbed Katcha. Of course, it's an approximation at best. The only reason I'm doing this is the odometer readings indicate a low overall métrage. That means point-to-point direct driving."

"Shouldn't we get the distance from here to that tramp freighter first while we're still here?" asked Kent. "I'm anxious to get a look at that Russian tub."

"Absolutely! That's what I had in mind," replied Ralph.

They drove to the waterfront and turned north, passing one warehouse after another on their left. Freighters and cruise ships were moored at the piers. The *MVC Maersk II* appeared on their right, broadside to the street. They saw a line of forklifts transferring goods from the warehouse across the street to a massive opening in the hull of the ship. They had to stop for a minute to let one of them cross in front of the car.

"I never saw a ship with so much red-lead and yellow primer before," said Kent. "Maybe too expensive to cover it over with a decent paint." His breath caught with a second thought. "Do you suppose my Katcha is being held aboard her?"

"I could almost bet on it," said Ralph, as he resumed driving. "But we need some solid proof before we can act."

"Can Finnish police search a foreign vessel?" asked Kent.

"I don't know much about maritime law," said Ralph. "Short of murder and cruelty, I assume the captain is the law at sea, but the ship's officers and crew have to abide by local law when they're tied to a pier. I'm pretty sure diplomatic privilege doesn't apply to ships' spaces. However, random or unnecessary invasion of privacy can raise a pretty big stink between countries."

"Oh hell. I guess we can't just barge in on them to search the ship for her," stated Kent. "We'll need some pretty convincing authorization to do it."

"You've got that right. We're at a dead end. I'm going to turn around and retrace our route." Ralph stopped the car in the next block long enough to record the odometer once more. He then drove to the cab company and did the same thing. During the ride back to the hotel he noticed that Kent was silent and distant most of the time. He dropped his friend off at the entrance and stayed parked long enough to acquire the last reading for his calculations. "I'm headed back to the embassy," he explained. "I need to pick up my messages and get to my computer to process all these odometer readings. I'll talk to you later."

"Maybe you can talk someone in authority at the embassy

into raiding that freighter before it gets under way," suggested Kent, knowing full well that the embassy had neither sufficient proof nor the juice to board a foreign-flagged vessel to conduct a search.

Ralph ignored the suggestion and the desperate mode in which it was made. He put the Opel in gear and drove off.

Kent went straight to his hotel room, shrugged off his suit jacket, and pulled off his tie. Stretching out on the bed, he plunged into some anguished thinking. What bothered him most was the thought of losing Katcha to Dmitri Federov and his henchmen. *I'm sure she's being held aboard that broken-down freighter, but I'm helpless to prove it. How are they treating her? Is she tied up? Are they torturing her to find out more about me? What does Dmitri have in store for her? I want to go to the police, but Ralph already brought them in. I wonder if they're doing anything useful, making any headway.*

Realization struck Kent like a slap on the forehead. He had become accustomed to spending entire days facing imminent danger with Katcha by his side. *We've become bonded well beyond friends with intimate benefits. Losing her, even for the short time she's been missing, I feel like something precious has been taken from me—like one of my limbs has been lopped off. Before meeting her, thoughts of marriage never crossed my mind. But now I can actually visualize being married to Katcha. The big question is: Can I face sitting behind a desk for the rest of my working life? And would I have to? Maybe Katcha could adjust to my being in the field. Right now there's only one thing for me to worry about. I've got to get her back to safety.*

Chapter 26
The Police

The Same Day and Next Morning

Two hours later Kent heard a knock on his hotel room door. He'd been trying to reach Ralph at the embassy without success. He put the phone down and opened the door to two men in dark blue uniforms and officers' caps. The one in front was husky, square-faced, and potbellied. He spoke in English.

"I am Komisar Eero Koskinen of the *Poliisihalitus*—Chief Inspector of the Federal Police. And this is Sergeant Jaakko Heikkinen, also of the *Poliisi*. We are investigating the disappearance of a Russian national by the name of Katcha Kroschenko."

"Have you found her yet?" Kent blurted out. "Sorry, come in." He held the door back.

They stepped inside. "No sir, she has not been found yet. We are merely collecting information at this point. A Mr. Ralph Ebernath of the U.S. Embassy informed us that you are the one most knowledgeable about this missing person and that you could explain why she was or is in Finland at all. We have the flyer he gave us, but perhaps you could give us a better description of her, yes?"

"I'll try. But does this mean you haven't made any progress at all?"

"Let me put it this way," said Eero. "In my profession, patience is a virtue. We have her picture posted, along with appropriate handling instructions for every mode of transportation out of the city. However, we cannot do much more unless we can grasp the greater picture. I am here to ask the questions now, if you don't mind."

"I'm at your service, and I apologize for my anxious behavior. Please have a seat."

"Your full name is Kent Brukner, that is so?"

"That's right."

Sergeant Jaakko whipped out a spiral notepad and began taking notes, which he dutifully did throughout the entire interview.

"I believe, Mr. Brukner, that you entered the country under the name of Oleksander Kroschenko," said Eero. "Is that correct?

"Yes."

"And may I ask why that was necessary?"

"Because I was a fugitive from Russian justice."

"Details, please, Mr. Brukner."

"Let's just say I was arrested by the FSB for being in the wrong place at the wrong time. They sent me to Camp Obuchat, a political prison, without the benefit of a trial or legal assistance. I managed to escape from Russia—over several thousand miles."

Eero's next question hinted of sarcasm. "Perhaps I can assume you were in that wrong place in the service of your country, yes?"

Kent simply shrugged.

"I can take that as a Yes?" asked Eero.

"I can neither confirm nor deny."

"I understand," said Eero. "Do you have proper identification?"

"Only temporary identification provided by my embassy," replied Kent. "It's obvious that I could not travel to Finland with my true identity. The embassy is also generating additional papers for me." He stepped over to the dresser, retrieved his current embassy pass, and held it up for Eero to examine.

Eero peered at it and nodded. "Now, was Katcha Kroschenko traveling under her own name?"

"Yes. There was no need to change her name. In fact, we traveled together as father and daughter. I used her father's papers to get out of Russia."

"Didn't her father need those papers?"

"Not while he was in jail for speaking out against the authorities," replied Kent.

"Miss Kroschenko entered Finland under a two-day visa. Did she leave Russia under duress?" asked Eero. "If not, why did she leave her home country?"

Kent eagerly explained how they had met at the family's Malen'koye Kafe. "We're in love. We intend to be married. Her mother is still a British citizen, an expatriate of sorts—she's also a Russian citizen. She supports not only our marriage, but made most of the arrangements so we'll be able to live in the Free World. Mavis Dowd Kroschenko, her mother, also hid me from the authorities for almost two months."

"Where do you intend to marry?" asked Eero.

"I'd like to be married and settle in Iowa in the United States, but if marriage is a requirement to enter the U.S., then we will marry here in Helsinki—if at all possible. The flyer Mr. Ebernath gave you has a good picture of her, but I'm sorry to say I have no idea what she was wearing. I left the room before she got dressed to go shopping."

Eero gave a deep sigh of annoyance, his potbelly expanding out and in. "I wish you every luck in your pursuit," said Eero. "We will do our best to locate her."

"Thank you, Komisar, but now I would like to ask you a question or two. "By any chance, have you spoken with Mr. Ebernath today?"

"No, I spoke with him yesterday," replied Eero. "I tried to phone him several times today, but he's been unavailable."

"I've been trying to reach him, too. He has some valuable

information that will help you in your search. Katcha got into a Helsinki Taksi cab out in front of the Villa Keirkner. When I questioned the doorman, he said he recognized the cab by its number, only the driver was a stranger to him. This particular cab cut in front of the regular queue of cabs down the block. At the cab company, the manager told Ralph and me that the regular driver had been hit over the head, and his cab had been stolen. The company recovered the cab a few blocks from where that Russia tramp freighter is moored." Kent's voice turned strident. "My Katcha has been kidnapped, I'm sure of it. She's being held against her will aboard that ship."

Eero raised one eyebrow almost imperceptibly, hinting at his disbelief. "But why would the FSB be so interested in a mere citizen seeking freedom? Who or what is behind this operation?"

Kent pressed his lips together before replying as he tried to contain his temper. "The truth is, Komisar, the FSB doesn't give a damn about Katcha. It's me they want. I'm an escapee from one of their prison camps. A Major Dmitri Federov feels cheated in letting me get away. He's using her as bait to land me. I'm certain he's behind this. He's a clever one, all right."

"What does this Major Federov look like?" asked Eero. "Can you describe him?"

"Oh, he's very recognizable," answered Kent. "There's a brown birthmark running from his right cheek to his ear. He's close to my height, maybe a little heavier, a sharp dresser, and has a round face. And he usually has two of his henchmen with him—thugs, in my opinion. A tall, skinny man and a red-haired guy with a red beard who drove the getaway cab. There you have it, Komisar."

"Thank you, we'll be in touch."

* * * *

Early the next morning, a Friday, following a fitful night, Kent picked up the room phone and tried Ralph once more. He sat on the edge of the bed in his boxer shorts while the phone rang and rang. As he was just about to give up, Ralph answered: "Ebernath."

"Where the hell have you been?" asked Kent. "I've been

169

trying to reach you since yesterday afternoon. Don't you answer your phone messages? You know how anxious I am to hear any news of the search. Besides, I have some news for you."

"Keep your pants on, man," muttered Ralph. "My computer's been down, so I used a coworker's machine in another office. I was so busy I forgot to retrieve my messages. Mea culpa. my friend. So, what's your news?"

"Two men from Finland's Federal Police paid me a visit yesterday afternoon. A Komisar Eero Koskinen of the Poliisihalitus and his sergeant, Janko Heikkinen, asked me a ton of questions. They were here for two hours."

"Did you tell them everything?" asked Ralph. "That is, what we learned yesterday morning."

"I told them everything I could remember—even our suspicions about Katcha being held against her will aboard that damn broken-down freighter. The komisar told me that all the police have done so far is to distribute her picture everywhere. He said his main purpose was to gather enough information from me to start their investigation. They also tried to reach you yesterday, but couldn't. Have you had any success with those cab scenarios?"

"I believe so, but it's hard to describe over the phone," said Ralph. "Why don't you walk over here to the embassy and I'll show you everything I've come up with. I'll notify security that you're coming."

"I'll be there in about an hour," said Kent. "I'm not even dressed yet and I need a shower."

* * * *

An early, brisk walk in the windy low-fifties air brought Kent to the front security desk at the embassy. Ralph came out to meet him and the two men walked downstairs to a small conference room next to his office. Kent was surprised to find a woman already seated there: the birdlike lady with the cane. The third agent. Up close, he found her features hypnotizing. Sleek gray hair in a perfect bowl cut, accentuating a sharp nose and cheekbones. Aging spidery lines around the corners of her mouth. Behind rimless glasses dark, penetrating eyes sized him up.

"Kent Brukner, I'd like you to meet Special Agent Lily Monahan," said Ralph. "She's been tailing the skinny guy who's been tailing you. She has new information that may shed some light on our search."

They shook hands, shocking Kent with her vise-like grip. He realized his first impression in the dining room had been mistaken. The cane was merely a prop to throw a target off guard.

Lily plunged right in. "In general, he and a second person, the driver, followed you two in a black Mercedes sedan everywhere you went yesterday. I managed to get several long-distance snapshots of the two along the way. I turned the mug shots in to the embassy's Who's Who Gallery in the hope of identifying them. When Ralph dropped you off at your hotel yesterday afternoon, the men tailing you drove right to a warehouse across the street from where that Russian tramp freighter is tied up. They drove straight inside through a truck delivery entrance."

"Wait! You said he drove the Mercedes inside the warehouse?" Kent interrupted.

"Yes," said Lily. "He must have used a remote. The steel door rolled up for them and down again behind them. The top floor of the warehouse appears to be either offices or maybe even residences. I saw lights come on a few minutes after they arrived. I staked out the place for another four hours. An hour and a quarter after their arrival, the short one walked out of a pedestrian front door and went around the corner to a small store a few blocks away. He returned carrying a brown paper bag. I followed him on foot. There was no other activity until I was called away by my boss. I think there's a good chance your missing person may be in the warehouse."

"My odometer calculations are still applicable," claimed Ralph. "The warehouse is across the street from the ship. The distances are the same."

"Based on your calculations," asked Kent, "have you come up with the most likely scenario yet?"

"Indeed, I have," said Ralph as he handed out a page of printouts to each of them. "You remember how we drove around and I collected the individual distances in the Opel? Well, this is what I collected." Ralph was in his element as he spoke. "Taking the odometer reading from the recovered cab and subtracting the last odometer reading entered in Tapio's fare log, we know the total meterage is 13.74 kilometers. Then it was a matter of finding the right kidnapping scenario and adding the correct segment distances to fit that scenario. The one scenario that came closest to what we believe happened is the five-segment one shown here. It starts with Tapio's last recorded odometer reading. In fact, the total error between the estimate and the actual distance turns out to be only about a third of a kilometer. Certainly, the warehouse and ship are interchangeable when it comes to distances."

Kent spent fifteen minutes studying the precise odometer readings and associated kilometers. "Hey, Ralph, great job." He turned to their new colleague. "And you too, Lily. I'm impressed. These figures dovetail neatly with what you told us. And Ralph, since the warehouse is on Finnish soil, do you think the police would have any problem investigating it?"

"Not at all," said Ralph. It's just a matter of presenting what we have to Eero."

Chapter 27
The Raid

Armed with their most recent intelligence, Kent and Ralph drove to Helsinki's Poliisi Headquarters, where they were met by a sergeant who escorted them to the modest office of Komisar Eero.

Standing at the head of a small conference table, Eero said, "Welcome, gentlemen. Let's be seated." Settling himself and his potbelly into a straight-backed chair, he leaned forward and locked his thick fingers together, as if prefacing a formal announcement. Which it was. "I wish I had better news, but unfortunately, I bring you an unproductive report. My *etsiväs*, my detectives, have turned up nothing new on your missing persons investigation. The whereabouts of Miss Katcha Kroschenko are still in doubt. And unless you have additional information, sufficient evidence, I do not have the authority to board and search the Russian freighter. Searching any ship, with its endless hiding places, is a difficult task requiring much manpower. Funding for that is extremely difficult to acquire."

"Ah, but we do have more information to work with," said Ralph. "Now we believe she is being held in a warehouse across the street from where the freighter is docked."

"Oh? Tell me exactly what you have learned."

"We've discovered that someone else was showing an extraordinary interest in what we were doing, so we assigned one of our people to tail that someone," said Ralph. "We pinned a tail on the tail, so to speak. Lily, our operative, followed two men in a late-model black Mercedes with Russian plates, ЖSЩ332Я. After I dropped Kent back at the hotel yesterday, Lily followed them to a warehouse directly across from the Russian freighter. In fact, the Mercedes drove right inside the place through an overhead door that was apparently remotely controlled by someone in the car."

"Doesn't that indicate that the warehouse is some sort of a home base for these guys?" suggested Kent. "Possession of a remote, I mean."

"One would think so," replied Eero. "But how do you connect the kidnapping to these men?"

"I know that Dmitri Federov drives a black Mercedes," replied Kent. "And I remember the plates started the same way as this one—at least the first few letters anyway."

"We have since identified the two men from snapshots taken by our operative using a long-range telephoto lens," said Ralph. He dug into his briefcase and came up with an eight-by-ten photograph, laying it on the table in front of Eero. "The tall, gaunt one is Vadim Ostanyuk. The short one with the red hair and beard is Adrik Troshevsky. Both men are known to have been henchmen for Major Federov in the past. The hotel doorman is pretty sure Adrik was the one who drove the kidnappers' getaway cab. He paid special attention to Adrik's face because his cabbie friend, a man named Tapio, should have been driving that particular taxi. We also got a pretty good look at Ostanyuk in the hotel dining room. I think that should be enough to connect these men to the kidnapping."

"You have put together a good argument," said Eero. "Is there more?"

"Ralph, why don't you tell him about how you put together a most probable kidnapping scenario using odometer calculations?" suggested Kent.

Ralph began to explain how he selected an intermediate

sequential distance scenario that most likely fit the cab's odometer readings from when the cab was stolen to the reading when the abandoned cab was returned to the company lot. "Either the freighter or the warehouse could be the kidnapping destination."

"Makes the warehouse seem even more plausible for holding Miss Kroschenko," said Eero. "What can you tell me about this warehouse?"

"Our operative surveilled the entire building from the outside only," said Ralph. "It's a two-story brick, stone, and steel structure, occupying one city block. The exits are the vehicle and pedestrian doors on the side facing the ship, and first-floor fire doors on each of the remaining three sides. There's a fire door and fire escape ladder on the left side of the building from the second story. Tall windows on all sides of the first floor are sealed. It appears that the second floor might either be offices or residences. Second-floor windows open, but it's a thirty-foot drop from there."

"Excellent. Couldn't ask for more," declared Eero. "I'll organize a team to go in." He picked up the phone and began barking instructions. When he finished, he informed Kent and Ralph, "We'll be gathering out front in thirty minutes."

* * * *

Aboard the freighter, still racking her brain for some way to escape, Katcha heard the padlock rattling outside her cabin door. The large steel door rested heavily on its hinges and squealed as it was pushed open. Sasha entered wearing a jeans jumpsuit and black boots. She carried Katcha's lunch in a white paper bag. Suddenly, the room electrified. Their eyes met, each woman searching the other—each looking to see the other's intentions. Sasha needed to know if there was any fight left in the prisoner and Katcha was desperate to know if there was any way she could get the upper hand. Her search of the cabin for some other kind of weapon had turned up empty. Sasha had treated the metal light-bulb cage as a mere toy to be deflected. Everything else was welded down except for the steel office-type chair, and that was far too clumsy to wield effectively against such a lithe foe.

175

With arm outstretched, as if she would get contaminated by coming too close to her prisoner, Sasha handed over the white paper bag. It bore the logo "Naughty BRGR." Katcha set it down on the writing desk and cautiously opened the bag. Head down, almost sticking her pert nose inside, she inhaled the delicious aroma as she carefully reached in and drew out the lunch. The toasted bun looked like a wide-open mouth, stuffed with spinach greens smothering a burger on a bed of melted cheese. Beside it was a small greasy pouch of sweet potato fries. She pulled out the desk chair and sat facing her jailer, who had chosen to sit on the bed across from her. Katcha was famished and couldn't wait to start wolfing down the tantalizing lunch, but Sasha made her mighty uncomfortable. *Why is she staying while I eat? There won't be anything but paper trash to take away. Does she want to taunt me further?* Katcha took a huge bite. Although she found it tasty, her eyes locked on Sasha across the top of the bun. Her intense stare was reciprocated with every bite of burger and fry. *What does this woman want from me? I wish she would leave so I can enjoy this in peace.*

The tension grew until it plateaued with the crumbling of the empty bag and its deliberate toss on the floor. Sasha interpreted the tossed trash as a medieval gauntlet thrown to the ground. She leaped off the bed and sprang into a wrestler's stance with both arms held chest-high and bent at-the-ready for either offense or defense.

The challenge had a simmering effect on Katcha. She was taller and heavier than her jailer, but her earlier experience had taught her there was no matching Sasha's nimbleness and strength. *I now know why she waited, what she really wanted. But I'd be foolish to take her on one-on-one. I wonder if this door can be a weapon of sorts.* Katcha continued to sit, shrugged her shoulders, and turned both palms out and upward in a gesture of "Not interested."

A disappointed Sasha relaxed her stance and started to leave the cabin. As she opened the door and took a step out, Katcha sprang from her chair and lunged forward, throwing all her weight on the door, pushing it closed, driving Sasha outside, off her feet, and against the corridor deck railing. Hoping to exploit her jailer off-balance, Katcha quickly opened the door again and darted through it, but the athletic Sasha held onto the railing and recovered enough to trip her. The two women, with Sasha on top, crashed to the deck outside the cabin. Katcha pinned Sasha's arms to her waist and held on for all she was worth, but Sasha brought her knee up into her opponent's crotch with such force that she had to let go. Sasha jumped to her feet and, within seconds, landed the heel of her boot in Katcha's vulnerable stomach, taking all the breath out of her. As Katcha struggled to sit up, gasping for air, Sasha finished her with two quick stinging face slaps and an uppercut that landed Katcha backward and unconscious.

Grabbing her opponent by the ankles, the victor dragged Katcha back into the cabin and left her lying in the middle of the steel floor. Sasha hurried out, padlocked the door, and hung up the key on the hook next to it. She left the ship, feeling pretty good about herself.

* * * *

Kent and Ralph waited in Eero's office while he organized the police raiding party. He returned for them and ushered them into the back seat of a black unmarked cruiser, leading two black vans toward the targeted warehouse. No sirens, no horns. Surprise was the key. The three-unit motorcade covered the four-mile ride through busy city streets in a quarter-hour. Arriving on the scene, the cruiser parked half a block away. One van disgorged its assaulting troops between the two front entrances. The second van distributed its police officers at four points of exits around the rest of the building.

The men had been ordered not to use their weapons unless fired upon, and then only if the target was clearly identified. They were cautioned that the primary reason they were there was to extract a female hostage without injury or loss of life.

From their position, Kent and Ralph saw two police batter in the pedestrian door. The next six men, wearing body armor and helmets, flooded through that door. Seven minutes later, a sudden burst of static on the cruiser radio was followed by a cryptic report:

177

the first floor of the warehouse had been secured without incident. The report also noted a late-model Mercedes parked on the first floor. Four minutes later, three shots rang out. The radio reported that the police had encountered resistance from at least two men, presumably armed, barricaded in a second-story apartment.

Eero took the time to translate all of the incoming messages for Kent and Ralph in the back seat. He also ordered the cruiser to take a new position closer to the warehouse entrance.

Next, a request to use tear gas came over the radio. "Not yet," ordered Eero over the radio mike. "Hold your position."

A minute later he ordered Sergeant Ksenia to mount the fire stairs on the left side of the building. The plan was for him and one other officer to enter behind the two armed men. The radio was quiet for almost five minutes and then two more shots were heard. A different voice was heard on the radio saying, "One dead and one suspect taken." Shortly after, the battered pedestrian door opened and two uniformed officers pushed Vadim Ostanyuk through it with his hands secured behind his back. They marched him over to one of the vans and shoved him inside. One of the officers climbed in after him.

Eero stepped out of the cruiser and called the other officer to him. Kent and Ralph got out as well to hear what this officer had to say.

"Sergeant Ksenia, what the hell happened up there?" asked Eero.

"I believe the unavoidable noise of our boots on the fire stairs spoiled any chance of surprise we might have had," said the sergeant. "The red-haired guy had been waiting for me in a large room just off the main hall. As I came up the hall from the stairs, he fired a quick shot directly at me and grazed the shoulder of my flack jacket." Ksenia pointed to the Kevlar on his left shoulder, ripped open and shredded. "I returned fire, and he dropped immediately to the floor. Fortunately, I had the advantage—he had to reveal himself in the hall to get his shot off. Unfortunately, my shot was fatal."

"But damn well necessary," said Eero. "Thank you. But are you hurt? Did the bullet graze your skin?"

"Not that I can tell, sir," said Ksenia.

"I must see for myself." Eero strode quickly to him and examined the jacket's frayed, tattered shoulder. He heaved an audible sigh of relief. "You lucked out, Sergeant."

"Eero, wait! What about my Katcha?" asked Kent. "Where is she?"

"Yeah, what about the hostage?" asked Ralph. "That's the whole reason for the damned raid."

"Yes. Any sign of the hostage, Sergeant?" asked Eero.

"Not so far, sir," replied Ksenia. "But we're still searching every inch of the second floor for any possible hiding place."

Thirty minutes later, another officer exited the warehouse and waved to them, but shook his head to indicate that their extensive search hadn't turned up a hostage.

"That can only mean one thing," Kent blurted out. "She's aboard that tramp freighter like we thought in the first place. Eero, you've got all the manpower you need right here on the pier. Why don't we just move the raid to the ship?"

"Getting permission to search a foreign-flagged ship is above my pay grade," retorted Eero. "Perhaps your embassy can handle this."

"But she's not a U.S. citizen yet," protested Ralph.

"What about our prisoner?" asked Kent. "Shouldn't he know where Katcha is?"

"Once we get him back to the embassy, we can probably squeeze it out of him," Ralph assured him.

"I beg to differ with you," snapped Eero. "The prisoner is mine to interrogate when we get him back to the lockup. May I remind you, it is *our* laws that have been broken."

Chapter 28
The Probing

At the Komisar's direction, the black van conveyed the prisoner, Vadim Ostanyuk, to the poliisi building. He was taken to a basement holding cell four floors below Komisar Eero's office. Much acrid discussion preceded this transfer. Ralph wanted the prisoner taken to the U.S. Embassy for questioning, but Eero convinced him of two factors. One, the kidnapping took place in Helsinki, his jurisdiction; and two, no American had been involved in this crime. He did concede that Ralph and Kent might witness his interrogation of the prisoner.

Kent fumed when he learned that Eero intended to wait two hours of "stewing time" before even starting the questioning, but neither he nor Ralph could sway the man. At eight that evening, a haggard Vadim was brought to an interrogation room down the hall from Eero's office. Ralph and Kent were ushered into an adjacent room outfitted with a one-way mirror and audio access to the questioning.

At first the prisoner was belligerent, demanding that the Russian Embassy be called. "I am a Russian citizen."

"But you do not enjoy diplomatic immunity," reminded Eero, who could tell that this man's testimony was going to be as oily and slithery as his snakelike appearance.

"I haven't committed any crime."

"That's not true," said Eero. "There's the theft of the taxicab for starters, driving that cab without a commercial license, and the more serious crimes of kidnapping the woman and assaulting the cab driver."

"What?" Vadim shouted. "I didn't kidnap anyone."

"You're lying," replied Eero. "We have a witness who saw you drive off with her."

"You're trying to trick me. There's no such witness."

"There's no trick. We have his sworn statement on file. And how do you think we tracked you down? Also, we have armed resistance to arrest. Why would you shoot at your arresting officers if you hadn't committed any crime?"

"That was Adrik that did the shooting. I surrendered right away."

"Where did you drive the woman?"

"I don't remember." Vadim began to sweat and tried awkwardly to wipe his brow with his two hands clamped together with tie wraps.

"You are definitely going to prison," cautioned Eero. "Having poor memory will only add years to your sentence. And that number is sizeable already. Just now you can only help yourself when you help us."

"I-I drove her to Pier 23."

"Where did you take her next?"

"I don't know, I don't know. Adrik drove her."

"Which direction? Toward the warehouse or the tramp freighter?"

"Toward the freighter, I think."

"You think?" pressed Eero.

"Toward the freighter. Yes, I'm sure now. I saw him take her up the gangway." Vadim shifted in his seat.

"Where is she now? Still held aboard the freighter?"

"I don't know. I never saw her again."

"You're not smart enough to engineer a caper of this size.

Who's your boss?"

"The major made me do it."

"What's the major's name?"

"Dmitri! That's what we call him."

"What's the major's *full* name?"

"Major Dmitri Federov. He ordered me to do those things."

"Is the major army or police?"

"Federation Police, FSB, I think.

"Who else is a part of this kidnapping conspiracy?"

"Just us three. The major, Adrik, and me. That's all I know about."

"Are you sure about that?" asked Eero. "Someone aboard that ship has to be in on this, too, don't you think?"

"Yeah, the captain gave his permission to keep her in a cabin on board, so he's in on it."

"Anyone else?"

"Oh, yeah," he muttered. "There's a woman we picked up here, but I don't remember her name. Wait…Sasha, I think."

"Does she have a last name?"

Vadim shrugged. "Never heard it."

"And what part does she play in the scheme of things?"

"I think she brings meals to the woman."

"What does she look like, this Sasha?"

"Straw-blonde, small, wiry," he replied. "A mean disposition, since you're asking."

"Do you know any reason why the victim was kidnapped in the first place?" asked Eero.

He shook his head. "No, but I think they're planning to take her back to Russia."

"Did Major Federov and this Sasha stay at the warehouse with the rest of you?"

"The major stayed at a nearby hotel," said Vadim. "I don't know which one."

"What about this Sasha?"

"I think she lives in an apartment somewhere around here.

She is from Helsinki, but she's Russian. Her family is in Russia. She has worked for us before."

"Is there anything else useful that you can tell us? Think hard before you answer."

"Not that I can think of," said Vadim.

"Thank you. I'll see that your cooperation is remembered."

Eero stood and left the room. He passed the guard officer standing by in the hall and told him to return the prisoner to the lockup.

The guard entered the interrogation room, undid the chain linking Vadim's foot to the floor, and led the prisoner back to the holding cell. Eero joined Ralph and Kent in the adjacent viewing room.

"Did I leave anything out?" asked Eero. "Was there anything more I should have asked him?"

"I think you got all there was from the man, including a full confession for his crimes," replied Kent. "We now know for sure she's being held aboard that tramp freighter against her will. Can't we extend the police raid to the ship?"

"I'm afraid not," replied Eero.

"I know that a captain rules his ship while on the high seas," said Kent, "but isn't a ship in any port subject to the laws of the land?"

Eero scowled as he thought, *These American agents are getting tiresome.* His voice grew hard. "We can't go aboard unless we are actually invited. There's no suspicion of contraband on board. Your young lady is a Russian citizen on a Russian ship. She was in Helsinki on a two-day visa. She has broken none of our laws. Nor has she applied for asylum. And we have no proof that she is in any kind of distress."

"Damn it, man!" Kent shouted. "Katcha was kidnapped in front of one of your hotels in your city and you wash your hands of her case?"

"Take it easy, Kent," warned Ralph, his high forehead lined with irritation. He yearned to be out on the tennis courts for his usual daily game. And right now, always aware that diplomacy ruled, he feared antagonizing the komisar. "The man is only trying to help us."

"But the ship is set to sail back to Russia soon," protested Kent. "We can't sit on our hands and watch that happen. I'll never see my beloved Katcha again."

Chapter 29
Dmitri and Sasha

Major Federov had just laid down the secure phone to his St. Petersburg office, where he had spoken to one of his police underlings. He sat in a temporary FSB office inside the Russian Embassy in Helsinki, pouring generous amounts of vodka into a water glass. Dmitri was feeling quite full of himself after the successful kidnapping, when he heard a loud, abrupt knocking at the door.

"Enter!" he yelled in Russian.

The door swung open, revealing an elegant and appealing Sasha. He had never seen her dressed up before. She closed the door behind her and stood in a somewhat taunting pose in her clinging pink satin blouse, black miniskirt, and pink stiletto heels.

Dmitri smiled broadly. "Sasha! Welcome!" She didn't reciprocate the pleasant humor he exhibited. He motioned for her to sit next to him, but she chose to sit on the opposite side of the desk. Her sour expression prompted him to ask what was wrong.

"Don't tell me the prisoner escaped?" spouted Dmitri.

"No, but the Helsinki police raided the warehouse yesterday. Adrik decided to shoot it out with the police. The idiot—he's dead. Vadim was taken into custody. I don't know what they can hold him on, but I'm sure he'll tell them everything."

Dmitri's panic subsided. "If they knew to raid the warehouse, they pretty much know everything anyway. Vadim and Adrik are expendable. We still have the prize, the bait. We'll get our hands on the escaped spy in a trade. We'll offer her freedom for his surrender. Isn't romance wonderful?"

"But Katcha says she won't cooperate in anything that puts him in danger."

Switching to a buttery voice, he said, "You needn't worry, my pet. I'll have a nice long talk with her. A few more days in captivity and she'll come around. And may I say you look lovely, quite fetching."

Dmitri held up his glass and tossed back a mighty slug of the vodka. He took a fresh glass out of the drawer, poured a hefty portion in it, and slid it across the desk toward Sasha. She began to sip, slowly at first, then with more purpose. Several minutes of silence passed while the alcohol went to work on the two parties, brewing newfound desire. Dmitri got to his feet, circled the desk, and stood before her, arms outstretched. She rose slowly and melted toward him. They came together and embraced until each wanted more. He lifted the petite Sasha off her feet, carried her to the leather couch on the opposite wall, and eased her down on the cushions. He began with the pearl buttons on her blouse as she undid his belt. And so it went, until two naked bodies came together with a driving passion—Dmitri with his generous endowment and Sasha with her dancer's moves and a gymnast's athleticism. The heat grew and grew fast and ended with fireworks. Afterward, the satisfied couple cuddled for a few moments, then began to dress. Suddenly a knock at the door sped their return to propriety. It was another FSB agent wanting to use this particular office.

Embarrassment and guilt found no place in Dmitri's temperament. Primed with a vodka buzz and sexual prowess, he ushered Sasha out into the hall without so much as a nod to the agent.

"We could go back to my place," she murmured in his ear. "I would make you some supper."

"Sounds fine to me," he said with a lascivious grin.

Chapter 30
The Romanov Plaza

Ralph and Kent returned to Ralph's U.S. Embassy office. Kent had lapsed into a funk and Ralph tried to cheer him up. "I've got an idea," he said. "Vadim told us that Dmitri is staying in a hotel here in town. We could check all the surrounding hotels and see if he's registered in his own name. If he is, maybe we could pick him up and squeeze him until he lets Katcha go."

Kent had to smile in spite of himself. "Listen to you, Mister straitlaced by-the-book guy. I like the idea, but we have no authority to break in on him. Maybe Eero would do us the favor?"

Ralph shook his head. "He has no solid evidence of a crime on Finnish territory. And I don't think he's permitted to squeeze like I had in mind."

"Just what *did* you have in mind?" asked Kent.

"You'll see." Ralph nimbly shrugged off his charcoal-gray suit jacket and tossed it over a chair. Loosening his tie, he sat down at the desk.

"Hey, man, I'm not into torturing anyone," declared Kent. "Besides, what if Dmitri's not dumb enough to register under his own name?"

"You have a point, but it can't hurt to try," said Ralph, as he pulled a city phone book from the single drawer in the desk. He flipped the book open to "Hotels" and started to dial the front desk at the first one. "Hello," said Ralph. "I'm trying to locate a Major Dmitri Federov. By any chance, is he registered with you? It's an emergency." Several minutes passed. "No? Thank you." He hung up and dialed the next hotel desk number. The result was always the same: "No" or "We're not allowed to divulge personal information." After dialing and querying more than a dozen numbers, the seventeenth call paid off. Federov had used his own name and was staying at the Romanov Plaza.

"Can you tell me what room he's in?" asked Ralph.

"Sorry, we can't give out personal information. Hotel policy." The desk clerk hung up.

"So now we've got the hotel, but not the damn room number," said Kent. "What do we do with this limited information?"

"Not to worry, my friend," assured Ralph. "I have the perfect solution." He slid his swivel chair over to the right and reached into the wastebasket. Fishing through it, he came up with a small cardboard box, four-by-four-by-two inches. Using white printer paper and Scotch tape, he wrapped the box and addressed it to Major Dmitri Federov, in care of the Romanov Plaza Hotel, Helsinki. He put a postage stamp on it. Then, with a magic marker, he simulated a postal cancellation so it would look like it had arrived in the mail. "This will do nicely," Ralph said, quite pleased with himself.

"Why are you going through all that trouble to make it look like mail?"

Ralph smirked. "You'll see."

Kent's anxiety kept pressing. "But what if he's in his room? What'll we do then?"

"We'll be able to tell whether he is or not, I promise you," said Ralph. "Let's go."

Kent and Ralph left the embassy by the side door and walked down the block to the rental Opel. Ralph, sitting behind the wheel, inserted the key in the ignition, but hesitated to start the car. He let his hand drop to his lap and leaned back on the seat.

"What's wrong?" asked Kent.

"Nothing's wrong," said Ralph. "It's just that I forgot to tell you something. I pulled Lily Monahan off surveillance of the warehouse."

"Do you really think that's wise? What if Dmitri or Sasha shows up there?"

"There's been no activity there since the police raid. I thought we could make better use of her talents if she shifted her surveillance to the lobby of the Romanov Plaza." Ralph's voice grew sharp. "And Kent, I'm cautioning you ahead of time. If you see her sitting there, do not acknowledge her presence!"

"Got it," said Kent, without being thoroughly convinced.

Ralph started the engine and pulled out into downtown Helsinki traffic. About two miles from the raided warehouse, they found the Romanov Plaza. They passed it, parked down the block, and walked back. The two-star hotel was less opulent and dignified than its name implied. The four-story, dark stone structure featured an arched swing-out entrance, three steps up from the sidewalk. No canopy to the street. No doorman.

Kent pulled open the glass door with the brass handle and followed his companion into a modest lobby outfitted with IKEA-style inexpensive sofas, settees, and chairs, all in subdued earth tones. Dim recessed lighting in the ceiling and the lack of plush, comfy furniture were meant to discourage hours-long visitors—or lingerers not registered. Ralph motioned for Kent to take a seat and wait. Kent settled into an armchair with a straight back, vinyl seat and arms, facing the desk.

Ralph, with a hand in his right suitcoat pocket, strode to the counter and engaged the desk clerk. "Any messages for room 303?" he asked.

When the desk clerk turned around to check the wall of wooden pigeonholes, Ralph removed his hand from his pocket and drew out the tiny white package he'd addressed to Dmitri. He set the package down on the opposite end of the counter from where he stood—not wanting the clerk to associate the item's arrival with him.

"You have no messages, sir."

Of course not. When first approaching the counter, Ralph had instantly surveyed the pigeonholes and chosen an empty one for his request. "Thank you," he said, as he walked away and joined Kent on an adjacent chair.

The desk clerk didn't discover the package on the opposite end of the counter right away, as he was engaged in some book-keeping in the workspace beneath the counter. As soon as he noticed it, he picked it up and realized the address lacked a room number. He scanned the guest list, found Dmitri Federov's name, and added room 419 in pen to the package. Assuming it was to be delivered immediately, he slammed his right palm down on the call bell several times. When it provoked no response, he repeated the motion.

An elderly man in a blue denim apron appeared out of a hallway. He limped toward the desk where he was instructed to deliver the package. The elderly valet received the package, took a few steps, and turned back to ask, "What room was that?"

"Room 419!" said the annoyed clerk. "I wrote it on the package, you old fool."

The valet started for the elevator, but the clerk scolded, "Take the stairs! The elevator is for our guests."

The stooped man adjusted his path and trudged toward the stairs.

Kent started to get up to follow, but Ralph restrained him. "We know the room now, so let's just take our time. We don't have to follow the old coot."

Fifteen minutes later, the two agents figured the package had been delivered. They rose from their chairs and moved to the elevators. Getting off on the fourth floor, they started down the hall toward room 419. Just then, the elevator door opened again, and the valet appeared with the package. He came limping toward them.

"Keep walking," whispered Kent, placing a hand on Ralph's

back for a slight shove forward past the designated room.

Ralph caught on immediately, and while they strolled farther down the hall, he whispered, "Cute. The old buzzard must have climbed to the second floor, had a smoke or something, and taken the elevator the rest of the way."

"Good for him," whispered Kent. "It's his way of beating the system." They turned the corner into a second hall to wait.

The valet stopped at room 419 and knocked on the door. Receiving no answer, he knocked again. Then he decided to use his master key and leave the package on the inside. When he was done, he relocked the door and returned to the elevator.

Hearing the elevator doors shut, the two agents moved back into the main hall to room 419. They now knew that their target was either not in the room or being extra cautious and lying low inside. Kent used a handkerchief to slowly push the door handle. and confirmed the door was locked. "Did you bring a pick set?" he asked.

"Like any good Boy Scout, I always come prepared," replied Ralph. He withdrew a thin black leather case from the breast pocket of his suit jacket. Flipping it open, he extracted two long needle-like instruments. Inserting them together in the cylinder's keyway, he manipulated the two until he reset and held each of the driver pins beyond the shear line. Practiced and precise, he heard the desired clicking sound that indicated the cylinder was ready to rotate and release the knob and latch.

The door swung inward, and both men spread across the room—Ralph, with his 9mm Glock in hand, to the bathroom, and Kent, with knuckled fist, to the closet to be sure that the room was actually clear. There was no sign of Major Federov, and an intensive search did not tie the few things left in the room to the man. The bed was made, so either housekeeping had come early or Dmitri hadn't slept there the previous night. However, Kent picked up a small pad near the house telephone. There was nothing apparently written on it, but he noted some impressions on its surface. On impulse, he ran a slanted pencil point over the impressions and the shading raised a string of numbers.

"Should I dial the number and see who answers?" asked Kent.

"No. An unresponsive phone call could tip off whoever it is," said Ralph. "I've got a better idea. We'll run a reverse telephone directory, a name-and-address trace, when we get back to the embassy."

"Then I guess we're done," said Kent, tearing the top sheet off the pad and sticking it in his pocket. Unless you want to stay and wait for him to return."

"No, that would be too risky—waiting for the unknown. Let's return to the embassy and run that trace. Maybe we'll get lucky."

Ralph reclaimed his phony package, and the two made a reasonable effort to leave the room precisely as they found it. They relocked the room and headed down the hall to the elevator. Coming out of the elevator into the lobby, in their peripheral vision they saw Lily sitting on a settee by the street window. Perusing a ladies' fashion magazine, she wore a beige suit and perky hat with a feather in the band, looking very much like a hotel guest. And very much in position to inform them if and when the major showed up and returned to his room.

* * * *

Sasha had made Dmitri dinner and invited him to spend the night, and they enjoyed a repeat performance in bed before breakfast. It had hardly been romantic between the two—rather, they were satisfying mutual physical needs. Neither fully trusted the other, but it was clear to both that each had a prominent place in the scheme of things.

Around eleven on Saturday morning, she left Dmitri behind in her apartment to head to the ship and feed their prisoner. In tan cargo pants and black polo shirt, Sasha trotted off to a fast-food shop, where she picked up fish and chips for an early lunch for both Katcha and herself. Dmitri left a half-hour later in his casual civilian clothes and headed back to his hotel to dress for work at his temporary embassy office.

Sasha walked briskly to the ship's quay. Up the gangplank to the main deck, she proceeded to the nearest ladder and climbed up to the next deck. Arriving at the makeshift brig, she unlocked the padlock and entered the cabin, where she encountered her prisoner pacing up and back like a caged tigress.

"What in the hell are you getting out of all this?" Katcha screamed at her captor and keeper. "How long is this imprisonment going to go on?"

"Whoa, calm down!" Sasha retorted. "I'm well-paid for what I'm doing. Besides, right now all I'm doing is bringing lunch. Afterward, we can talk about what you can do to gain your freedom."

Katcha grabbed one of the white bags from Sasha and sat down hard on the bed. Sasha seated herself in the chair at the shelf-like desk, facing her, and ripped open her bag. Keeping their eyes on one another, instead of on the food, they reached inside and snatched bite by bite, fry by fry until nothing remained.

Swallowing her last mouthful of fish, Katcha crushed her empty bag into a ball, and broke the silence. "What's this you're telling me? You're planning to let me go after all?"

"Let's put it this way," started Sasha, smoothly. "If you do us a favor, we'll reciprocate and do you a favor as well."

"And, what favor would that be?" asked a suspicious Katcha.

"A small one. Are you aware that your boyfriend is an American spy, a despicable enemy of Mother Russia, your birth country?"

"Perhaps."

"All I'm asking is that you remain loyal and help your country."

"Get to the point," demanded Katcha.

"The major and I would like you to arrange a rendezvous with your boyfriend. Think about it. Wouldn't you like to see your lover again?"

"Of course. But I'm not stupid. You want to send him back to that prison camp where they originally threw him without even a decent trial. My answer is No!"

Sasha lapsed into her soft, endearing mode. "We could get you a legitimate exit visa, so you can go and live anywhere outside of the Motherland. You could go to France, England, or even America. Isn't that what you want most?"

"What happens if I don't cooperate and say No?"

"You will return to the Motherland on this ship. The major will decide your fate after that. And I can't imagine his decision will be pleasant." Sasha's eyes bore into hers. "Has your boyfriend even asked you to marry him yet? Or is he planning to ditch you in Helsinki?"

Color rising in her cheeks, Katcha hesitated, unsure how to answer. "N-n-no, he hasn't asked me yet. But he's not like that. He'll eventually marry me, I'm sure of it. He's planning to take me to America with him. He told me that much."

"That's what they all say," said Sasha with a smirk. "How is he going to get you an entrance visa to the U.S. without marrying you? Think about that. It takes years to get into the U.S. otherwise."

"I don't care. Even if he doesn't marry me, I love him enough not to betray him. My answer is still No!"

"The major isn't going to like this one bit and he's got one hell of a temper."

"Why is the man so damned fixated on bringing Kent back to Russia?" asked Katcha. "Surely, escapees have gotten away before."

"I've gotten to know him a bit," said Sasha. "He's a perfectionist. Doesn't like to fail at anything. He's angry that your Kent outsmarted him. Any escapee, especially an American spy, puts a black mark on his record. It bruises his ego. Dmitri is very sensitive."

Katcha snickered. "That's a joke. *Ruthless* is more like it."

Sasha stood and walked toward the door to leave. Just as she opened it, Katcha raised her right arm and hurled her crushed greasy bag like a quarterback throwing a desperate Hail Mary pass. It sailed out onto the open deck. Sasha laughed out loud, slipped outside, and locked up.

Chapter 31
Sasha's Place

Ralph and Kent met at Ralph's office that afternoon and engaged a duty secretary to use one of the embassy's valuable resources: a reverse telephone directory of Helsinki. While in Dmitri's room, Kent had discovered the small notepad next to the telephone. The top page was blank, but a note had been written on the pad and left an impression. By rubbing a pencil's graphite over the impression, he had cleverly lifted a phone number. The reverse directory revealed the name for that number—Sasha Puttonyos, and an address not too far from the warehouse and pier.

Back in the Opel, the two agents drove to that address and parked across the street a few doors away. The address was a three-story, red-brick apartment building similar to many others along both sides of this street. While they sat in the car casing the building and deciding on their next move, a portly middle-aged man exited the building of interest and turned to walk in the opposite direction from where they were parked. As soon as the man turned, Kent saw the brown blemish on his cheek.

"It's Dmitri Federov! I never expected to find him here."

"Why not?" Ralph asked. "They're in this conspiracy together. And they might even be having an affair."

"Can't we pick Federov up and put the squeeze on him?"

asked Kent.

"We don't have the official authority to detain him even for questioning," replied Ralph.

"Couldn't we do it unofficially?"

"Let's face it, Kent, the man's a professional and has little or no reason to cooperate with us. Besides, Eero wouldn't like it one bit, and we still need him on our side."

"But why can't Eero act on our behalf?" pressed Kent. "He does have Vadim Ostanyuk's confession to the whole kidnapping conspiracy. And didn't he implicate Federov as the one master-minding the whole kaboodle?"

"Sure, but Eero's already said No," replied Ralph. "There're some delicate international negotiations going on with the Russian Embassy right now. His superiors are afraid of rocking the boat. The guy's hands are tied."

Kent shrugged. "Well, the subject is moot now that Federov is out of sight and out of our grasp. Let's go see what Sasha has to tell us."

The two left the car and crossed the street to her apartment building entrance. Just as they arrived, a young mother with a baby in a stroller was struggling to push the door open. Kent hurried to hold the door open for her. She thanked him and pushed on beyond the two men to the sidewalk. Kent continued to hold the door while Ralph scanned the mailboxes for the Puttonyos apart-ment number. With no elevator in sight, they climb the three flights of stairs to reach apartment 303. Again, Ralph picked the simple lock with ease.

"Nice," said Kent.

"They say there's no key lock that's completely secure," said Ralph, pushing the door open. "The more difficult ones just take a little longer." After re-locking the door, he drew his 9mm Glock. The two men entered the tiny foyer and Sasha's living room, then spread out to the remaining two rooms, encountering no one in either the kitchen or bedroom. But they found the bathroom door almost shut. Ralph approached with his Glock at the ready and kicked the door open—no one was in there either. They began to search her rooms in earnest.

"Just what are we looking for?" asked Kent.

"I'm not sure," replied Ralph. "But we'll know if and when we find something." On a small wooden desk in a corner of the living room, he saw a little stack of envelopes and shuffled through them, finding nothing more than utility bills and ads. The living room looked bare, impersonal, with a sole picture of a seascape on one wall. The floral-patterned drapes were faded from sunlight. He decided, *Nothing, not even the furniture in here, appears to be new, so maybe the place is a furnished rental.* Every drawer he pulled out, cabinet opened, and cushion flipped yielded nothing of interest.

Meanwhile, Kent searched the bedroom. The first thing he noted was the double bed. It was unmade, with head-dented pillows on both sides and both edges of the covers tossed inward. *That old devil. Federov slept here last night. The daylight in this room is dim. Ah, the window needs washing. Sasha's not much of a housekeeper.* To his right, next to the window, he saw a stationary bike. His foot bumped into something on the window side of the bed. When he bent to check, he found a pair of crossed twenty-pound barbells lying on the carpet. *This Sasha must be quite a weightlifter. I'm not sure I want to run into the woman, but, hey, isn't that why I'm here?*

Kent opened the nightstand drawer. Amid several white handkerchiefs, he saw a Taurus 85 snub-nosed revolver, a gray-green popular self-defense weapon. As a precaution, he removed the rounds and stuck them in his pocket. Kent then turned his attention toward the closet. On the outside of the door, a pair of two-foot-long rubber stretch bands with handles hung over a hook. *More exercise stuff.* Opening the closet door, he found two plain-Jane dresses, and a trendy outfit typical of young Finnish women: a pink satin blouse with pearl buttons and black miniskirt. The rest of the clothes were more unisex—jeans, khaki pants, and a fleece-lined parka. On the floor were two pairs of sensible shoes, a pair of well-worn high-top sneakers, and a striking pair of pink leather stiletto heels.

Ralph had finished searching the living room and headed to the kitchen. In the refrigerator he found small jars of salted herring and pickled vegetables, a chunk of honey cake, and half a round rye bread. His mouth watered at an array of savory-looking leftovers: an almost-empty jar of borscht and a casserole dish half-full of pirozhkis. *From a dinner with a guest?* The freezer on top held three boxes of single-meal Russian-style dinners. The two ice cube trays were filled, not with cubes, but with wads of cash: markkas in one tray and rubles in the other. Ralph smiled. *So common a place to hide cash that a professional thief knew to look in the freezer before anyplace else in the target's house.*

While checking out the medicine cabinet in the bathroom, the two men heard clinking sounds at the front door—someone was unlocking it. Kent pulled the bathroom door almost, but not completely, shut so they could see who came in.

A woman they presumed to be Sasha entered the living room. The two agents were somehow dumbstruck, unprepared. A short rather attractive woman with straw-blonde hair. An angular face with large dark eyes and a hard expression. For her size, she nevertheless emanated sinewy strength and lithe movements resembling those of a dancer. Flinging her canvas shoulder bag onto the sofa, she headed straight to the kitchen as though she knew exactly what she needed.

Sasha opened a tall cabinet and brought down a nearly full liter-sized bottle of Grey Goose vodka. She set it on the counter next to a water glass and was about to unscrew the top of the bottle when she felt a tingling sense that someone was watching her. She spun around and faced two men—one pointing a gun directly at her chest.

Sasha knew full well how to use her boots as a weapon—and relished an encounter. With split-second timing, she jumped sideways, spoiling the Glock's aim. Ralph had no chance to fire his weapon—and actually had no intention of doing so. Sasha leaped forward, landing on her left foot, and with her flexed right heel used a karate move to kick the gun from Ralph's hand. A spasm of pain shot through his knuckles. As he winced from the impact, she grabbed the bottle of vodka and flung it straight at his head. Ralph yelped, "Son of a bitch!" and ducked. The Grey Goose sailed past him, bounced once on the tile floor, and crashed. A river of vodka surged out amid shards of glass. Sasha exploited her remaining momentum by shoving Ralph hard into a kitchen chair.

Kent, stunned seeing his former instructor and friend whipped by the little lady, moved forward to tackle and contain her. He didn't expect to be confronted with the reflexes of a cheetah. She came at him, landing a solid boot-kick to his midsection. He doubled over in pain. While the two men gasped for breath, she reached the front door in three long strides, grabbing her purse on the way, and disappeared from view, slamming the door behind her.

"Jeez loueez," moaned Kent. "She's half my size. I feel like a goddamn fool and my gut still hurts. And we don't even get to sample the vodka. Should we give chase?"

Ralph didn't answer. Picking his way around the sodden, slippery floor, he bent over to retrieve the Glock, now swimming in Grey Goose and glass shards. "Shit! We don't have a chance in hell of catching her the way she moves. She's gone, all right."

"She's quite an athlete," Kent reluctantly admitted.

"Yeah. And if we had contained the woman, what information did you hope to get from her?" asked Ralph. "We already know Katcha's aboard that ship."

"If Sasha's the one feeding her, then Sasha knows exactly where Katcha's being held. Didn't Eero say his problem with searching an entire ship was the manpower required? Sasha could lead us straight there."

"What makes you think she'd cooperate?" asked Ralph.

"Most do when they think the game's really up."

Ralph did a double-take. "Listen to you! I think we've exhausted our search here."

"And turned up nothing we can work with," added Kent. "Let's head back to the embassy and regroup."

"Hey, man," Ralph said, "my knuckles still hurt like hell.

You drive." With wobbly steps, they made their way through the potent puddles and left.

* * * *

Forty minutes later, Dmitri sat in the basement office of the Russian Embassy, reviewing boring communications from his St. Petersburg office. He leaned back in his chair, with both feet crossed and resting atop the desk. A seventeen-inch computer monitor stared back at him. He glanced at it from time to time to see if anything new had turned up. He had finished reading one printed document after another and now his mind dwelled on the painful slowness of his current operation to lure the escapee back to prison.

A sharp knock came unexpectedly. The repeated sound shook him from his dark thoughts. He dropped his feet to the floor. Another knock and a female voice. "Major Federov, are you in there?"

"*Vigh-tee*, Enter," he called out.

A somber woman with jet-black hair stepped into the borrowed office. "Comrade Major? A young lady by the name of Sasha Puttonyos wants to see you."

"Where is this insistent young woman now?" he demanded in a gruff voice.

"In the main lobby, Comrade Major. Shall I escort her back here, sir?"

He thought for a moment. "Yes, but first provide her with an uncleared visitor's badge."

"Of course, Comrade Major." She did an about-face and left the room.

Dmitri swore aloud in the office where no one would hear him. *I warned her. She knows better than to come to the embassy.*

Another knock. "Enter!" he called in Russian.

The usually pert Sasha burst in, looking haggard, disturbed, and red-eyed.

He rose from his chair and came around to the front of the desk. She rushed into his arms and managed to leave a wet kiss on his birthmarked neck. He pushed her away to arm's length, and

201

stared eye to eye. It was then that he saw her tears, the desperation in her dark blue eyes.

"I've warned you not to come here," he said. "Why are you here now? You left me this morning in good spirits and now you are crying. What's wrong?"

"I had no place else to go," she sobbed, dropping into the chair in front of the desk. "They came for me at the apartment. I can't go back there. I need a place to stay."

"Who came for you?" he demanded as he returned to his swivel chair.

"Two men—searching my apartment."

"What did they want? Were they police?"

"I don't know. I don't think so. They weren't in any kind of uniform."

"Can you describe them?"

"One was medium height, brown close-cut hair and pleasant face. He held a gun to me. The second man was bigger, more like a football player. Real good-looking with wavy thick hair."

"Did the second man sound like an American?" asked Dmitri. *Could be the very escapee I'm looking for.*

"I don't know. The second one never spoke. I suppose the first one could be. He could also be a Brit. I didn't hang around long enough to have a conversation with either of them."

"How did you get away?"

Sasha perked up, always delighted to brag about her skills. "By surprising them in the kitchen. I quick-kicked the gun out of the first one's hands and pushed him into a chair. When the big guy came at me, I kicked him good in the gut. While they were both nursing their wounds, I beat it out of there. Nobody followed me—I checked."

"I see, my dear," Dmitri said. "You did well. Now tell me about Katcha. Is she willing to set up a rendezvous with her boyfriend yet?"

"The bitch said No!"

"Didn't you threaten her? Tell her she'd wind up in prison

herself?"

"I did my very best to frighten her."

"Did you at least find out the boyfriend's real name?"

"Katcha called him Kent. That's all I know."

Dmitri brooded for a moment. "I think I'll bring her the next meal myself. I'll get her to open up to me."

"You haven't solved my problem yet," whined Sasha. "I don't have an apartment to go home to anymore. You created the problem. How about some help?"

"Temporarily, you can stay with me at the Romanov Plaza, room 419. In a day or two, or even once the ship has sailed, your visitors will no longer have any interest in you and then you can go home."

Her lips compressed in a stubborn response. "Dmitri, I left there with only a little cash in my purse. I need a loan."

He removed a key from a ring and laid it on the desk in front of her. Then he dug into his wallet and retrieved a thin pile of markkas and rubles, which he laid on the desk next to the key. "There! That should do for now."

Sasha scooped the key and bills up and stuffed them into her canvas shoulder bag. Feeling more cheerful, she rounded the desk, and plopped onto his lap. She kissed him deeply on the lips before getting up. On the way to the door she said, "I'll see you when you get back to the room."

"I'll be there shortly," he whispered.

Chapter 32
Katcha's Move

Katcha sat on the bed listlessly thumbing through an old issue of *Nauka i Zhizn*, a Russian science magazine that Sasha had brought her. Her shoulders slumped as she brooded. *Will I ever get free? Will I ever get to wear fresh clothes again? Brush my teeth?* She had been in the same underwear, skirt and blouse, socks and shoes for four days. The snaky kidnapper had grabbed her purse in the taxi, with her simple cosmetics and, most important, her papers, including her Helsinki visa. She felt not only grubby, but that she had lost her identity.

Suddenly, she heard someone handling the padlock outside her cabin door. *Sasha just fed me an hour ago, so who could this be?* Then she heard a vaguely familiar male voice. "Back away from the door." A chill shot through her. It was the voice of Dmitri Federov—the police officer who tried to stop them from boarding the *Princess Anastasia*. Although his voice was calm—the same voice he had used to converse with Kent on the bus, she wasn't fooled. He was still issuing an order. Her body stiffened.

The door swung wide and Dmitri stepped inside with a broad smile. She thought the smile itself seemed out of character—insincere, calculating. He was not in uniform, but dressed casually in a blue and gray checkered flannel shirt and tan slacks. He had deliberately changed to look less intimidating and throw her off guard. He pulled the chair out from under the welded steel shelf and turned it so he could straddle it, facing the bed where she sat. He still held the padlock in his right hand, repeatedly spinning it around his index finger and catching it in his palm. For the first time she noticed how large his hands were while he toyed with the brass object.

Her eyes were drawn hypnotically to the unguarded door. It was a temptation, a prize. When she glanced back at him, he smiled and merely shook his head.

Mixed signals, she thought. Pretending to be friendly, but virtually slamming the door on her thoughts of escape.

"I trust they are treating you well enough here," he said.

"How can I be treated well when I am held here against my will?" she snapped.

"Let's just say it's necessary. It suits my purposes, my dear."

"Your purposes?" she retorted. "I don't care one lousy bit about your purposes. Why am I here? I have committed no crime against the Motherland, yet you make a prisoner of me."

"You are mistaken, my dear. You *have* committed a crime. Aiding and abetting a known foreign spy, an escapee from one of our prison camps. But you are, as the American expression goes, *small potatoes*. I could spare you a life of future grief if you would lure the American back into our country. You, my dear, are already the bait and George Thermon, AKA your Kent, is my big fish."

"There is no way that I will help you," she shouted with tears in her eyes. "I will not betray Kent and there's no way you can make me betray him. Your stupid ego can go to hell."

Not use to being insulted and disobeyed in one sentence, Dmitri's double-chinned face turned red, toothy, and eye-bulging, the face of a madman. He stood up and slammed the padlock down on the steel shelf so hard the resounding sound took seconds to dampen. He lunged toward her, raised his right arm, and with an open palm struck her left cheek with a blow that sent her reeling against the head of the bed. He thought about striking her a second time but changed his mind. "You will do as I instruct you," he snarled. Disgusted, Dmitri turned away, stomped toward the door, and stepped out to the open deck beyond. As soon as the cabin door swung shut behind him, captor and captive had a simultaneous epiphany—the padlock had been left behind.

Observing the padlock left on the shelf, Katcha sprang up and raced toward it with no idea what to do with it once it was in her possession. The door swung open just as she wrapped her hand around the prize. Dmitri rushed in and toward her. She had no time to hide the padlock. She turned her body slightly to the right with her right arm outstretched and, like a discus thrower, flung the padlock at him as hard as she could.

His left hand tried to deflect the speeding missile but missed. It struck just above his right eye and landed on the floor several feet away. Staggering, stunned, he fell down on one knee.

This gave her a second or two to plot her next move. The day before, with Sasha, Katcha had considered the steel chair too heavy to wield as a weapon. But at this moment, facing her most dangerous adversary yet, her adrenaline pumped furiously. She was able to hoist the chair only a couple feet, but it was enough to swing it sideways. With Dmitri still on one knee, the chair slammed against his left shoulder and the side of his head. He collapsed on the floor. The vicious Russian policeman was still breathing, but not moving. He was out cold. His right hand had dropped the key to the padlock next to where he lay.

Katcha picked up both key and padlock, flew outside to the open deck, and swung the cabin door shut behind her. With trembling fingers, she flipped the hasp in place, slipped the open padlock through the loop, and snapped it secure, ensuring that the roles of captor and captive had been reversed. Her next order of business? She gleefully threw the key overboard. It instantly disappeared into the brown-green water.

But by no means was Katcha free yet. Getting off the ship without being detected was her next challenge. In front of her lay the Gulf of Finland. From her position, there was no telling fore from aft. In any case, the ship's pier side and gangway seemed to be her next target.

Moving to her right, she discovered that she had gone as far forward as she could on this level. Hearing an ear-splitting din below, she halted. Looking down, she saw the main deck one level below where she stood. A crane, with its enormous arm, was lowering pallets piled with crates into the open hold. Sailors then removed the crane's hook, and a forklift conveyed the pallets farther into the freighter's hold. Katcha decided she would be too exposed trying to cross the ship to the port side amid all the workers. She turned around and headed aft until she found a midship passageway, but she jerked to a stop. A crewman about thirty feet away emerged from the passageway, walking toward her. She quickly ducked behind an air vent cowling until he passed. At midships, she encountered a second crewman almost head-on. Terror raced through her brain—there was no place to hide. Katcha needn't have worried. The sailor smiled, barely acknowledging her, and continued on his way.

Reaching the port side, Katcha could see the pier, the tractor-trailer rigs unloading, and all the warehouses beyond. Looking over the railing at the main deck, she located the gangway directly below her. There were crewmen carrying cases aboard and a bearded man with an official-looking white peaked cap that seemed to have sway over the others. *Is it possible to leave via the gangway while it's so busy?* she wondered. *Is the gangway always manned? The man in the cap must be a ship's officer, probably privy to my imprisonment. Sasha told me the ship is scheduled to sail sometime tomorrow, but I have no idea what time. Which means my escape has to be tonight when there are fewer people moving about.*

Another crewman exited a compartment and leaned over the port-side rail to shout down to someone ashore. His very presence forced her to retreat to the starboard side with its view of the Gulf of Finland. She looked down at the dark brownish-green water, choppy enough to break with whitecaps. It gave her a chill just thinking about diving into that cold, cold water. She would probably freeze to death and drown within minutes. She looked at her watch. It would be several hours to the time when Sasha usually brought her evening meal. She would discover that the key and padlock were missing and figure out the rest—enough to raise the alarm. Katcha faced three dilemmas. Escaping now was risky enough. Escaping after Sasha sounded the alarm could prove even more risky. But hiding and trying to escape when things died down presented an additional problem. She might wait too long and end up sailing with the ship.

A burly crewman carrying a seabag on his shoulder came up the ladder from a lower deck. He stopped and laid the seabag on the deck while he fished around in his pockets for something. Katcha had retreated behind a lifeboat to avoid being seen by him. Then she spied a fire extinguisher and fire axe strapped to an outside bulkhead only a few tempting feet away.

The crewman would never know how much she needed what he possessed. He proved so preoccupied that he didn't see her move out of her hiding place, steal across to the bulkhead, lift the fire axe from its hooks, and sneak up behind him. Not wanting to kill an innocent man, Katcha turned the axe around and struck him in the back of the head with the pole handle end. Her thumping heart almost burst out of her chest and her stomach spasmed with the thought of what she'd done, what a rotten person she'd become. The man folded forward and rolled over on his side, completely out cold. She dragged him, and then his seabag, behind her lifeboat refuge. On her knees, she unzipped and unbuttoned and tugged to pull off his clothes as quickly as she could. Frantically slipping out of her own outfit, she donned the sailor's black cargo pants, gray T-shirt, and black fleece jacket. Surveying her new look, she noted they fit her ample body quite well. *Even his boots fit! Now I won't be so recognizable.* She folded the pants cuffs up to her own ankle length and tucked her hair inside his black woolen watch cap. With a pang of regret, she stuffed her blouse, skirt, sweater, and shoes into the seabag.

Katcha was ready. She shouldered the bag on her right side

because she remembered that the ship's officer stood to the right of the gangway. The bag would hide her face from him. She descended the ladder to the deck below and crossed to the portside via a midships passageway. When she got to the gangway, the ship's officer was arguing with a crewman. He broke away from the to-do long enough to challenge her. Fright struck her harder than if it were a fist. She stopped. The argument restarted and the ship's officer waved her on through. She continued down the gangway to the pier and the city street below. At the second street corner, she turned right—out of ship's sight.

Katcha got rid of the seabag in a narrow alley. She started to walk, then picked the pace up to a trot—zigging and zagging through several blocks to confuse any would-be pursuers. She looked at her watch. *Surely, by now Sasha has found Dmitri locked in and given the alarm. They will be out looking for me any time now. I can't let them find me. I've got to get away.* Each time a car passed, she shrank into the nearest alley or behind a parked car or, at a minimum, a wide-trunked tree. The trot slowed to a walk as exhaustion reared its ugly head. Now stumbling every few feet, she eventually collapsed altogether on the sidewalk of a dark street.

* * * *

Meanwhile, Sasha returned to the cabin and could not find the key to the padlock. It wasn't on the hook beside the door where it should have been. There was also blood on the lock. She set the bag of Chinese food down on the deck and hurried to the captain's quarters, hoping he had a spare key to the lock. He didn't. The captain sent her to the ship's boatswain for a set of bolt cutters and a new lock and key. Sasha had no idea what to expect once the boatswain cut through the lock.

Inside the cabin Dmitri heard the metallic sounds outside. The door swung open. He came charging out. His temper had reached the explosive mode and he began shouting curse words. "That infernal woman knocked me unconscious and escaped," he bellowed. "See if she's still aboard or if she already left the ship."

Sasha raced to the gangway and interrogated the ship's officer there. He told her that no woman had left the ship. Only two of the crew had gone ashore in the last four hours, the length of his watch. The last one about an hour and a half ago. *Then the bitch is still aboard,* she thought. She hurried back to Dmitri with what she believed was good news.

While she was gone, Dmitri paced on the starboard side deck, waiting for her. His left shoulder ached, and his head throbbed from the huge purple-blue knot on his forehead. He heard moaning coming from behind one of the lifeboats and went to explore. The victimized crewman was just tottering to his feet when Dmitri discovered him. The vulnerable man was standing there, sheepish, in his red long-johns underwear.

"What happened to you?" asked Dmitri.

"Someone came up behind me and clobbered me, knocked me out." The crewman rubbed the back of his head and his fingers came away with a few drops of blood. "He took my clothes right off my back and stole my seabag. I was going home on leave. I don't know what I'll do now."

"You simpering fool," said Dmitri. "You've been worked over by a damn woman."

"So have you, Dmitri," lashed out Sasha, coming up behind the two. "*You* let the woman escape. But the good news is, the gangway officer says she's still on board. Only two crewmen have left the ship in the last four hours."

"You're wrong, dear," sneered Dmitri. "According to this fellow, she stole his clothes. She must have left the ship dressed as crew."

"Damn it, Dmitri! This is all your fault. That means she has an hour and a half head start on us. She has no bus or cab fare money. We had better get the car and go after her."

Chapter 33
Collision

Another corner, another street. Should she stagger across a street or turn into it? Katcha's decisions became both frightening and random. She desperately needed an alley to rest in and hide. Her legs couldn't go on much farther. The fatigue had become painful. The few pedestrians who paid attention to her probably assumed she was some drunk person. She had already seen the black Mercedes cruising the streets looking for her and twice managed to avoid them.

Sinking onto one knee next to a lamppost, she peered across the street to the narrow alley between two buildings—a temporary sanctuary, perhaps. *The trash bin at the end of that alley would make the perfect hiding place for me.* Katcha used the lamppost as a crutch to haul herself upright. At the curb, she stepped out into the street in front of a parked truck. There was no way she could have anticipated the Toyota Camry cruising toward her from behind the truck. Another two steps out into the street and the two collided, sending Katcha four feet in the air. She rolled another two feet before losing consciousness.

The Camry came to a screeching halt, the door flew open, and the driver emerged. Middle-aged, in a well-tailored suit and tie, he appeared to be on his way to or from an important meeting. The man rushed to the victim and soon realized he'd struck down a young woman—the seaman's black watch cap lay beside her, leaving her abundant hair with bloody strands. He knelt down beside her to see if she was still breathing, and shouted out, "She's alive! Somebody call an ambulance!" He then realized that she was unconscious and bleeding, but not so much. Paying no attention to his smudged trousers on the dirty pavement, he held her hand while he tried to find the source of her bleeding. His search was limited because of his fear of moving her.

A crowd of onlookers began to gather on the sidewalk. The black Mercedes, cruising the streets in search of its prey, slowed and pulled over to the opposite curb some distance away.

Sasha screamed. "It's Katcha! I'd recognize that face any-where. She's dressed in the crewman's outfit. Shouldn't we go and claim her? We can't just leave her like that, can we?"

"Forget it!" snapped Dmitri. "There would be too many explanations required. We need to keep a low profile here."

With downcast eyes, Sasha muttered, "You're all heart, aren't you, Dmitri?"

He ignored her.

The ambulance responded several minutes later. Its medical technicians provided a quick examination where she lay, then an IV hookup and transfer to a gurney. They loaded Katcha into the ambulance and drove away, sirens blaring.

In silence Dmitri and Sasha drove back to the Romanov Plaza. All the way to room 419 she expected him to suddenly im-plode with anger. His face had already reddened, his eyes bulged, and his jowly cheeks were full. It was only a matter of time now. She thought it best to keep her distance and not speak until he calmed down. Inside the hotel room the seething major fell into the upholstered armchair. She eased into the chair at the small desk to watch him, steeling herself for the tirade she knew was coming. Five minutes later he got up, walked to the cabinet holding the minibar, and extracted a half-dozen tiny bottles of assorted liquors before returning to his chair. He twisted off the screwcaps and gulped down the contents of each bottle, one after the other.

Dmitri finally broke the silence. "What took you so damned long to unlock the friggin' cabin door?"

An enraged Sasha glared at him. "Are you kidding? The key was missing from the hook. The captain didn't have an extra one. He sent me to the boatswain to open the padlock with bolt cutters. It took a while."

Dmitri retorted, "If you hadn't been so easy on her, delivering her meals, she would have caved hours ago. Some warden *you* made!"

"It was *your* fault, Dmitri. Don't you dare pin this on me! You went to visit her and left the padlock in the room. The key, too."

Dmitri boiled inside. He knew she was right, but couldn't let her have the last word. He continued with a whole series of blaring accusations ending with, "Now the ship will sail in the morning without her."

An hour passed. Then she saw the tears of frustration melt in his eyes and his face soften as the tension left his body. An exhausted and drunk Dmitri had trouble getting to his feet. Sasha jumped up, helped him to the double bed, and sat down on the edge next to him. He grabbed her around the waist and buried his head between her tiny breasts. After a few moments, she wiggled out of his embrace. With effort, she picked up his heavy legs, laid them on the bed, and pulled off his shoes. A gentle shove to his meaty upper chest sent him on his back. He fell asleep as soon as he hit the pillow. After several hours of television watching, Sasha joined him on the opposite side of the bed.

Chapter 34
Lily Monahan

Sunday morning Lily Monahan had important information to convey to her controller, but no one had picked up the phone in either Ralph's embassy office or Kent's hotel room the night before. She called both places repeatedly, finally gave up, and turned in for the night. What Lily didn't know was that the two men had eaten their evening meal in the Villa Keirkner dining room and moved to the hotel's bar to nurse the day's failures. At six o'clock in the morning, even before she had dressed, Lily tried Ralph's office again, but he hadn't come in yet.

Ninety minutes later, Ralph was sitting in his office, his brain a little fuzzy, when an anxious Lily pounded on his door. He called her in and she sat down across the desk from him.

"What brings you out so early?" he asked, wishing he'd had two fewer scotches last night. "What's so all-fired important?"

"I wanted to tell you about the major and his girlfriend. Their comings and goings."

"Girlfriend?" he asked. "You mean Sasha, don't you?"

"Yes." Lily replied. "I assume they were intimate."

"We knew it was more than just a business arrangement," said Ralph.

"Yesterday morning," Lily continued, "Federov returned to

214

his hotel room around eleven o'clock looking disheveled in casual shirt and pants, and left again at 11:30 in his uniform to go to his embassy office. I assume he spent the night at her place. Oddly, Sasha showed up at his hotel alone at 1:30 yesterday afternoon and didn't leave until 6:10 p.m."

"I get it," said Ralph. "She feels she can't go back to her apartment anymore. Kent and I raided the place yesterday morning. In fact, she walked in on us unexpectedly and gave us quite a fight."

"What happened?" asked Lily.

Ralph sighed and slumped in his chair, wishing he could avoid this conversation. "Well, I pulled my gun on her and thought she'd surrender. Boy, was I wrong. She was wearing ankle-high boots. Would you believe it if I told you that, with one foot, she kicked the gun right out of my hand and pushed me into a chair? I felt like a friggin' fool. A step or two later she planted her left heel in Kent's breadbasket and doubled him over in pain. She's one quick, powerful, and adept woman. To make a long story short, she slipped out of the apartment, leaving us to lick our wounds and egos. She was just too damn fast for us to pursue."

"Too bad," said Lily, thinking *How unprofessional can you get, guys?* "Just to finish up my report, Dmitri and Sasha returned to the hotel at 11:55 p.m. last night. From the look on his face, he seemed awful angry about something."

A knock on the door surprised them both.

"It's open," called Ralph.

Kent appeared in the doorway and nodded. "Lily. Ralph."

"What's wrong?" asked Ralph. "You look terrible, man. And why are you in jeans and a sweatshirt?"

"I went down to the pier this morning, hoping I'd find a way to sneak aboard the tramp freighter as one of the deckhands, but when I got there it wasn't in its berth. What I did see was the ship's stern already several miles out in the gulf. I stood there like a damn fool watching the ship grow smaller and smaller as it sailed farther out. All I could think of was I'd never see Katcha again. I've failed her and I don't know what to do."

"Maybe there is a way," said Ralph. "From what Lily just told me, there's an excellent chance that both Dmitri and Sasha are still in his hotel room at the Romanov Plaza. They got in late last night." He checked his watch. "It's only 7:55. Maybe we can get Eero's assistance this time and take them both by surprise and by force."

"Why would Eero agree to raid Federov's hotel room now?" asked Kent. "What's so different?"

"To begin with, this raid involves neither a ship nor an embassy," said Ralph. "And these two have been implicated already by Vadim, our jailbird ace in the hole."

"Then by all means call the man," whined Kent. "The longer we wait, the less chance we have to swoop in and grab the two of them before they leave Helsinki. But what I don't understand is how this is going to bring Katcha back to me."

"Don't you see? If we have them in custody, we can bargain with Federov," said Ralph. "He can have Katcha on the ferry back to us within a day."

Kent scowled. "You're dreaming, guy."

Ralph spent the next five minutes on the phone convincing Eero of the raid's worthiness. The chief inspector finally agreed. He and three other policemen would meet them in the lobby of the Romanov Plaza in fifteen minutes. When Ralph hung up, Lily had already left. He reached into his top left drawer and handed Kent a 9mm Glock pistol. Kent tucked it into the back of his jeans belt. The two were out the door and out in the embassy parking lot in a flash.

"You okay with this, Kent?" asked Ralph as they slid into the Opel. "You don't seem totally on board."

"I'm wondering whether Eero will agree to trade Federov for my Katcha. Does he even have the authority to make such a swap?"

"I think we're getting a little ahead of ourselves here," said Ralph. "We don't even have Federov in custody yet."

When they arrived at the Romanov Plaza, Eero and three of his men were waiting in the lobby. Lily had resumed her usual position in a chair by the window to the street. When Ralph stared in her direction, she hand-signaled back that she hadn't seen either one of the targets this morning.

Eero turned to the desk clerk and showed him his badge. "How long have you been on duty?"

"Since 5:30, sir."

"Have you seen anyone from room 419 go out this morning?" asked Eero.

"I haven't seen anyone leave, except the guest in 205. She checked out at 6:30. Said she had to catch a train," said the nervous clerk.

Eero demanded the house master key. The clerk started to make an excuse, but fearing the consequences, he complied, and handed it to the komisar. Eero positioned one of his men outside at the bottom of the fire escape. He sent the remaining two men to the staircase while he and the Americans took the elevator. Arriving at the fourth floor, he positioned the two men at opposite ends of the hallway. Eero inserted the master key in the lock, and he and the two American agents drew their weapons. The unlocking hardly made any noise. The three men charged into the room, catching the two targets by surprise. Dmitri had one foot in a leg of his trousers and Sasha stood in the open bathroom doorway without a stitch on. Her nudity didn't seem to disturb her as much as being trapped in a room without a window.

"So…What can I do for you, gentlemen?" asked Sasha, her cherubic lips curling up at the corners. She stepped into the room and casually picked up a short terry hotel robe at the end of the bed. Slipping her petite athletic body into it, she slowly tied it shut, while her calculating eyes darted about the room looking for some advantage.

Eero moved toward her with his restraints at the ready.

"Watch out—she's trained in the martial arts," warned Kent. "She has a mean kick."

Sasha half-turned away from Eero and timed her round-house kick as he came close, but a hair too late. When she tried to whirl about with a barefoot kick, he shoved her in the small of her back and knocked her onto the bed face-down.

"Wait!" she screamed. "I have to get dressed!"

Eero hesitated for a moment. "You can go into the bathroom, but leave the door open. Don't try anything stupid."

Sasha snatched her cargo pants, T-shirt, and underwear off a chair, ducked into the bathroom, and in a lightning flash got dressed. She sauntered out of the bathroom, seeming to surrender, but with eyes darting everywhere. Sliding into her black leather boots, she darted toward the door in one last attempt to escape, but Eero was waiting. He grabbed her and flung her back down on the bed. Instead of placing the restraints on her wrists, he chose to put them on her legs, just above her ankle boots. Suddenly, with two feet tied together, she managed to kick the big man in his chest with all the power she had left. His Kevlar vest absorbed the brunt of the blow.

Dmitri, standing at the far side of the bed, was busy pulling up the second leg of his trousers. He grabbed yesterday's white dress shirt and slipped into it. *Son of a bitch,* he thought. *I should be in my uniform.* Ralph allowed him to button up before putting on plastic tie-wrap restraints.

Sasha still wasn't giving up. She lay on her back on the bed swinging her fists wildly and powerfully, rebuffing any attempt to put restraints on her wrists. It took Eero on one side and Kent on the other to pin her arms down on the bed. Eero slipped a metal cuff on her right wrist and the two men pushed her arms together so Kent could snap the cuff about her left wrist. Without removing the restraints on her ankles, Eero slipped a new tie-wrap around each ankle and a third one interconnecting the two ankle restraints. The third one was a long enough loop to allow mini-stepping, and short enough to discourage any damaging acrobatics. He then stood her on her feet, placed a hand on her back, and pushed her toward the door.

Sasha couldn't do anything but shuffle her feet. She spit at anyone who came within range. There was still too much fight in her. She shuffled forward as rapidly as she could, knowing she had no choice or she would fall on her face.

"Where's Katcha?" Kent confronted her. "Is she on the ship?"

Sasha flashed him a mocking smile.

Kent turned to Dmitri with the same question. The major merely pressed his bulbous lips together as he was marched into the hall. He knew he had a valuable commodity to trade.

"Don't worry, friend," boomed Eero to Kent to be sure he was heard. "We'll break them both when we get them back to the station."

Dmitri parried in a calm, sugary voice. "Of course, you'll notify the Russian Embassy of my awkward situation, won't you?"

"Why should I?" asked Eero. "You don't have any diplomatic immunity to speak of."

"I'm a Russian citizen in distress and entitled to my government's assistance."

"As far as I'm concerned, you are a criminal."

"What about me?" asked Sasha.

"You're no angel either," said Eero. "We know all about you. You'll get your turn."

My turn? Sasha didn't like the sound of that.

Chapter 35
Confrontation

The poliisi conveyed prisoners Dmitri and Sasha to the holding cells four floors below Komisar Eero's office. They were placed in separate cells some distance from the one that Vadim Ostanyuk occupied. The cuffs were removed from Sasha's wrists, but the triple restraint was kept on her ankles as a precaution—her feet were lethal weapons. After an hour of simmer time, Dmitri was removed from his cell and taken in the elevator up to Eero's office. Eero was already sitting at the bare table when he arrived. Ralph and Kent were ushered into the adjacent room equipped with video and audio presence of the interrogation room. Dmitri took a seat opposite Eero and the escort guard cuffed Dmitri to the table before leaving the room.

"We have a solid witness who will testify that you directed a conspiracy to kidnap Katcha Kroschenko. Conspiracy to commit kidnapping carries with it a substantial prison term. I can promise you a lesser charge if you cooperate fully with us and return Ms. Kroschenko to us unharmed."

Dmitri glared at Eero and droned a rehearsed response. "Before we go any further, let's assume that I know all the questions you are about to ask me, and that I have all the right answers to them. A lesser sentence simply won't cut it. I will need full immunity from any and all crimes and I will need free passage back to my country in return for what I have to tell you."

"How can I determine the truthfulness and completeness of your information?"

"You have my honor as a Russian soldier. Let me stipulate first that Miss Kroschenko suffered no harm while she was my guest."

Eero's face turned stormy. "*Was your guest?*"

"A minor slip of the tongue, I assure you."

"A slip of the tongue?" Eero retorted. "Don't lie to me, Major. But you said "was." Are you telling me that you are no longer holding the woman against her will?

"Yes," said Dmitri.

"What is it you want from us, Major?"

"I will provide all the information you need just as soon as I am on the *Princess Anastasia* to St. Petersburg."

Eero turned silent to gather his wits and suppress his anger, realizing that once the major was on the ferry the Finnish poliisi would lose complete control of him. "You must think I'm a babe in the woods, Major. Your so-called negotiation is ludicrous. No, that won't do. However, I could hold you and offer your girlfriend, Sasha, her freedom if she tells us everything first. What do you think of that, Major?"

"You wouldn't do that," said Dmitri.

"Why not? Sasha's only a conspirator, not the ringleader like yourself."

"So how do you propose to establish trust for the trade on your terms?" asked Dmitri.

"I will provide you with documents that guarantee your safe passage to St Petersburg if and when you return Miss Kroschenko unharmed to us."

Dmitri smiled. "If I am locked up here, I can hardly bring her to you, can I?"

"But you can tell us where she is, and we can go get her."

"I can't do that?"

"Why not?"

"I can't tell you why until you guarantee my safe passage out of here."

"That's an unreasonable answer, Major. You are talking in circles. You leave me no recourse but to prepare a long-term cell for you. Perhaps I should turn my attention to Sasha now."

"No, wait!" said Dmitri, losing some of his staunch military stature. "Miss Kroschenko is no longer a guest of ours, so I simply cannot release her to you. But if I tell you how to find her, will you still allow me to get on that ferry?"

"Let me put it this way, Major. It's time you dropped the phony word guest. Your cooperation would be duly noted at your kidnapping trial."

"That's not enough," Dmitri countered. "No trial. What would it take to grant me my freedom and no charges?"

"First of all, you would have to tell me all that you know about Miss Kroschenko's whereabouts and welfare. Now! If she is returned to us unharmed and in good spirits, my superiors and I will reassess your current circumstances."

"I can assure you that while she was in our care no harm came to her," pleaded Dmitri. "She was kept in a first-class cabin aboard ship and fed only restaurant meals. All her needs were attended to."

"Nevertheless, you kidnapped her and held her against her will," said Eero. "What has changed that you cannot tell me where she is?"

"During one of my friendly visits, your young lady hit me on the head and locked me in the cabin."

"So, you have no idea where she is now?"

"That's not exactly true," Dmitri admitted. "Several hours later, Sasha returned with her evening meal and released me from the cabin. That's when I found out that the young lady managed to escape off the ship in seaman's attire. We took the car and searched the surrounding streets."

"Did you ever find her or even see her?" asked Eero in an

impatient tone.

"I'm telling you all that I know."

"I doubt that. Just answer the question."

"Yes, we did," surrendered Dmitri. "She had fallen down, but when she saw us coming for her, she got up and darted out into the street. A car coming from her blind side hit her and threw her body through the air several feet. It wasn't our fault. It just couldn't be helped."

"Yes, it damned well was your fault," declared Eero. "Stalking her forced her into that street. But was she hurt? Was she still moving? What did you do then?"

"We were too far away to help or do anything but watch. She lay there in the street not moving. The driver got out, and a crowd began to gather. Someone must have called for an ambulance because a few minutes later one arrived and took her away."

"Do you know where they took her?"

"Not exactly, but how many hospitals can Helsinki have? I'm sure a few well-placed phone calls will locate her."

The disgusted komisar turned to face the one-way glass wall and gestured to those on the opposite side. The ball was in their court now. He got up, went to the door, and spoke to the guard standing there. "Take the prisoner to his cell and bring the woman to me."

* * * *

Kent and Ralph had soaked up every word spoken on the other side of the one-way window. Kent experienced every emotion, from heart-beating suspense to red-faced rage to nerve-wracking anxiety over Katcha's welfare. He had come to know how much he really cared about her. Ralph tried to calm him. When Eero actually forced Dmitri to reveal that she was hospitalized, Kent wanted to leave immediately and search for her. They now had the means to locate Katcha, but what kind of condition would she be in? Was she even alive?

The two men rushed out into the hall and headed for Eero's office to use his telephone. The calls were frantic, and her name meant nothing to any of the four main hospitals. But their fifth call produced a glimmer of hope. The night before, in the early evening, the Helsinki University Central Hospital admitted a nameless female auto accident victim. The mid-twenties victim had remained nameless because she was comatose and had no identifying papers. The hospital would give no additional information over the phone.

"It's got to be Katcha," said Kent, his voice cracking. "We've got to go to her."

"Sounds like it might be her," said Ralph. "Let's go. I know the way."

Ralph drove to University Central Hospital and dropped Kent off at the front door. He rushed inside and up to the reception desk.

"You admitted an unnamed auto accident victim last evening," he said to the young receptionist sitting behind the desk. "I believe she is my fiancé, Katcha Kroschenko. Can you tell me what room she is in?"

"I'm terribly sorry, sir," she replied, "I am not authorized to give out that kind of information." Seeing the crushed look on his face, she pointed to his right and added, "Talk to the head nurse in Trauma Unit Two. It's on the third floor of the next building over. She might be able to help you."

Kent thanked her and started down the corridor, when she called him back.

"Sir! Wait! You need a visitor's pass to access any part of this hospital."

Kent returned to the desk and had to fill out a half-page form before she handed him a visitor's pass. He hurried through the inter-building connections to the elevator that took him to the third floor. When the elevator doors opened, Kent stopped an orderly pushing an empty gurney and asked where he would find Trauma Unit Two. The orderly pointed down one of the corridors. With fear stealing most of his breath, Kent approached the counter at the end of the corridor.

A fiftyish nurse, granny glasses perched low on her nose,

looked up from her computer screen. The young man standing before her looked frazzled. "I am Head Nurse Valerie Huhta. How can I help you?"

"I understand you have an unidentified comatose patient who was admitted last evening, a car accident," said Kent.

"That may be true," said Nurse Huhta. "What exactly is your interest in this patient?"

"She's my fiancé Katcha Kroschenko. I would like the opportunity to verify her identity. Can you tell me what room she's in?"

"If you will follow me, I will take you to her room—for identification purposes only. Do you agree?"

"Of course."

Nurse Huhta led him down a hall to the last room on the left. The door to room 324 was wide open. His anguish and doubts peaked as he entered the room. *What if I'm wrong? I can't be. It has to be her.* The patient lay on her back, her substantial body filling one of the two beds. The second bed was empty. He recognized Katcha's profile almost immediately. *It's her!* The round cheeks in her peasant face looked pasty, Her thick, normally glossy, ash-blonde hair flopped around the pillow looking like it needed a good shampooing. Her normally swelling bosom flattened out under the white hospital gown. Her eyes were closed, as if the long light-brown lashes had sealed them shut.

Kent spun around to the nurse. "Yes! She's is my beloved Katcha! Please tell me she's going to recover."

"There are no guarantees, of course, but many do," said Nurse Huhta, trying to be hopeful, but treading carefully.

His voice quavered as he dared ask the dreaded question.

"She's not just sleeping, is she?"

"No," said Nurse Huhta. "She's in a coma."

"But will she come out of it?"

The nurse paused to frame her words. "You'll have to talk with the doctor for a prognosis. Hospital policy prohibits me from giving out that kind of information." But then she saw the pitiful, puppy-dog look on his large square face and relented. "She's suffering from a severe concussion. The scans show quite a bit of swelling in the back of the brain. We'll know more when the swelling subsides. We're hopeful, but there's no way of knowing for sure. And if she does come out of it, we'll perform tests to determine whether any permanent damage has occurred."

"Damage?" Tears welled up in Kent's eyes. *Oh my God, I've failed to keep her safe. I failed in my promise to Katcha's mother. Mavis, please forgive me.* "Can I stay a little while in her room?" he pleaded. "I just want to be near her."

Nurse Huhta hesitated for a moment. "I don't suppose it can do any harm as long as you don't interfere with hospital routine. You can stay until visiting hours are over."

"Can she hear me when I speak?"

"Who knows? Possibly. It might speed things along." Nurse Huhta gave him a sympathetic nod as she left the room.

Chapter 36
The Prisoners

The prison guard left the interrogation room with the cuffed Dmitri and called to a second guard in the basement to bring Sasha upstairs from her holding cell. The elevator doors opened in the basement. Dmitri and Sasha met face to face.

"Don't tell them anything!" Dmitri bellowed. "Don't take their lousy deals." His face turned red and there was something in his voice that was neither genuine nor convincing.

"You bastard!" she spit out. "I bet you took a deal and it doesn't include me!" She tried to shuffle closer to him, but her guard kept her in check and pushed her into the elevator.

In the fourth-floor hall, as the guard prodded her forward toward the interrogation room, she jerked to a stop. In a small, appealing voice, she said, "I'm not going another step unless you take these nasty ties off my legs." She bent over to rub her left shin with her cuffed hands. The guard, new to his job, hadn't been informed how lethal her legs were. Seeing the ugly red marks on the pale skin just above her boots, he undid the restraints in an innocent moment of compassion.

"Thank you," she murmured.

The concrete-walled corridor was lined with waist-high windows every ten feet. The guard walked behind his prisoner, convinced that he had pacified her with his act of kindness. In a flash Sasha spun around, raised her knee, and landed her first kick straight into the unsuspecting guard's groin, sending him flat on his back. Doubled over in pain, he struggled to get up and retaliate. The second kick caught him just under the chin, knocking him out cold.

Hopping a few steps away from him, Sasha's next move was a powerful third kick placed in the center of the thin glass window pane next to her. It shattered into numerous shards and sounded so loud that it alarmed workers in nearby offices. With bent elbows, she cleared the shards off the frame, and with the skill of an acrobat, she climbed onto the windowsill. Poised and controlled, Sasha readied herself to leap to the fire escape on the next building some ten feet away and four stories above ground. Ordinarily, this feat would have been well within her athletic capabilities, but with cuffed wrists, her jumping range was shortened by mere inches. She bent her knees deeply, then leaped through the air. Her fingernails scratched at the fire escape's wrought-iron guardrail, but couldn't find a grip at anything substantial. With a desperate scream, Sasha slipped away into nothingness and fell the four stories to a concrete walk between the buildings.

Hearing all the noise, Eero rushed into the corridor, discovering first the unconscious guard and then the smashed glass pane. Other workers flowed into the corridor from adjacent offices. A courthouse clerk poked his head out the broken window and peered down between the buildings. "Someone jumped through the window and landed on the sidewalk!" he cried.

"Oooh!" the guard on the floor moaned as he regained consciousness. "What happened? I hurt all over. Where's the prisoner?"

"She took a leap through the broken window," cried the clerk.

Eero approached the broken window and looked down for himself. "It's Sasha, my prisoner," he confirmed, shaking his head at the tragedy.

"Well, look at it this way," said the clerk. "There won't be an expensive trial, nor will we have to feed her for the next umpteen years."

"Damn it, man, this is a human being you're talking about," scolded Eero.

The clerk said nothing, stole away to his office, and shut the door.

Chapter 37
The Long Wait
Thursday, September 3

Kent spent the next four distressing days with Katcha in her hospital room, hearing only the sound of his own droning voice while speaking at levels meant strictly for her ears. He spoke of hope, love, and marriage—subjects he'd avoided until now. But tragedy can strengthen the urgency of the heart and the weakness of the will, and here he was, knowing these were the words she wanted to hear most. But he wondered, *Does she even hear what I'm saying?*

He stepped aside when the nurses came and went, checking vitals, changing IVs, and extracting fluids. Two excursions to the cafeteria for lunch and supper and three trips to the vending machine for coffee were the only times he was absent from her side during hospital visiting hours. He was always the first to arrive in the morning and the last to be shooed out at night.

On his arrival the fourth morning, he discovered that her arm was in a different place. He didn't dare hope that she had moved it voluntarily. *It could have been a nurse's aide fussing around her, changing sheets, fluffing the pillow.* At times he noted evidence of other small changes, too, but had never witnessed any actual movement with his own eyes.

By cell phone Ralph kept him abreast of embassy activity and the disposition of Major Dmitri Federov while he awaited trial. By his own admission of guilt, Dmitri was certain to be convicted. Because of his cooperation, his prison sentence would probably be reduced to ten-to-fifteen years.

During the endless hours sitting with Katcha, Kent brooded about Sasha—how she had returned to her apartment while he and Ralph were searching it. Yeah, she had slammed her booted foot into his stomach. Nevertheless, he was deeply disturbed to learn about the manner of her death. He did not believe for an instant that she committed suicide. He'd heard how she overcame her prison guard escort—with wits and martial-arts skills. *I'm guessing her final leap was a desperate failed attempt to escape imprisonment. The way Ralph described her fall, in handcuffs, she missed the railing on the adjacent building's fire escape only by inches.*

Kent had plenty of time to think about his career while he sat next to the bed. On his first mission, he'd been caught in the corridor of the Russian Federation's Army Annex Three—and arrested. But only after he had successfully planted a bug in the base of the lamp in the general's office. The transmissions from that bug were providing the West with valuable intelligence. Because Kent had accomplished his mission, he was entitled to thirty days of paid leave. He wasn't going anywhere.

My career, a brand-new assignment? Whoa, one more thing I haven't considered is that my face has been plastered across the Russian news media for more than a month. Of course, it's only a sketch, but the risk of my going under cover in Russia has become unacceptable. Any advantage in field work, my knowledge of the Russian language and culture, has certainly lessened in value. I can only foresee a series of desk jobs in my future if I remain with the agency. This makes my decision to take up the law profession so much easier. Katcha will be glad to know this.

He was thankful that the doctors had declared Katcha stable. Plenty of bruising and abrasions, but at least no broken bones. According to the radiologist assigned to her case, the swelling had subsided significantly. *But is it enough?* Kent couldn't suppress his fears. *And will she be my very same Katcha? Or will she only be a fragment of the woman I love?*

* * * *

On the fifth morning of her hospitalization, Kent saw her right foot wiggle back and forth. His body tensed with anticipation. As she lay on her back, he saw additional signs, too, and then, when he returned from lunch, he noticed Katcha's eyes were open and staring up at the ceiling. A lump grew in his throat as he assembled appropriate words for her ears. But she didn't seem to respond to what he said. His heart missed a few beats while he envisioned her emerging from the coma in a catatonic state. He bit down hard on his lower lip and felt tears rolling down on his cheeks.

A half-hour later, Katcha's eyelids began to flutter and blink. Her cheeks rose to force her eyes into a squint, followed by an intense stare that melted into a softer look. A faint guttural sound emerged as she cleared her throat.

"Sweetheart, you're awake," he almost shouted.

Her head turned toward him, responding to his voice. In a raspy whisper, she asked, "Where am I? Who are you?"

A jolt of despair shot through him like an electric shock. His chest tightened and his throat closed up, choking him with dashed expectations.

"It's your Kent, sweetheart. You're in the hospital. You were in a car accident five days ago and you hit your head. You've just emerged from a coma." He held his breath.

A blank look spread over Katcha's face. Her normally expressive gray-blue eyes reflected nothing. She turned her head away. *Maybe she's digesting my words*, he told himself.

But when she turned back again, she whispered, "I'm sooo tired." Her eyelids fluttered, then flapped shut as she drifted off to a nether place once more.

Crushed, Kent tried for another fifteen minutes to talk Katcha back to an awakened state. His fingers trembled as he pressed the button for help. Nurse Huhta arrived moments later, and he babbled, telling her of Katcha's all-too-short return to reality.

She took Katcha's vital signs. "Mr. Brukner, this is not an uncommon experience. It's encouraging and hopeful. Possibly the beginning—gradual improvement that might include more recognition and understanding."

An hour later, Katcha was still asleep when Kent left the room for supper in the cafeteria. He knew he needed to eat, but could barely get down a turkey sandwich and small carton of milk. Upon returning, he took one step into the room and stopped short.

Katcha was sitting up! But not *just* sitting up. She was carrying on a conversation with Nurse Huhta, who was standing next to the bed.

"Kent!" she squealed when she caught sight of him in the doorway. The nurse backed away and slipped out. Startled but overjoyed, he rushed to the bedside, leaned down, and kissed her gently on the lips.

"Nurse Huhta told me you've stayed with me the whole time," she said.

He pulled up the vinyl-padded wooden armchair he'd occupied for five days and took one of her soft hands in both of his. Momentarily speechless, he finally gathered his wits about him and said, "Katcha, I can't believe this. An hour ago you didn't recognize me. I thought I was going to lose you. I didn't want to let you go."

"That's so sweet," she said with a smile.

He noted that color had returned to her cheeks. Still clasping her hand in his, he said, "Darling, I've finally found out what's most important to me in my life and I'm going to rearrange things to fix some mistakes I've made."

"What mistakes, dear?" she asked.

"One, these agonizing seven days without you have taught me that you, Katcha Kroschenko, are my top priority, so I'm asking you formally. Will you be my wife?"

"Of course, dear," she said. "It's all I ever wanted—to be your bride."

"Two...well, it's not a mistake, Katcha. It's more like a decision." He noted the confusion in her eyes. "There's an in-house, spook expression: 'I've been made.' My face and name are too well known now to be an effective spy anywhere, anymore. So, rather than become some dull contract manager at the organization, I plan to leave and return to law school."

"That's wonderful, sweetheart," she said. "Then I won't have to worry about where you are and whether you are in danger. I love that decision."

"Three! I will patch things up with my dad, and we will live in the big house on my father's farm near Jefferson, Iowa, until I actually start practicing law."

"Iowa? I'll have to look at a map and see where that is," she said. "This is getting better and better. But is there anything in Iowa except corn and cows?"

He grinned and assumed she was joking. Or was she? His expression turned serious and businesslike. "The way I figure things, as soon as you're discharged from the hospital we should be married here in Helsinki. If you're my wife it'll be easier for you to enter the United States. If we're not married, Ralph says you could make a case for political asylum, but that might take a whole lot longer to arrange."

Katcha's face lit up. "Of course I'll go as your wife! Nurse Huhta told me my doctor will want to observe me for a few more days to see if there are any aftereffects and to see how I adapt to real food and a normal sleep pattern again. About the wedding, what did you have in mind?"

"Well, I've always been a believer, but I'm not keen on organized religion. If it takes a priest or minister to do the trick, it's fine with me. Otherwise, a judge, or court clerk, or a justice of the peace—whatever it takes to tie the knot in Helsinki."

She looked relieved. "I've only been to church twice in my life and I was frightened both times by the enormity of it. Besides, the Soviet government was very hostile to religion in general, and I don't know how much the new government has changed. I'd just as soon have a civil ceremony."

"Okay, then, a civil wedding it is." He bent over and kissed her on the lips. She hugged him tightly.

"Now that was easy, wasn't it?" she asked. But her mood suddenly changed. "Kent, I have to call Mama. She must be so worried, not hearing from me for so long. And I do have one requirement if I marry you. That Mama gets to come visit us in your dad's house or wherever we live. And Papa, too."

"Absolutely, dear! After all, Mavis made this whole thing, our entire relationship and everything else, possible. Without her kindness and generosity, we wouldn't even be together. And your papa played a big part, too, without even knowing it. His papers made our escape possible."

But Kent couldn't keep the mood light. He dropped his arms, his posture stiffened, and he opened the subject that had obsessed him from the moment Katcha went missing. "Darling, I have to ask you…. Hell, you don't need to respond if it's too traumatic. But what exactly do you remember of your kidnapping ordeal?"

A flush rose from her neck to her cheeks and her eyes turned an intense hue. "No, no, it's not too traumatic. I *want* to tell you. I want you to know everything. I was actually worried that you weren't going to ask me. So… I remember leaving the hotel for my shopping trip. I was all dressed in my purple-flowered skirt and blue blouse. The doorman got me a taxi. But it was strange—the one that came wasn't the one he waved for that was next in line. This taxi did a U-turn from across the street, like it was waiting just for *me*. And a few blocks later, this guy forced himself inside the back seat next to me. He was skinny and had slicked-back hair, and whenever he moved, he slithered like a snake."

For the next hour, Katcha talked nonstop. At some points, Kent wondered if he was taxing her too much. But her story never flagged. In fact, he was startled by her recall ability. Ironically, he even thought she would have made a first-rate agent. Midway through, he listened to her describe Sasha—with respect and a certain gratitude for the meals she selected to bring her.

Winding down, her voice filled with pride as she described throwing the padlock at Dmitri's head, hitting him with the chair, and locking him into the freighter cabin where she was imprisoned.

He saw that her eyelids were flickering, a sign of fatigue. "Dear, would you like to stop for a while and take a nap?"

"No, no. I need to tell you everything right now while I still remember stuff."

"Okay, sweetheart, but let me know if you get too tired. But how did you manage to get off the ship?"

"Kent, you'd have been proud of me. I'm pretty strong, you know—from carrying trays loaded with dishes in the café. I was hiding behind the lifeboats trying to figure out what to do next, and I saw a seaman with his bag, like he was ready to leave the ship. I hit him over the head with a fire-axe handle. The poor guy collapsed. I hope I didn't kill him. After all, he was just an innocent bystander. But he was also my passport to freedom. I dressed myself in his shirt and pants and jacket and boots and cap and took his seabag. I had the seabag hoisted on my shoulder so the gangway officer couldn't see my face. Once ashore, I hid in an alley.

"I had no idea where I was going, just wandering through alleys to keep hidden, and then I tried to cross a street. Too many cars. That's all I remember. I woke up here. But what happened to those horrible men who kidnapped me? Did they ever get caught?"

During the next half hour, Kent told her about the Finnish police, Komisar Eero, and their investigation. "The snake-like guy, as you described him so well, is in custody, and so is Dmitri. The other one was shot dead by the poliisi."

"What about Sasha?" Katcha asked.

Kent hesitated. "On the way to interrogation in the courthouse hall, she overcame the guard and took a nosedive out of a fourth-floor window, trying to escape. Even though she was still in handcuffs, she tried to leap to the next building, where there was a fire escape. She couldn't make it. She fell and went splat on the sidewalk.

A sob caught in Katcha's throat. "Oh no! That's terrible!"

She wasn't a bad person. She just got in with a bad man."

* * * *

A week later, Katcha left the hospital to pursue her new life. A receptionist at the embassy accompanied them on a Helsinki shopping spree to acquire the semblance of a wardrobe for her. With many months of back pay fortifying Kent's credit card, they picked out a simple pastel wedding dress and several travel outfits for their honeymoon and the trip to the United States. Kent applied to the Civil Registrar's Office for the necessary marriage paperwork, including affidavits stating "Both parties are acting of free will," and a scheduling date for the actual marriage. Another week passed. On the following Monday, the receptionist and Ralph witnessed the nuptials of Kent and Katcha as they became Mr. and Mrs. Kent P. Brukner.

The three-week honeymoon to Berlin, Paris, and London passed blissfully. The lovebirds were intoxicated with their new-found freedom.

Chapter 38
Iowa

Friday, September 25

A British Airways plane out of London to Chicago, a connecting plane to Des Moines, Iowa, and a taxi ride deposited the newlyweds at the front door of Kent's childhood home, a large farm just outside Jefferson. Kent rang the bell. The door was opened by a man much older-looking, balder, and grayer on the fringes than Kent remembered him. Even though he had wired ahead that they were coming, his father's face displayed surprise.

"Ahh, so you finally remembered that you had a father," said Clinton Brukner.

"Sorry, Dad. I know we didn't part on the best of terms, but I want to make that up to you."

"So, you've up and come home to roost and you've brought someone with you," said Clinton. "A pretty one she is."

"Katcha is not just someone, Dad. She's my loving wife. We were married in Helsinki, Finland. I was hoping we could stay here while I finish law school over in Ames."

"Law school, eh! I thought you gave up that grand idea to go galivantin' and stickin' your nose in all over God's green earth. What do you want from me now? Free rent and a free meal ticket while you become a shyster lawyer? You made your own wild decision and it didn't include me. You didn't want to help out on the

238

farm neither."

"What about Greg?" asked Kent. "Doesn't he help you with the farming?"

"My *good* son runs the whole farm by himself now."

"Dad, I have plenty of savings—money I can contribute for our keep here. Or, if we're not welcome here and you prefer to forget that you have a second son, we can easily go elsewhere. It's up to you, Dad. Son or no son. Mom taught us to love and respect one another. If you can't find a way to love me, I think I at least deserve your respect."

The mention of his late wife triggered something in Clinton's brain and tears appeared in his tired gray eyes. He took a deep breath and slowly mouthed the words, "You can stay. She would have wanted us to be a family again."

As soon as these three words—"You can stay"—came out of his mouth, Katcha surprised Clinton by throwing her arms around him and hugging him hard. On tiptoe, she kissed him on his unshaven cheek. "Thank you," she said.

Somehow his hands went around her back to complete the hug. "You sure know how to soften up a mean old man, young lady. You are welcome here. As for you, Kent, you can earn your way back into my good graces."

The Paco and Molly Mystery Series (#1)

Locks and Cream Cheese—In scandal-ridden Black Rain Corners, a Chesapeake Bay mansion harbors locked rooms and deadly secrets. A wily detective and a gourmet cook tackle the case.

The Paco and Molly Mystery Series (#2)

Hot Grudge Sunday—Bank robbers and conspirators derail the sleuths' blissful honeymoon at the Grand Canyon. Can they nail the suspects after they themselves become targets?

The Paco and Molly Mystery Series (#3)

Boston Scream Pie—A teenage girl's nightmare triggers a sinister tale of twins, two feuding families, and a blonde bombshell who hates being called "Mom."

Available on Amazon.com and all e-readers.

The Dan and Rivka Sherman Mystery Series (#1)

Death Goes Postal—Rare 15th-century typesetting artifacts journey through time, leaving a horrifying imprint in their wake. Dan and Rivka risk life and limb to locate the treasures and unmask the murderer. Not quite what they expected when they bought The Olde Victorian Bookstore. (**Also available as an Amazon Audible Audiobook.**)

The Dan and Rivka Sherman Mystery Series (#2)

Death Takes A Mistress—A young Englishwoman is murdered by her lover. Years later, her daughter, seeking revenge, journeys from London to Annapolis, MD to find the killer and her father. But to which family does he belong? Dan and Rivka set out to expose the true villain.

The Dan and Rivka Sherman Mystery Series (#3)

Death Steals A Holy Book—Dan and Rivka inherit a rare Yiddish translation of a 14th-century holy book, but it is stolen and their book restorer is murdered. Can they recover the book and nail the culprit?

Available on Amazon.com and all e-readers.

The Dan and Rivka Sherman Mystery Series (#4)

Death Rules the Night—Dan wants to know why all copies of an important book are missing, not only from the bookstore, but also from all the local libraries and the author's bookshelves. Who is trying to hide the book's secrets and what are they? Can stalking, threats, and even murder sway Dan from solving this mystery? Rivka fears for their lives.

Cry Ohana, Adventure and Suspense in Hawaii—A car accident, blackmail, and murder tear apart a Hawai'ian *'ohana* (family). Kekoa, the teenage son, witnesses the murder and is forced into life on the run. Danger erupts at a Filipino wedding, a Maui resort, and the Big Island's volcanic steam vents. Can the family re-unite and bring down the killer?

Honolulu Heat—Leilani and Alex Wong anguish over son Noah, an idealistic teenager who teeters on both sides of the law. He meets Nina Portfia, his dream girl, but they unwittingly share horrific secrets. Noah finds himself immersed in a bloody feud between a Chinatown protection racketeer and a crimeland don who, ironically, is Nina's father.

Available on Amazon.com and all e-readers.

Murder, Fantasy, and Weird Tales

—Delve into tales of the brave, the foolhardy, and the wicked on their journeys to the unknown in Hawai'i, Japan, Cambodia, Italy, and elsewhere. Art lovers, hit women, a vampire, a lively hologram, and others reveal their secret compulsions.

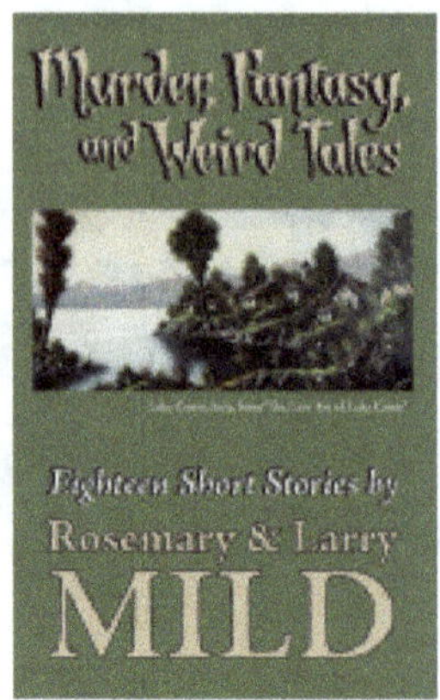

The Misadventures of Slim O. Wittz, Soft-Boiled Detective—

"If you're looking for a truly bumbling gumshoe, you want me, Slim. I'm frequently behind the eight ball and seldom paid. In eight complete mystery stories I always bump into criminals. And you're right: my case record is remarkably shaky."

Copper and Goldie • 13 Tails of Adventure and Suspense in Hawaii

—Sam, a disabled ex-cop-turned PI, and his canine sidekick, Goldie, ply the streets of Honolulu in a Checker Cab, looking for fares and solving crimes.

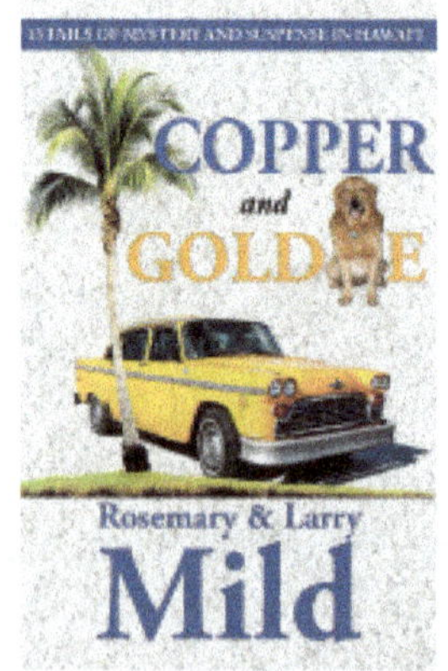

Available on Amazon.com and all e-readers.

Miriam's World—and Mine
—Miriam Luby Wolfe, a junior at Syracuse U., spent her fall semester in London exploring her talents: singing, dancing, acting, and writing. But she never made it home. A terrorist bomb destroyed her plane over Lockerbie, Scotland. Learn about Miriam, the Pan Am families, the bombers, and the political fallout.

Love! Laugh! Panic! Life with My Mother—Don't we all have mixed emotions about our mothers? Rosemary Mild's mom was super-achieving, but tough to live with. Luby Pollack was a journalist, popular book author, and psychiatrist's wife. Always the heroine, and sometimes the villain, from the viewpoint of her loving but ornery daughter.

In My Next Life I'll Get It Right— is a collection of personal essays ranging from the hilarious to the serious—keen, sometimes wicked, observations on everyday life. And… wishful thinking mixed with tough reality, See how Rosemary views her two marriages, the good and the not so good. Join her as she takes on sailing, skating, Jazzercise, football, and more—and feel for a mother's heart-wrenching loss.

- **Available on Amazon.com and all e-readers.**

Unto the Third Generation—Two young people, each unaware of the other, volunteer to become cryonauts—physically frozen in a life-suspension experiment. Leonard, a steel worker, and Francine, a waitress, postpone their destinies for untold generations. But their lives are in jeopardy —depending upon two world-shaking events.

Charley and the Magic Jug and Other Stories—Climb the mountain to the secret cave with Charley. Watch three brothers face a sweet but certain death. Learn how a tiny pill can changes lives. Get away through time with thieves. See what the winds reveal in "Tsunami!" Follow Casey as he chases the ladies in "On the Prowl." And so much more.

Also by Larry

No Place To Be But Here—It is not only Larry's own story, but that of his family. Join him as he tells how his two wives, three children, and five grandchildren have shaped his life as much as he has molded theirs. Tragedy is certainly no stranger as he deals with death, cancer, murder, and global terrorism, not only on the written page, but in his own life.

Available on Amazon.com and all e-readers.

On the Rails, *The Adventures of Boxcar Bertie*—What's a young teacher to do when she is jobless and homeless in 1936—the heart of the Great Depression? Bertie Patchet dresses as a male, takes to the rails, and rides boxcars into a hobo's life of peril, thrills, and maybe even romance.

Kent and Katcha, *Espionage, Spycraft, Romance*—Kent Brukner, a rookie American spy, is sent to Moscow on a dangerous mission, and meets innocent, passionate Katcha. Stalked by the evil Major Dmitri Federov, the lovers must escape from St. Petersburg to Helsinki, Finland, or face life in a Russian prison.

Coming Soon!

The Moaning Lisa, *A Paco and Molly Mystery IV*—The LeSotos retire to Next to Heaven, an assisted living community. But it's not all relaxation and serenity when a sleepwalker stumbles on a serial murder scheme. Are Paco and Molly up to unraveling this medical and financial conspiracy that will lead them into harm's way?

Photograph by Craig Herndon

Larry grew up in New Haven, Connecticut, and served in the U.S. Navy during the Korean War. After earning a BS in Information Systems Management from American U. he became a field engineer riding Navy ships for RCA. He spent most of his career at Honeywell/Alliant Techsystems, designing electronic equipment for the U.S. Government. Larry feels fortunate to have wed two terrific ladies. Losing Hannah to leukemia in 1986, he married Rosemary some time later. Together they launched their career coauthoring mystery, suspense, and fantasy fiction in their Honolulu condo overlooking the Pacific Ocean.

Rosemary, a Smith College graduate and former *Harper's* assistant editor, also writes personal essays, many published in the *Washington Post, Baltimore Sun, Chess Life*, and elsewhere. She was divorced when she met Larry on a blind date. He told her, "When I retire, I'm going to write a novel and I want you to help me." She knew he was Mr. Right, so she chirped, "Okay!" Twenty books later, Larry still conjures up their mysterious plots while Rosemary adds the pizzazz. And they haven't killed each other yet!

Email the Milds at: roselarry@magicile.com
Visit them at www.magicile.com